Bridge to Nowhere

Bridge
to
Nowhere

Gerald Names

The E. B. Houchin Company
Est. 1992

The E.B. Houchin Company
Salt Lake City, Utah

Trade Paperback ISBN: 978-0-938313-03-8

Printed in USA

1

DACHAU

Dachau was a quiet little town just outside of Munich and likely would have stayed that way had it not been selected by *Reichsführer-SS* Heinrich Himmler as the site for the first concentration camp in 1933. The camp itself was the die from which all the others were struck, a model of German efficiency. It was situated near the main railway tracks between Munich and Nuremburg, and the guard towers and rows of barracks could easily be seen from the passing trains.

Himmler had his own personal train that he usually traveled in, but this time he had chosen to fly in to the *Luftwaffe* air base at Fürstenfeldbruck west of Munich and drive the short distance to Dachau. As Himmler's staff car and accompanying entourage pulled up to the gate house on the west side of the compound, the sentry gave a smart salute and waved the car on. Himmler's only acknowledgement was a slight nod. The signature motto of the concentration camps, *Arbeit macht frei*, work will make you free, adorned the metal gate

The crematorium smoke stack could be seen above the trees northwest of the prison compound. Billows of thick black smoke poured from the stack and the stench was indescribable. Himmler seemed oblivious to the odor and to the hollow-eyed prisoners. They were mostly political prisoners, from all walks of life and from all over Europe. Each had his own reason to hate Heinrich Himmler, but their faces did not betray their feelings.

Himmler had organized the camps as a business enterprise with an abundant supply of dispensable, cheap labor, and Dachau had been the first. He was reputed to be one of the richest men in the *Reich* and he had recognized early the two sources of real power: money and political position. Himmler was the master of both.

Accompanying the *Reichsführer* was Wilhelm Nordhoff an official of the *Reichsbank* from Berlin. Nordhoff was the type of man Himmler preferred: efficient to a fault and easily awed by anything authoritative.

The camp commandant, an *SS* toady named Wilhelm Weiter stood in front of the administration building waiting to greet the *Reichsführer*, but Himmler was not in the mood for formalities. When the car stopped, he rolled down the window and leaned out. "Where is it, Weiter?" asked Himmler.

"I will take you there, *Herr Reichsführer*."

Weiter opened the car door and stepped aside for the two men. He led the way into the administration building and escorted Himmler and Nordhoff to a guarded room, which they entered alone.

In the far right-hand corner of the room was the object of Himmler's hurried trip from Berlin: a stack of 80 wooden crates. Each crate was four inches high, 16 inches wide and 12 inches deep. A huge swastika was painted on the lid of each wooden box and an official seal was stamped on every side.

"Open one," said Himmler.

Nordhoff retrieved a small pry bar and removed the lid of one of the crates. Packed in straw were three bars of gold. Each bar of gold was numbered serially and stamped on each was the figure of an eagle clutching a wreath in its talons. Enclosed in the wreath was a swastika. Each bar weighed exactly thirty-five troy pounds. It was a fortune by any standard. Yet it only represented a minute portion of the gold fillings, rings and other jewelry extracted from the millions of European Jews who had perished in Hitler's quest for racial purity.

Himmler stood for several moments gazing at the gold. Nordhoff stood beside and slightly behind him. Neither spoke. From his placid expression one could only guess at the thoughts coursing through Himmler's mind. Were it not for his uniform, this little weasel of a man, with his awkward gait, receding chin, and rimless glasses, would have looked more like a store clerk than the second most powerful man in the German *Reich*. Himmler silently congratulated himself for having the gold stored at Dachau. There couldn't be a safer place in all of Germany. A concentration camp was the one place people wanted to stay out of, not break into.

Apparently satisfied with what he had found, Himmler turned and wordlessly left the room with Nordhoff trudging dutifully behind. Weiter was waiting outside the door like a faithful hound. "Was everything in order, *Herr Reichsführer?*" he asked.

"How many are there?"

"Eighty boxes, *Herr Reichsführer*. Two hundred forty bars in all."

"Well done, Weiter," replied Himmler, then added, "This is *Herr* Nordhoff from the *Reichsbank*. He will be my representative in this matter. Do what you can to accommodate him."

"As you wish, *Herr Reichsführer*," said Weiter with a salute, which Himmler, hurrying to his staff car, hardly seemed to notice. The *Reichsführer's* mind was obviously preoccupied. The one thing he had wanted most and had previously not dared to dream of was now within his grasp.

During the short trip back to Fürstenfeldbruck air base, Himmler's thoughts turned to the Bavarian scenery as he silently gazed out the window. He always enjoyed the trips to his native Bavaria, the scene of his early political activism and his subsequent rise to power. He had come a long way since his boyhood days in Landshut. For five years he had occupied an office at Nazi Party headquarters in Munich. As his car cruised through the countryside, he thought of the contrast between Munich and Berlin. Munich had fared much better under the onslaught of Allied air power.

Nordhoff had made the trip only because gold came under the authority of the *Reichsbank*, and even Himmler had to observe certain aspects of German law. Nordhoff's attempts to make conversation were politely rebuffed, so he sat back and enjoyed the ride. As the car arrived at the air base, Himmler turned to Nordhoff and finally spoke.

"*Herr* Nordhoff," he said softly, "I want the gold shipped on the 17th of March."

"To Berlin?" asked Nordhoff.

A telling smile replaced Himmler's normal expression.

"No, *Herr* Nordhoff. There's a war going on in Berlin. You are to ship the gold to my villa in Gmund on the Tegernsee. Someone will be there to receive it and take it to its ultimate destination. I trust you can handle the details?"

"Gmund, *Herr Reichsführer?*" Several thoughts raced through Nordhoff's mind. What he was being ordered to do was questionable, if not illegal, but he didn't want to debate the point. As leader of the *SS,* Himmler could do most anything he wanted to do. The *SS,* or *Schutz Staffel,* had started out as a small band of men who were Hitler's personal body guard. Himmler had gotten himself appointed head of the *SS* and in short order had consolidated his power by bringing all of the police in Germany, including the *Gestapo,* under his control, wresting that power from Hermann Goering. In practical terms Himmler was second only to Hitler in power and authority in the German *Reich.*

Himmler gave Nordhoff an icy stare. "The destination of the gold is a state secret, *Herr* Nordhoff. I'm sure I needn't explain what that means."

Nordhoff began to sweat in spite of the cold weather. "I'll see that it's taken care of, *Herr Reichsführer.*"

"See that you do," responded Himmler.

"Yes, *Herr Reichsführer.*"

On the flight back to Berlin Nordhoff sat alone with his thoughts, many troubling thoughts.

2

BERLIN March 2, 1945

Berlin was like an elegant lady who had fallen on hard times. To the casual observer she was just another broken-down hag, a creature of the streets, the product of a life of excess and dissipation. However, those who knew her most intimately, who had experienced her grace and beauty, who had exulted in her days of glory, now felt a painful sorrow to see her reduced to such a pitiful condition. A facelift would not be sufficient. Only major reconstructive surgery could repair the damage. Nevertheless, her basic character still remained.

Twelve years before, she had gone whoring with the Nazis, and though having now been brought so low, her final degradation was yet to come. More than seventy-five times during the previous three months the Allied air raids had rained death and destruction on the inhabitants of Berlin. Reportedly fifty thousand Berliners had already been killed. Though staggering from the blows of Allied air might, daily life went on: shops opened, telephones still worked, garbage was collected, and even public transportation still functioned. Germany was like a punch drunk boxer, reeling under the relentless assault of its opponents, yet unable or unwilling to recognize that the war was lost, or perhaps just too worn out to care.

A feeling of weary resignation had settled over the people and only the German need for order and discipline seemed to be holding everything together. For most, war was a disaster, a tragic smudge on the pages of history. But for an enterprising few it was a time of unparalleled opportunity. Some men created their own opportunities and carefully orchestrated their plans to a successful conclusion. Others just happened upon favorable situations. The less timid seized upon them, while those of lesser vision just muddled along, content to wish their lives away.

Wilhelm Nordhoff had lived forty-two mundane years, hoping for much, expecting little, and willing to settle for whatever leftovers fate might provide. This was all about to end. Opportunity, in the form of two hundred forty gold bars, had grabbed him roughly by the collar and had fired his mind with images of wealth, power, and social respectability. Nordhoff was not a canny thief, but simply a man too weak to resist the temptation. He nevertheless recognized his own limitations. He needed an accomplice, a man in the right position, not given to a false sense of political idealism, and just as hungry as

Nordhoff for the things money could buy. Therefore, it was only natural that he should turn to his nephew, *SS-Untersturmführer* Karl Schweizer.

Only 22, Schweizer had been in the *SS* for more than four years. He had been an excellent candidate, a marvelous specimen of Aryan manhood: blond, intelligent, and in outstanding physical condition. On the surface he was loyal to the *Führer* and the Party, but he was not a fanatic.

Initially, Schweizer had served with the *Waffen-SS*, but his intelligence and leadership potential had landed him in the *Sicherheitsdienst*, the *SS* intelligence service, where he had served for the past eight months. His assignment with the *SD* brought him in contact with valuable information, and offered him a degree of freedom of movement not enjoyed by the average citizen. But best of all, and most important as he saw it, Schweizer was exempt from combat duty.

When Nordhoff had called that morning, his voice betrayed a degree of suppressed excitement. Would Schweizer be interested in a post-war business proposition? Schweizer was a little leery, seeing how the war was going. Still, he had nothing to lose. The proposition was at least worth listening to. Besides, Uncle Willi's position as an official of the *Reichsbank* suggested a wealth of possibilities.

As the streetcar rumbled toward his meeting with his uncle, Schweizer reflected on the progress and likely outcome of the war. All around him were the grim reminders. No part of the city was left untouched. Often the streets were merely a pathway through the rubble. Day to day existence was more or less regulated by the wail of air raid sirens. Such conditions could easily persuade one to look out for himself first. No one expected the war to last much longer.

Schweizer got off at his stop and waited for the streetcar to move on before he crossed the street. Under the circumstances, it was a wonder that public transportation functioned at all.

The *Gasthof zum schwarzen Bären* was a nondescript little restaurant on the outskirts of Berlin. Its stucco exterior was the usual pale yellow, and above the door and windows was painted a sylvan setting with the images of two rather large black bears. Inside, Schweizer found his uncle in a corner nursing a cup of ersatz coffee. It wasn't really bad stuff, some kind of concoction made out of grain. Schweizer looked quite smart in his *SS* uniform as he made his way to Nordhoff's table, but he was hardly noticed. Uniforms were commonplace these days.

Nordhoff rose and extended his hand. "Hello, Karl. It's good to see you again. How goes everything with you?"

Schweizer accepted the proffered handshake and reciprocated with a kind of half bow as he clicked his heels. He seated himself took out a package of cigarettes and offered one to Nordhoff before he spoke. "Things are not so good these days, Uncle. I suppose you heard about Pforzheim."

"Yes, I did, Karl," he answered, shaking his head. "Those lousy British bastards! There's no reason why they had to bomb Pforzheim, no reason at all. I'm sorry about your mother. She was a good woman, a good sister. I loved her dearly. I hear more than 40,000 people were killed. Such a tragedy!"

The protestations of outrage and regret made no impression on Schweizer. He knew his uncle had not gotten on well with his mother for several years. He had been able to put her death out of his mind, and now he realized it had been a mistake to bring it up. Somehow, the mention of his mother by Nordhoff seemed almost a profanity, and Schweizer felt a deep resentment toward his uncle. He sat silently looking at his hands for several moments, overwhelmed by the need to master his emotions. Nordhoff remained silent, perhaps embarrassed by the realization of his own hypocrisy. Finally, Schweizer let out a sigh, looked up and smiled. "Well, Uncle Willi, how are things in the banking business?"

"As well as could be expected, I suppose," said Nordhoff with a shrug. "In a manner of speaking, that's why I asked you here, Karl, to talk about money." Only a slight flicker of interest showed on young Schweizer's face. Nordhoff continued: "What do you think is the world's hardest currency?"

A faint smile crept across Schweizer's lips. "It certainly isn't the *Reichsmark*," he said. "I would guess the English pound or the American dollar. Which would you say, Uncle?"

"There is a better one, but let me get back to that later. Tell me, Karl, a man of your position is privy to a lot of information we ordinary people never hear about. Are there any serious possibilities of winning this war? You know, the secret weapons and all that?"

Schweizer's first impulse was to spout the usual, the expected Party rhetoric, but all at once a feeling of heaviness descended upon him. "No, Uncle Willi, Hitler is not Fredrick the Great. There will be no last minute miracle."

Nordhoff pressed a little harder. He wanted to be sure of his man. "But, you know, just the other day I heard Dr. Goebbels say ..."

"Uncle, uncle," snorted Schweizer, "if I ever become a salesman, I hope you're my first customer. Goebbels says what the people need to hear."

Nordhoff held his finger to his lips. "Not so loud, Karl! The waitress is coming."

The waitress, a middle-aged *Hausfrau*, came over to their table. Schweizer leaned back and looked up at her. It was then that he noticed that several people were looking in their direction. He wondered just how much they had heard.

The waitress was bracing a tray of empty beer steins against her waist, which was very ample. The *dirndl* she was wearing emphasized her overly large breasts. In all, it didn't appear she had been hired for her comeliness. Schweizer concluded she must be the wife of the owner.

"May I get you something, sir?" she asked.

Schweizer looked at his watch. It was almost noon. "Bring me two bratwurst and a stein of beer." Schweizer waited until the waitress was gone before resuming their conversation. Folding his arms on top of the table, he leaned forward and spoke in an intimate voice. "Listen, Uncle Willi. Helga Schweizer raised a very rowdy boy, but she didn't raise a fool. The war was lost a long time ago, probably at Stalingrad. Maybe we lost it when the *Führer* declared war on the United States. Anyway, only the fanatics and the ignorant fail to see it."

Nordhoff leaned back in his chair. He was visibly more relaxed as he eyed his nephew tentatively. The contrast between the two men was very marked. Schweizer was tall, blond and ruggedly handsome, while Nordhoff was short and dark with the bespectacled look of the bookkeeper he had once been. Finally, Nordhoff leaned forward again.

"Karl, I'm going to take a chance on you. I don't believe you would betray a member of your own family." Schweizer only shrugged. "Karl," he continued, "how would you like to be a very rich man when the war is over?"

Their eyes locked. Schweizer mustered his most piercing look and held it until Nordhoff nervously looked away. When he looked back, Schweizer spoke: "A rich man, huh? I suppose this has something to do with your question about hard currency. Am I right?"

Nordhoff nodded, then took a deep breath and plunged ahead. "Last Friday I was in Munich with Himmler. At Dachau there are two hundred forty gold bars awaiting shipment." Nordhoff had taken out his handkerchief and was wiping his brow. His hand trembled slightly as he lifted his coffee cup to his lips. "I think Himmler is going to steal it."

Schweizer's eyebrows shot up. "Himmler? Are you sure? Why would he steal gold from the *Reich?*"

Nordhoff threw up his hands. "How the hell should I know? Maybe he's just greedy! What difference does it make, why?"

Schweizer looked around nervously as he placed his hand on

Nordhoff's arm. "Don't get excited, Uncle Willi," he said reassuringly, "people can hear you."

Nordhoff jerked his arm from his nephew's grasp. "God in heaven, man ..."

It was not like his uncle to get so upset, thought Schweizer. "Just be calm, Uncle Willi," he said quietly.

Something seemed to go out of Nordhoff. His shoulders slumped and he had a tired, dejected look. "All right, Karl. I'm sorry, but this is serious business."

"I'm sure it is, Uncle. These are serious charges. Now, what makes you think Himmler intends to steal the gold?"

Nordhoff grimaced and stared at the floor. "Well," he said slowly, "actually, all he said was that I was to transport the gold to his villa in Gmund."

"On the Tegernsee?"

"Yes."

"Is that all?"

"No. He said someone would then take it to its final destination."

Schweizer saw nothing wrong with that. "Maybe that's all there is to it. Maybe the stories of a National Redoubt in the Alps are true. After all, it takes money to conduct a war."

The look of exasperation returned to Nordhoff's face, "Karl, you're missing the point. First of all, it isn't enough gold to finance a good battle, let alone a war."

"Maybe it's just a small amount of ..."

"No, no! You're missing the point, Karl. The war is lost. You say so yourself. This is a golden opportunity that will never come our way again. We can't afford to let it pass us by."

Schweizer smiled at the unintended pun. The young officer glanced quickly around the room. No one seemed to be interested in them or their conversation. "Just what are you saying, Uncle Willi?"

Nordhoff closed his eyes and swallowed hard. "Karl, I am proposing that we transport the gold elsewhere." Nordhoff opened his eyes and looked at Schweizer. His expression was unchanged. "Well, Karl?" he sputtered.

The younger man just looked down at his left hand and began picking at a hangnail. Nordhoff looked ready to burst. Schweizer was about to speak, but he saw the waitress returning with his order. When she had left, he said: "Let's see if I understand you correctly, Uncle." Schweizer took a bite of the bratwurst and followed it with a mouthful of beer. "You are suggesting that I help you steal gold that belongs to the *Reich*?"

Nordhoff averted his eyes and, nodding his head, said, "It doesn't

12

sound very good, but I guess that's the simplest way to put it."

Schweizer looked away and scratched his head before returning to his bratwurst and beer, which he proceeded to devour with gusto. The tension Nordhoff felt was becoming, unbearable. He knew Schweizer was just playing with him. "Damn it, man!" he exclaimed through clenched teeth. "What are you going to do?"

Schweizer set his mug of beer down and wiped his mouth with a napkin., "Well," he replied thoughtfully, "if you mean, am I going to betray you, the answer is no. If you mean, am I going to help you, that depends on several things. First of all, why me?"

"For one thing, Karl, you're a relative, the least likely to turn me in." Nordhoff was smiling now, like someone about to share a great secret. He continued: "And you are an authority figure in your *SS* uniform. People look up to you, fear you, jump when you say jump. My plan could not succeed without someone in your position."

"You flatter me," said Schweizer. "But I am just a junior officer. I have no real authority."

"That may be true, maybe not," rejoined Nordhoff, "but you wear the *Totenkopf* on your cap. The people fear it. Take my word for it."

"I'll accept that," said Schweizer. "But now the most important point: do you have a workable plan?"

"I think so. The gold is to be transported on the 17th of March. It will be turned over to whoever has the proper authorization. I can get you the necessary papers."

"Then what?" asked Schweizer.

"You transport the gold to my summer home on the Austrian border and deposit it in the cellar. I'm going to build a false wall to conceal it until we can come and get it when the war is over."

"And that's it?"

"No, there's more. You will need five men to do the work. I would suggest getting them from a prisoner-of-war camp. You might try *Stalag VII-A* near Moosburg. It's only about an hour away from Dachau."

"Prisoners? Why not just some of our own people?" asked Schweizer.

"I thought about that," replied Nordhoff. "We wouldn't want too many people to share our little secret. Prisoners are expendable."

"You mean ..."

"When you're through, just take them into the woods and shoot them." Nordhoff now seemed very businesslike. He could have been talking about auditing the books instead of the routine murder of POWs. "You will also need a driver," he continued, "and two or three armed guards."

"What about them?" Schweizer had now grown quite serious.

"We don't want any witnesses, Karl."

"I see." Schweizer had a frown on his face. This was lunacy. Steal from the *Reich*? It was a deadly game his uncle was proposing. "How much is the gold worth, Uncle Willi, that I should be so willing to kill for it?"

"About fifteen million *Reichsmarks*."

"How much in a hard currency, such as dollars?"

"About three and a half million."

Schweizer had a far away look in his eyes as he assessed this dramatic proposition. Nordhoff leaned forward, his eyes very intense. "Are you with me, Karl?" he asked softly.

Schweizer reflected for a few moments. He thought it would be great fun to let Nordhoff dangle for awhile. "As long as we are talking about money, I wonder what the reward would be for turning you in?" Nordhoff felt an electric shock go through his body as the color drained from his face. "Don't worry, Uncle Willi," said Schweizer with a reassuring grin. "Relax! Let me buy you a beer."

Nordhoff wasn't sure what to make of it all, but he had become very thirsty from all the conversation. "Sure. Why not?" he said.

After the two steins of beer arrived and the waitress was out of earshot, Schweizer raised his drink as if to make a toast. "Uncle Willi," he said, smiling broadly, "to us, to peace, to good health, and to post-war prosperity!"

Nordhoff touched his glass to that of his nephew. Something worthwhile was going to come out of this war after all.

3

STALAG VII-A March 17, 1945

Hauptsturmführer Georg Wetzel had never been fond of clerical work, and now that the war was lost he liked it even less. As the Nazi regime was crumbling into chaos the only thing that remained constant was the bureaucracy. As adjutant to the commandant of *Stalag VII-A*, Wetzel was still expected to get his reports in on time, but with the shortage of clerical personnel that meant he had to do it himself. He wasn't very good at figures, though, having been a waiter prior to the war.

What a bloody waste of time, he said to himself as he threw down his pencil in disgust. Wetzel leaned back in his chair and swiveled to face the window. His thoughts turned to his present circumstances. At least he hadn't been sent to the Russian front like every other member of the *Einsatzkommandos* he had served with. There seemed to be a silent conspiracy to eliminate the participants in the Final Solution by putting them into the thick of desperate situations. Wetzel had wondered for several months why he had been spared the same fate.

He thought back to those days in the Ukraine and then later in Poland. What an experience it had been! Others in the *SS* had been sickened by the slaughter, but not Wetzel. He particularly liked the shootings, the closer the better. He felt a perverse satisfaction in seeing flesh being ripped apart by bullets. Then one day it was over. Some technocrat had devised a system of slaughter with phony showers and Zyklon B. What a pity! They could kill Jews by the thousands, but it was so impersonal, so efficient.

In June, 1943, Wetzel was assigned to the camp at Treblinka and served there until August of that year, when the Jews revolted and burned the camp. More than a hundred broke out, but only a handful made good their escape. The rest were captured and shot on the spot. Wetzel led one of the parties of security forces and had particularly enjoyed the hunt.

Wetzel's initial assignment at Treblinka had been to classify the new arrivals, those who would work and those who would die. Most of those who died at Treblinka did so within an hour of their arrival. They were ordered to strip naked in two large buildings and were then driven by *SS* men with whips along a barbed-wire enclosed path some one hundred yards to the gas chambers. Someone had dubbed this path, *Himmelstrasse,* the road to heaven.

This method was too clean, too cowardly to suit Wetzel. He felt it was unmanly to let a machine do the killing. Wetzel had been at Treblinka only two days when he learned about the "hospital," a three-sided enclosure painted white with a large red cross on the side. Behind it was a trench with a fire that was kept burning day and night. Prisoners who were too sick to work or who had offended an *SS* man in some way were taken to the "hospital," where they were forced to kneel in front of the ditch. A bullet in the back of the neck was their ticket out of Treblinka.

Wetzel made frequent use of the "hospital" facility, perhaps too frequent. On one occasion he had been reprimanded by Franz Stangl, the camp commandant, for having killed one of the many craftsmen that Stangl was so fond of.

After the revolt, Wetzel was given the task of obliterating all traces of the camp. Trees were planted, and the gas chamber was dismantled and the bricks used to construct a farmhouse. A Ukrainian and his family were installed on the farm and remained there until the Russians came. No visible trace of the camp's evil past remained. In fact, *Gruppenführer* Globocnik, the *SS* general in charge of the Jewish extermination in Poland, had been quite pleased and congratulated Wetzel personally. Perhaps that was why Wetzel had not been sent to the Russian front.

But this! To be relegated to a prisoner-of-war camp! For a dedicated *SS* officer, it was unheard of. Sometimes Wetzel wondered if it would have been better to have been sent to the front with the others.

"*Hauptsturmführer* Wetzel," said a voice softly.

Startled, Wetzel jumped to his feet, knocking over his chair. "Damn it, Ansbach, don't you know how to knock!" he shouted.

Ansbach retreated a couple of paces and stood at attention, fully expecting a blow that never came. "I'm sorry," he said timidly, "but I did knock and when you didn't answer ..."

"That's enough!" snapped Wetzel. "Now, what do you want?" Wetzel had a capacity for deep concentration and he almost regretted his harsh words ... almost.

"At the gate, sir, there is an *Untersturmführer* Karl Schweizer, who wants to requisition five prisoners."

Wetzel glanced out the window and saw a truck at the gate with an *SS* officer leaning against it. A few moments before Wetzel had been staring right at it, but had seen nothing, so great was his concentration. "What kind of papers does he have?"

"That's just it, sir," said Ansbach, "he says he has papers but won't show them to me."

Wetzel flopped down in his chair. Suddenly he felt very tired. "Tell him to go away," he said.

"Sir?" said Ansbach tentatively.

"Yes," replied Wetzel, trying not to sound weary and annoyed.

"He says he is on personal business for *Reichsführer* Himmler."

Wetzel closed his eyes and frowned. "Why me?" he muttered.

"Sir?"

"Never mind," said Wetzel. "I guess I'll have to see him. Tell him I'll be out directly."

"*Jawohl!*" Ansbach popped a smart salute and disappeared through the office door.

Wetzel walked over to the wash basin on the table against the wall. He reached into the water pitcher and pulled out his bottle of real Irish whiskey. It had cost plenty, but it was worth it. He pulled the cork and raised the bottle to his lips. As he was about to take a drink the reflection in the mirror above the wash basin caught his eye. Wetzel was shocked by what he saw. Looking back at him was a caricature of an *SS* officer, clad in trousers and boots, and a soiled undershirt. With unkempt hair and red-rimmed eyes, the unshaven Wetzel looked considerably older than his twenty-six years. A feeling of self-consciousness came over Wetzel. Suppose this visitor really was from Himmler. He put the whiskey back into its hiding place and sent for some hot water. The man at the gate would have to wait.

Twenty minutes later, Wetzel stepped through the front door of the *Kommandantur*. A remarkable transformation had taken place. The myth of the master race was born anew as Wetzel appeared dressed in *SS* black. Even Schweizer, irritated as he was by the delay, was suitably impressed. Wetzel stood with his elbows bent, his hands clasping his pistol belt as he slowly turned his head. His visage was hawk-like, his eyes cold and clear. He was the overseer, surveying the plantation, the monarch overlooking his kingdom. At last his eyes rested on Schweizer. Wetzel's face had a passive expression. Schweizer frowned and looked away. In a few moments he heard the crunch of footsteps on the gravel and when he looked up, Wetzel was standing in front of him. Wetzel's expression hadn't changed. The two men exchanged salutes.

"My aide tells me you wish to borrow some of my prisoners," said Wetzel. "Is that correct?"

"Yes, *Herr Hauptsturmführer.*"

"He also tells me you refuse to show your authorization to requisition prisoners."

"That is correct," replied Schweizer. "I have no papers for the prisoners, it is true, but I do have papers for the rest of my business."

17

"May I see them, please?"

"I'm afraid not," replied Schweizer. "State secret. You understand."

The expression on Wetzel's face hardened. "Then I'm afraid our business is concluded, *Herr Untersturmführer*." Wetzel spit the title out like a piece of rotten fruit as he turned and began to walk away.

"Wait!" Schweizer was in a panic.

Wetzel stopped but didn't turn around. The gold had to be picked up without delay. Schweizer made the only decision possible under the circumstances. "Could we perhaps discuss this in private? When I tell you everything, I think you may change your mind."

Wetzel hesitated for several moments, then resumed walking toward his office. A sinking feeling flashed through Schweizer's body. *Now what?* he thought. At that moment, without breaking stride or looking back, Wetzel raised his right hand and, motioning with his index finger, said, "*Kommen Sie mit.*"

Inside Wetzel's office Schweizer was directed to a chair next to the desk, while Wetzel retrieved the bottle of whiskey from its hiding place. Schweizer was puzzled by the sudden change in his host's demeanor.

"Do you drink?" asked Wetzel, as he set the bottle and two glasses on the desk.

"Well, not usually ... uh, that's Irish whiskey, isn't it?" Wetzel smiled for the first time since they had met.

"Indeed it is," he said gleefully as he began to pour.

Schweizer was more than a little surprised. "Yes, I'll have one, thanks."

With drink in hand, Wetzel leaned back in his chair and smiled warmly at Schweizer. "Don't let that business at the gate bother you," he said. "It's just part of the image. You know, something to impress the others. They should be at the front. As a matter of fact we all should." The hard look came back into his face. "Why aren't you at the front?" Wetzel asked accusingly.

"Well, as I told your aide, I'm here on business for *Reichsführer* Himmler ..."

"Oh, that's right," said Wetzel, his manner softening. "Why don't you tell me about that."

"Certainly." Schweizer then proceeded to tell Wetzel about the gold shipment and the need for secrecy. The destination of the gold aroused the same suspicions in Wetzel that Nordhoff had felt that day in Dachau.

"I don't understand why, if you have papers for the gold, you don't have papers for the prisoners. It just isn't done. Why am I asked to stick my neck out? No, I can't do it. It's out of the question."

Schweizer looked at his watch. Something had to be done to break the impasse, if the gold was to be picked up on time. "Why don't you call Himmler and ask him?" suggested Schweizer.

Wetzel shrugged his shoulders and reached for the phone. "Why not?" he said.

As Wetzel tried to pick up the phone, Schweizer clamped his hand on top of Wetzel's. "However, I wouldn't advise it."

"And why not?"

"Because the whole reason for using prisoners is so there won't be anyone around to tell where the gold is. Do you catch my meaning?"

Wetzel nodded.

"If Himmler finds out that you know ... well, I don't think I would like to be in your place." Now Schweizer was smiling. "On second thought, go ahead and make that call. Could be interesting."

Wetzel's face was ashen. Everything Schweizer said was logical. Why risk everything over some lousy prisoners? Besides, if Himmler were stealing the gold, it just might be possible to get some of it for himself.

"How many do you need?"

"Five."

"We have nearly 80,000 prisoners. Russians, Poles, French, English, Americans ... what's your pleasure?"

"No Russians or Poles. They're unreliable."

Ten minutes later Schweizer and Wetzel stood in front of a group of prisoners in the work yard where the coal stocks were kept, three hundred sixteen in all from one of the American barracks. Schweizer leaned over and spoke quietly to Wetzel. "Do you have any who speak German? I don't speak English."

"Mmm, yes, I have just the man for you." Wetzel looked the group over and quickly spotted the man he was looking for. "Lieutenant Lindner," he called out in heavily accented English, "please step out and stand over there."

A tall, athletic looking youth stepped forward. Though only nineteen, Eric Lindner was a natural leader, commanding respect even from those of higher rank. In matters of military discipline the other prisoners jokingly said that he even out-Germanned the Germans.

"All right," said Wetzel, "I need four more volunteers for a special assignment."

Lt. Colonel Bruce Morgan, the senior officer of the prisoners, stepped forward.

"Sir, I must protest," he said. "We are all officers here, and the Geneva Convention forbids the use of officer prisoners for work details."

"I acknowledge your protest, colonel, now get back in line," said Wetzel.

Lindner started back for his place in the formation.

"Where are you going?" asked Wetzel.

"Colonel Morgan said we didn't have to volunteer, so I'm not."

"Get back over there," said Wetzel, "or I shall make life very unpleasant for you."

It was not an idle threat. Several months before, a prisoner who had tried to escape had been beaten and confined on half rations. The Geneva Convention didn't seem to mean much to Wetzel. Lindner returned to the spot where he had been told to wait. The prisoners, angered by Wetzel's threat, began to boo and catcall.

"Hear me out," shouted Wetzel. "This is a very important mission. Those men who volunteer will be taken to the Swiss border and released when the mission is completed."

"Do you really expect us to believe that?" asked Col. Morgan.

"The war's almost over, you jerk," yelled one of the prisoners.

"And when it is, we're going to hang your ass from that flagpole," shouted another.

Wetzel's face turned bright red. Four years before the Germans had been masters of all Europe, and now this!

He looked for the source of the last remark, and his eyes fell on Lieutenant Mike Erickson. "Bring that man to me!" said Wetzel.

Erickson looked around, bewildered. "Who, me? I never said anything!"

Two guards took Erickson by the arm and began pulling him toward Wetzel, who was now walking toward the flagpole. "What are you going to do?" he shouted. "I didn't do nothing! Let me go!"

Several of the prisoners made a move to go to Erickson's aid, but a burst of machine gun fire at their feet stopped them. Erickson was kicking and struggling so hard that four more guards were needed to subdue him. At the flagpole Wetzel looped the rope three times around Erickson's neck. For a moment the two men's eyes met, Erickson's wide with terror, and Wetzel's bright and excited-looking.

"Hang him," said Wetzel. The guards were too shocked to respond. "I said, hang him!"

Wetzel pushed one of the guards out of the way and grabbed the rope himself. As he began to pull it, lifting Mike Erickson off the ground, two of the guards grabbed hold and began to pull, too. Erickson struggled with the rope, trying to free himself. He tried to pull himself up the flagpole in a vain attempt to relieve the pressure of the rope, managing to get one of the loops from around his neck before he weakened, but in a few minutes it was all over. His lifeless body hung before his horrified comrades.

Schweizer turned around and vomited several times. *Surely,* he thought, *Wetzel must be insane.*

"Now," said Wetzel, turning back to the prisoners, "I want five volunteers or there will be a repeat performance!"

Colonel Morgan stepped forward again. "You'll have your volunteers," he said. "Just give us a few minutes to make a decision."

Wetzel turned and headed back to his office. Schweizer, still retching, followed behind.

"I can see you've never had to kill a man," said Wetzel over his shoulder in tones of disgust. "What did you expect? Killing is what war is all about."

Eric Lindner stood rooted to the ground, stunned by what had just transpired. He didn't know whether to follow Wetzel or rejoin the other prisoners. Tears were beginning to roll down his cheeks. Erickson had been his friend, his very best friend. Had it been only five months since they had met in October at *Stalag Luft III*, just after Lindner's arrival? Mike had been like an older brother, helping Lindner to adjust to life in the camp. Mike Erickson was always smiling, never critical. Nothing phony about him. He had helped Lindner to forget those unhappy days growing up in Indiana.

A feeling of melancholy came over Lindner and his mind began to fill with thoughts of home.

Eric Lindner had grown up in Mishawaka, a small town in northern Indiana. Life had been very pleasant for his family until the war broke out. His parents were native Austrians and everyone with a German accent was suspected of being a Nazi. At school Lindner was taunted by the other children. His father had run a small but successful sporting goods store. By 1942, though, he had had to file bankruptcy. Nobody wanted to buy from the *kraut*. The only work his father could find was as the janitor of Battell Elementary School.

After graduation Lindner joined the army and entered the air cadet program. In just eight months he went from private to second lieutenant and was on his way to England to join the 375th fighter squadron of the 8th Air Force as a P-51 pilot. It was a very heady experience for someone only nineteen years of age. The men who flew the Mustangs considered themselves the very elite. Their airplanes were the best, and with the long-range auxiliary tanks they could provide escort for the B-24's all the way to Berlin.

Lindner's career as a fighter pilot ended on August 6, 1944, on only his third mission. They were somewhere over central Germany, when a flight of Messerschmitts arrived. These were the first enemy planes Lindner had ever seen. On his previous two missions, they had met no resistance except sporadic anti-aircraft fire in the Berlin area.

In no time at all Lindner began to feel like the man in the middle of a game of keep-away. Every Messerschmitt he went after managed to outrun or outmaneuver him before he could even fire a shot. Just as he was about to give up in frustration, another P-51 flashed in front of him with a Messerschmitt in hot pursuit. Lindner turned to follow and lined up on the Messerschmitt's tail. *God, this is going to be easy,* he thought. His finger tightened on the trigger, but before he could shoot, a dark shadow came out of nowhere. It was another Mustang, in a power dive. Lindner was filled with horror, when he realized the Mustang was on a collision course with the Messerschmitt. "Pull up!" he called out. "There's a ..." It was too late. The P-51 impacted right on the Messerschmitt's cockpit. The German's wings folded up, and a brilliant orange ball of flame erupted from the tangled wreckage as the two planes began a dance of death to the ground below.

Lindner could only stare in shock and disbelief. His knees were shaking so badly, he could hardly work the rudder pedals. Suddenly, Lindner felt his plane being buffeted about. Thunk! Thunk! Thunk! It sounded like someone was pounding the fuselage with a hammer. He remembered what a veteran pilot had once told him, "All you hear is your own guns and the roar of the engine. You never hear the other guy's guns. That's only in the movies." Shreds of metal and slivers of glass began to fly as the Instrument panel began to disintegrate. Lindner looked at the convex mirror mounted above the panel. A Messerschmitt was right behind him. Lindner saw the flash as the German pilot fired off another burst. He felt a sharp pain as one of the slugs ripped through his flight suit and bounced off of a rib on his right side. Oil began to spray along the cowling and onto the canopy, partially obscuring his vision. Lindner's reaction was more instinct than anything else.

He pulled the stick back into his lap, putting the Mustang into a steep climb. Then he pushed the stick to the left and all the way forward, at the same time practically standing on the right rudder pedal. The Mustang nosed over and began screaming toward the ground. Lindner checked the mirror. The Messerschmitt was gone. Then he looked below. It was a solid overcast, nothing but fluffy white clouds.

The Mustang began to vibrate badly as Lindner surveyed the damage to the instrument panel. He only had needle, ball and airspeed for flying. The oil pressure said zero, and the temperature gauge was in the red. Black smoke was pouring from the engine as Lindner eased the throttle back. The oil leak had stopped, but maybe that was because there was no oil. Lindner ran through his options. He could set it down here, but he would certainly be captured. Besides, it was overcast. The clouds had been known to have solid objects in them. His other option was to try for home. However, if his engine quit, he would have to take whatever he could get for a landing field. On the other hand, at least now he had power, so he would have some control over where he landed. THUNK! A hole appeared in the canopy just above Lindner's head. He looked in the mirror. It was the Messerschmitt again. "You sonofabitch!" he shouted. "I'm going down anyway! Give me a chance!"

Lindner advanced the throttle to full power and the Mustang began to shake violently. The temperature gauge was off the scale. The overcast was coming up rapidly. Lindner checked the mirror again. No Messerschmitt. *Better get this bird level before I enter the soup,* he said to himself. He reduced power and pulled back on the stick. In seconds he was in the clouds.

Even on reduced power, the plane still vibrated. Perhaps he had lost an engine mount. Several minutes passed. Lindner was applying everything he had learned about flying the basic instruments. He had never been this scared before in his life. He felt a funny sensation in his crotch. It was only then he noticed the circle of wetness on his flying suit.

When Lindner broke out of the overcast rain fell steadily. He was only about 500 feet off the ground, and below him were patches of farmland bordered by trees. It didn't look too promising, but the decreasing RPM told him he had better find a good place to set it down.

Drained of its oil, the engine shuddered to a stop. Lindner slid the canopy back and pointed the Mustang into a grain field. He later would recall the sound of the airplane swishing through the grain just before the jolt of the impact.

For several moments Lindner was stunned. The P-51 had dug into the mud as it tipped up onto its nose at a crazy angle, and the fuel tanks had ruptured, spraying gasoline everywhere. Some of it had gotten into his eyes and he could barely see. The fear of fire was overpowering as he unbuckled his harness and tried to climb out.

Lindner screamed and fell back into the seat. He had broken his left leg and the pain was excruciating, but he knew he had to get out quickly. He grasped the frame of the cockpit and hauled himself up, then tumbled out onto the wing and rolled off onto the ground. Lindner crawled and scrambled as fast as he could away from the wreckage. When he was about fifty yards away he heard a muffled explosion and looked back over his shoulder. The Mustang was engulfed in flames.

By the time some German troops arrived, Lindner had managed to prop himself up against a tree. He was cold and wet, and considered their arrival more of a rescue than a capture. His trail through the grain field was easy to follow and soon he was on his way to internment, first a field hospital for seven weeks, and then to *Stalag Luft III*. To avoid liberation by the advancing Soviet army *Stalag Luft III* was evacuated and Lindner arrived at *Stalag VII-A* on February 2, 1945, after a forced march.

Lindner looked up at Erickson's body, but all he could see was Wetzel's sneering face. *Someday I'm going to kill that bastard,* Lindner said to himself.

Inside the *Kommandantur,* Wetzel was pouring himself another drink. "You see," he said, "getting what you want is easy when you deal with men like those. They have no respect for authority like we do, eh, Schweizer? But every man fears death."

Schweizer sat slumped in a chair. *Is this what it will be like, when I have to kill the guards and prisoners?* he asked himself. Then he thought of the gold. *Survival is everything,* he thought, *and these men ... well, every war has its casualties.*

Someone knocked on the door and then it opened. It was Ansbach with Colonel Morgan. "Ah, Colonel Morgan. Do come in," said Wetzel. Morgan took two steps into the room and stopped. He looked very grim.

"Well, aren't you going to salute me?" asked Wetzel.

"I heard you," said Morgan, barely able to contain himself.

"Are you being disrespectful?" asked Wetzel.

"No sir," said Morgan and slowly raised his right hand and touched his forehead.

"Not a very good salute," said Wetzel. Morgan looked him straight in the eye. Wetzel could feel the burning hatred and looked away. "Well, no matter. Who do you have for me?"

Morgan handed him a list of five names: Lindner, Stagg, Lutz, Kabello, and Hashimoto. "Now, here's an interesting story," said Wetzel to Schweizer. "Major Frank Hashimoto ... the Americans intern his family at some camp in Utah and he comes to Europe to fight against us. He doesn't know who his enemies really are. And you should see how he is treated by the other prisoners." Wetzel laughed and shook his head. "Where's Lindner?" he asked Morgan.

"Outside."

"Send him in on your way out. Dismissed."

Lindner entered and stood in front of the two men. He had a very tired look about him.

"This is Lt. Lindner," said Wetzel. "His parents are Austrian and they have sent their boy to make war against the *Reich*. I can't understand what a good Austrian boy is doing here. Why are you here, Lindner?"

"I came here to kill Huns," said Lindner, biting off each word.

For a moment anger flashed in Wetzel's eyes. "Well, no matter. You will be liaison between the other prisoners and *Untersturmführer* Schweizer."

"Pardon me," interrupted Schweizer as he looked at his watch, "but I really must go. I have a schedule to keep."

"All right," said Wetzel. "Lindner, assemble the other four and meet us at the front gate."

Five minutes later, the truck was rumbling down the streets of Moosburg that led back to the highway B11, the road to Freising. Schweizer was having serious reservations about the entire affair, but it was too late to turn back. He glanced at the driver, Hans Eberts, a swarthy looking man of about fifty with a bushy moustache. A pipe was clutched tightly between his teeth. Eberts had witnessed the hanging, but had said nothing. Schweizer didn't feel he should bring it up.

Then Schweizer thought of the three guards in the back. They couldn't have been more than sixteen or seventeen. *Old men and young boys,* he thought, *that's all that's left now.* Could he kill them when the time came?

4

HOHENLYCHEN March 17.1945

The forest near Hohenlychen had a serenity that belied the fact that a war, a total war, was raging throughout central Germany. The winter snows had gone and the first buds of spring were beginning to appear. Some said that it was the warmest spring of the twentieth century. A stroll in the forest was a traditional German pastime, but the forest was also a good place to get away from inquisitive ears, and *Reichsführer-SS* Heinrich Himmler had come to the forest this day for that very purpose. *Gruppenführer* Fegelein, Himmler's personal representative at the *Führer's* headquarters, had brought news earlier that the secret negotiations Foreign Minister von Ribbentrop had sought with the Western Allies had been a complete failure. Accompanying Himmler on his walk in the Forest was *Brigadeführer* Walter Schellenberg, his most trusted advisor and head of the Foreign Section of the *SD*.

The two men strolled silently through the trees, hands clasped behind their backs. Himmler's head was bowed and occasionally he would gently kick a rock or a dead tree limb. Schellenberg glanced at his superior from time to time, but said nothing. Himmler was obviously very troubled about something. Eventually, they reached a small clearing where the first new blades of grass were beginning to appear. Himmler stopped at the edge of the clearing and looked from side to side. The last rays of the setting sun were illuminating the tops of the trees, painting them a golden brown. Himmler had a rather pensive look about him. The famed coldness of his eyes was not in evidence. He looked almost sad.

"I don't know what we are going to do, Schellenberg," he sighed. "Fegelein brings news that von Ribbentrop has been trying to negotiate peace on the western front also. It was a complete waste of time. Of course he shouldn't have used a man like Hesse. I think the British really hate that man and besides, he's such a dolt anyway."

"Perhaps if you were to approach the Americans, *Herr Reichsführer* ..."

"I have considered it, believe me I have. Do you remember when Count Bernadotte came from Sweden in February? I was going to ask him to act as intermediary for me with Eisenhower, but I sensed the time just wasn't right." Himmler fell silent again. What he wanted to say died on his lips. He had spent too many years in the service of

Adolf Hitler, "the greatest genius of all time," to say what was really in his heart. But somehow the words formed anyway, and he was astonished to hear himself speaking them.

"The problem, Schellenberg," said Himmler hesitantly, "is that the *Führer* is the major stumbling block to peace. I'm afraid there can be no peace short of total defeat as long as he is Chief of State. Somehow he must be removed."

Schellenberg only nodded his assent. Himmler fell silent and his gaze slowly swept over the sylvan setting. When Himmler finally spoke again there was a certain awe in his voice. "Beautiful, isn't it? So peaceful and quiet. One wouldn't think a war was going on only a few miles away."

Schellenberg did not respond.

"Sometimes I wish I hadn't entered politics," the *Reichsführer* continued. "When I was a young man I was a chicken farmer. 1 was poor, but happy. But fate has cast me in this role and I suppose I must play it out to the end. The war is lost, God help us, and the people are tired. You can see it in their eyes." Himmler paused. The hardness returned to his eyes, and in an instant the magic was gone. Once more he was the canny politician. "When was the last time you saw the *Führer?*"

"I think it's been more than a month ago."

"What did you think? Did you notice how stooped and stiff he is? His hearing is shot and I think his eyesight is failing, too."

"Yes, I noticed that," answered Schellenberg.

"Even Dr. Crinis says the *Führer* is no longer able to fulfill his duties," continued Himmler. "I don't think we can work any longer with the *Führer*. Do you agree?"

Schellenberg hesitated. Could this be some kind of loyalty test? Finally, he said, "Yes."

"But, what should I do?" asked Himmler anxiously. "I can't simply have him murdered, or poisoned, or have him arrested at the Reich Chancellery ..."

"There is only one possibility," said Schellenberg. "You must go to the *Führer,* tell him the facts, and compel him to resign."

"That is out of the question!" replied Himmler terrified. "The *Führer* will go into a rage and have me shot on the spot!"

"Well, you can take measures against that possibility," urged Schellenberg reasonably. "After all, you are the superior of higher *SS* leaders who could readily arrange his arrest. And even if that didn't work, you could always use the doctors."

"I don't know," said Himmler in a worried tone as he turned around and headed back. "I just don't know."

As they walked along Himmler began to assess his situation. Considerable infighting among the inner circle of Hitler's associates had always been the norm, even as far back as 1934 when Ernst Röhm and the other leaders of the brown shirted *SA* were ruthlessly murdered at the behest of Himmler, Goering, and Goebbels. Now, Martin Bormann, by seizing on Himmler's oft expressed wish to have a combat command, had succeeded in diminishing the *Reichsführer's* influence with Hitler. At Bormann's suggestion, the *Führer* had appointed Himmler on January 25, 1945, to command Army Group Vistula, which had been hastily put together from elements of Army Group Center and Army Group South for a last-gasp defense of Berlin. Thus, by getting Himmler out of Berlin, Bormann now had the *Führer's* ear and was able to take increasing advantage of Hitler's paranoia.

From the outset, General Guderian, Chief of Staff of the *OKW*, had opposed Himmler's appointment, but Hitler had been adamant. After a shouting match between the two, Hitler had relented a little and agreed to a military adjutant being appointed. But now the Russians were less than fifty miles from the German capital and Guderian was pressing the *Führer* for the appointment of a real military commander to lead the defense of the city. No one wished Guderian success more than Himmler himself.

Just as they were reaching the edge of the forest Himmler stopped and turned to Schellenberg. "You know, Fegelein also tells me that the Americans have announced that unconditional surrender is not enough. They intend to occupy and govern the entire *Reich*. There seems to be no end to their thirst for revenge."

"They are madmen!" said Schellenberg emphatically. "Don't they realize how many lives will be lost by pursuing such a course? Surely they realize the Bolsheviks are the real enemy, don't they?"

Himmler stood silently looking at the ground. The only sound was the tapping of his fingernails on his teeth, a nervous habit that had become well known among his immediate subordinates. It was time for the decision he had put off for so long. When he finally spoke, it was with a heavy feeling of resignation. "Schellenberg, I believe the time has come to put Operation Golden Adler into motion."

"You are going to flee the country, then?"

Himmler gave Schellenberg a piercing look. "No, I don't think so," he replied. "I think instead I am going to remove myself from the *Führer's* reach and proclaim a new government with myself at the head. Negotiations for a separate peace have been fruitless thus far, and because the *Führer* has pledged to stay in Berlin to the very end, there can be little doubt that he will be dead within a few weeks, perhaps even days. Naturally, the country will need a strong leader to succeed the *Führer*. By establishing a new government at this time, we can perhaps save the country from total defeat, and at the same time protect ourselves from the *Führer's* wrath. What do you think?"

Schellenberg chose his words carefully. What Himmler was suggesting was treason. He didn't want to be caught with his pants down if Himmler backed out. "I think it is a reasonable plan, *Herr Reichsführer*. When will the operation begin?"

"I am ready now," replied Himmler. "A large amount of Jewish gold was shipped to a safe place today and we could be ready to form the new government in a week to ten days. There is a very important position for you if you support me in this, Schellenberg."

"You may rely on my loyalty. *Herr Reichsführer*."

It was easy for Schellenberg to agree, considering he was talking to the chief of the German police. Himmler's mood had visibly changed for the better. He resumed walking, now at a brisk pace.

At Himmler's headquarters, a very animated military aide came running to meet them. "*Herr Reichsführer!*" he called out. "There is a telephone call waiting for you. They say it is extremely urgent."

"Who is it?" asked Himmler.

"*Oberführer* Viertel is calling from Gmund."

Himmler hurried into the building with Schellenberg close behind. He picked up the phone and motioned for the aide to leave.

"Heinrich Himmler," he said in his high-pitched voice.

"*Herr Reichsführer*, I have bad news. The shipment we were expecting from Dachau has not arrived. It was picked up, but has disappeared"

"Are you sure?"

"Yes, *Herr Reichsführer*. It was due more than five hours ago."

Himmler tried not to appear concerned. "Perhaps it has only been delayed."

"I don't believe so," said Viertel. "I have driven to Dachau and back, but there is no sign of the truck or the shipment. What do you wish me to do?"

"I ... I will call you back," said Himmler as his stomach began to twist into a knot. He replaced the receiver and slumped down into a chair. He turned slowly and stared blankly at Schellenberg, the color drained from his face. "We are undone," he said weakly.

"What is the matter?" asked Schellenberg.

"The gold ... it's disappeared."

"What happened to it?"

"I don't know," answered Himmler, his voice becoming a whine. "What are we going to do?"

"Who was assigned to transport the gold and who else might have known about it?"

Himmler's indecision left as quickly as it had come. He rose to his feet and strode to the window. He raised his right hand in front of his face with the index finger extended as if to make a point. "Ah, yes," he said. "Wilhelm Nordhoff. Yes, that's it!"

"Who is Wilhelm Nordhoff?" asked Schellenberg.

"An official of the *Reichsbank*," replied Himmler as he looked at his watch. "I put him in charge of getting the gold shipped. It's after seven. I think we had better have a talk with *Herr* Nordhoff."

"I would also suggest," said Schellenberg, "that we find out who picked up the gold and put out an alert for his apprehension."

"Yes, of course. You are quite right." Himmler walked over and picked up the phone. "Get me *Gestapo* headquarters in Berlin," he said, his voice firm and authoritative. Himmler turned and looked at Schellenberg. "We'll have our gold back before morning," he said confidently.

5

BERLIN March 17-18, 1945

The all-clear had just sounded in the German capital and the Berliners began emerging from the shelters. The British sent their bombers to Berlin every night that the sky was clear, and on this particular night the British raid had followed on the heels of an American raid by 1300 bombers earlier in the day. Even for a city grown used to airborne destruction over the past several months, this had been an especially bad day. In spite of it all, the people never seemed to lose their sense of humor. A standing joke among the weary inhabitants of the shattered city was that the constant bombing of Berlin was good for the German war effort. It was costly for the Allies to waste good bombs blowing up rubble.

Klaus Dieter Berndt, the night duty officer at *Gestapo* headquarters, could hear the phone ringing as he was returning from the air raid shelter. He was in no particular hurry, because he felt if it were really important, they would call back. Besides, the phone would probably quit ringing just as he got there.

Berndt was no more remarkable than any other *Gestapo* officer. In his middle thirties, he had been a policeman all his adult life, beginning in his hometown, Neuburg an der Donau, and then in Nuremburg. He had been present at many of the early Nazi rallies there and had been an early convert to National Socialism. When the Nazi party had come to power in 1933, the *Gestapo* did not yet exist. The police in the various German states were loosely organized, with the Prussian police being the largest. The *Geheime Staatspolizei* was the creation of Hermann Goering, who was head of the Prussian police, but he had been unable to control it because of constant infighting. Berndt could recall a time when things were so bad that an agent who had to go to the lavatory would tell a close friend, just in case he didn't come back.

It was left to Heinrich Himmler, the master organizer, who had quietly applied his bureaucratic skills in the police of the other German states and in the process getting himself appointed Chief of the National Police, to transform the *Gestapo* into the efficient instrument of political terror necessary to the survival of a totalitarian regime. Berndt had eagerly sought admission to its ranks and had been an outstanding student at the *SS* academy in Bad Tölz. The *SS* was the parent organization of the *Gestapo*. His first assignment was Munich, which he now called home, and he was finally transferred to Berlin in

31

1943. Berndt suffered from the typical police mentality: nothing is intrinsically right or wrong. Right, truth, and justice are only what the state defines them to be.

The ringing of the phone was becoming insistent, and when it didn't stop after several rings, Berndt quickened his pace instinctively, just in case. "*Gestapo,*" he said into the receiver, out of breath.

"*Hier ist Himmler,*" said the voice on the phone.

Oh my God, said Berndt to himself, *why couldn't it have been someone else.*

"Where were you?" demanded Himmler. "I've been calling for more than an hour!"

That wasn't quite correct, thought Berndt as he looked at the clock. He had left for the shelter only thirty-seven minutes earlier. However, the question of time was merely academic. "I'm sorry, *Herr Reichsführer,* but there was an air raid and I ..."

"Idiot!" shouted Himmler. "Someone has stolen millions in gold from right under our noses and you are cowering in a hole in the ground!"

Berndt knew it was pretty serious, because he had never known Himmler to shout in the two years he had been assigned to *Gestapo* headquarters. "I'm sorry, *Herr Reichsführer,*" said Berndt, his mouth suddenly dry.

"Never mind!" snapped Himmler, his tone softening a little. "Get the file on Wilhelm Nordhoff. Find out where he lives and arrest him immediately. I'm leaving for Berlin now, and I want to see him when I get there. Find out what he knows. Don't be overly severe, but I want answers. Do I make myself clear?"

Himmler's tone had changed from rage to menace and Berndt couldn't decide which was worse. "Yes, *Herr Reichsführer,* but what should I ..." The phone went dead before Berndt could finish his sentence. It didn't take long for him to recover from the initial shock and set the *Gestapo* machinery into motion. Within twenty minutes, he and another agent were on their way to Nordhoff's last known address.

Nordhoff had been pacing the floor and chain smoking for more than two hours. When the bombs had begun to fall he didn't bother to go to the air raid shelter for fear he would miss the call he was expecting. Frieda, his wife, was finally out of patience. She had been pleading with her husband for several weeks to get her out of the city, and she couldn't understand why they now had to wait for a call from their nephew before they could leave.

"For God's sake, Wilhelm," she said in her most weary voice, "why can't we just leave? It's almost nine o'clock. How far can we get, starting out this late? Where are we going to stay tonight?" She let out a heavy sigh. "I really don't see what's so important about getting a call from Karl."

"Shut up, woman!" snapped Nordhoff. The firmness of his response was unusual, to say the least. In nineteen years of marriage he had gradually grown into the role of henpecked husband. It had become increasingly easy to ignore her rather than to get into an argument. Though surprised by her husband's unexpected outburst, Frieda Nordhoff didn't let it intimidate her. After all, he had always been so ... *so* average.

"Wilhelm, please!" she pleaded. "Let's go!"

Nordhoff threw his hands in the air and, cursing to himself, walked over to the window shaking his head. He wondered how he had put up with it for so long. Perhaps if all went well with the gold, he wouldn't have to put up with it much longer. Absentmindedly, Nordhoff pulled the blackout curtains back a few inches and peered out. Just then a car turned the corner and the glimmer from its hooded headlights immediately caught Nordhoff's attention. The drone of his wife's nagging faded away as his every sense focused on the approaching car. Who would be coming down his street this late? The car was moving very slowly and Nordhoff wasn't sure if it was because of the reduced illumination of the headlights or if the driver was looking for a particular address. Frieda must have sensed his concern, for she stopped in mid-sentence and just stared at the back of her husband's neck.

"Is something wrong, Wilhelm?" she asked. She couldn't know how wrong things really were. Just then the car stopped and Nordhoff could see the two men who got out. "*Gestapo,*" he said in a hoarse whisper.

"What was that you said?" asked Frieda, not wanting to believe her ears.

Nordhoff turned to face his wife, his face totally void of expression. "*Gestapo!*" he said emphatically. "Karl has betrayed me"

"But how ..."

"He wants it all for himself! That's why he never called, the greedy bastard! I'll kill him! I swear to God I'll kill him!"

Frieda was on her feet and moving toward her husband. "Wilhelm! What is this all about? You must tell me!"

"Wait! I have to think this out and there's not much time." Nordhoff bit his lower lip and raised his right hand to his forehead. With no rear exit and no fire escape, he was trapped in his second floor apartment and his only chance was to play the role of loyal citizen, innocent of all charges. *The suitcases! My God, the suitcases!* he thought.

"Quick! "said Nordhoff in a restrained voice verging on a shout. "Get the suitcases into the bedroom!"

In spite of her bewilderment, Frieda Nordhoff began to gather up the luggage. "Please, Wilhelm, tell me what's happening," she pleaded.

Nordhoff could hear footsteps on the stairs. They would soon be at the door. Would they knock, or just politely break it down? What would happen to his wife? *Damn,* he said to himself, *why had he waited so long? What about Schweizer? Had he simply fled with the gold, or had he been caught and implicated Nordhoff in an effort to save himself?* Nordhoff knew he must tell his wife as much as possible before he was taken away so she would not feel inclined to wait around for his return. If he was in danger, then so was she. "Frieda, now listen carefully. Himmler put me in charge of a lot of gold bars that he wanted shipped to his villa on the Tegernsee."

"Oh, my God!" *Frau* Nordhoff was visibly shaken. Her eyes were filled with terror, like an animal caught in a trap. Nordhoff raised his finger to his lips. "Karl and I planned to steal it and hide it away in our villa. Well, it appears as if my sister's boy has failed me. Either way I am in for a pretty rough time. But you must not wait around for me. As soon as they take me away, you must get out of the city. I will contact you as soon as I am able."

The knock at the door had a gentle, almost considerate sound to it, as if to apologize for the intrusion. "Quick," said Nordhoff urgently, "hide in the closet! Maybe they won't think to look for you."

She threw her arms around his neck as tears began to flow down her cheeks. "Oh, Wilhelm," she cried desperately.

The knocking became more insistent. Soon they would break the door down. Nordhoff tried to free himself from his wife's grasp, but she only held him tighter. Somehow she knew she would never see him again. "Frieda," he said quietly, "it's time for me to go. I'm afraid they won't wait any longer."

Gently he pushed her toward the closet and softly closed the bedroom door. As Nordhoff crossed the room to the front door he tried to compose himself. No need to look guilty before being formally accused. He opened the door a crack. "Yes?"

The larger of the two men pushed the door open and stepped into the room. In his hand he flashed the silver disk the *Gestapo* used for identification. "*Gestapo,*" he said matter-of-factly as he quickly surveyed the room.

"What do you want?" asked Nordhoff, trying to appear unconcerned.

"Are you Wilhelm Nordhoff?" asked the first man as the second agent began to move around the room as if looking for something. Nordhoff turned his head and followed him with his eyes as the man approached the bedroom door. "Well?" asked the first man.

"Uh, yes, I'm Nordhoff, and who are you?" The agent frowned. This was a real cool customer and a cheeky bastard at that. "*Hauptsturmführer* Berndt, *Geheime Staatspolizei*," said Berndt, trying to sound official. If his intent was to invoke fear, Nordhoff didn't seem at all impressed.

"I'm happy to meet you, *Herr* Berndt," said Nordhoff as he extended his hand. "Now what can I do for you?"

Berndt ignored the proffered handshake. He was more than a little irritated, now, and was not sure how to proceed. This was not your usual arrest, by any means. The other agent had opened the bedroom door and stuck his head in. "Where is your wife?" he asked.

"She has gone to the country," said Nordhoff, turning away from Berndt as if he wasn't there. "The bombing and all that – you understand." The agent didn't answer. After a quick look around the bedroom, he closed the door and joined the other two men.

"*Herr* Nordhoff," said Berndt, "*Reichsführer* Himmler would like a word with you."

"Really?" said Nordhoff, trying to sound surprised. "What about?"

Berndt was a bit nonplussed by Nordhoff's exterior coolness. Had the man no fear at all? "I'm sorry, *Herr* Nordhoff, but the *Reichsführer* does not take me into his confidence," said Berndt sarcastically.

Nordhoff only nodded. "Would Monday morning be convenient?" he asked.

The agent who had been nosing around in the bedroom responded with a savage blow to Nordhoff's left ear, sending him crashing to the floor. The ear had a fiery hot feeling and after a few seconds it also felt wet as it filled with blood. As Nordhoff tried to rise the agent delivered a vicious kick to the kidney. The pain was excruciating. Nordhoff collapsed on the floor and lay there moaning.

"That's enough, Koerbler. You never were one for protocol. Let's get him downstairs."

The ride to *Gestapo* headquarters was like a dream as Nordhoff drifted in and out of consciousness. He knew that if they would treat him so brutally on suspicion only, then it was hopeless if they had conclusive proof of his complicity in the theft.

The *Gestapo* headquarters on the Prinz Albrechtstrasse was like an oasis of evil in a desert of destruction. It had come through relatively unscathed by the Allied bombs, as if some unseen power had decreed that it fulfill its perverted destiny to the very last. Interrogations were conducted in the basement, and few who entered ever returned.

Berndt and Koerbler took Nordhoff directly to one of the subterranean rooms, where two other agents were waiting. They had been specially called in for this phase of the interrogation, and were well suited for the task. Both weighed more than two hundred pounds and one had been an Olympic wrestler before becoming a policeman. For nearly fifteen minutes they beat him with their fists, in the process cracking three ribs. During the entire time neither of them spoke. Their sole purpose was to convince Nordhoff of the seriousness of his circumstances. When they had finished, they strapped him securely to a chair and left.

Nearly thirty minutes passed before anyone came. The idea was to allow the prisoner sufficient time to consider what he had just been through, and to speculate on the likely course the rest of the interrogation would take. Nordhoff had spent the time imagining the possible questions and rehearsing his answers.

At last Berndt and Koerbler returned and wordlessly began to lay out the implements of the interrogator's art. Among the items put on display for Nordhoff's benefit were a thumb screw, various sticks and leather straps, a device for crushing testicles, and a hand-crank generator with two leads for applying a charge to the prisoner's genitals. With such an inventory of tools at their disposal, the *Gestapo* usually got the answers they wanted, or killed the prisoner in the process.

As they were about to begin, the door opened and a solitary figure stood silhouetted against the brightly lit corridor. His appearance was a contradiction. His *SS* uniform, bearing the rank insignia of *SS-Gruppenführer*, made him look rather impressive, but a closer examination revealed a rather unimposing individual. One was left to wonder whether or not the Nazis would have succeeded as a political movement if they hadn't gone in so heavily for uniforms, swastikas, and the like. It was Heinrich Mueller, Chief of the *Gestapo*. He had come immediately when he learned that Himmler was due back in Berlin. Nodding toward Nordhoff, he asked: "Who is he?"

"His name is Wilhelm Nordhoff," replied Berndt. "He's an official of the *Reichsbank*."

"Why are we questioning him?"

Berndt turned his head and looked at the prisoner. Nordhoff was a pitiful sight. His lips were blood-caked and swollen, and his left eye was beginning to close. Droplets of blood had dried on the front of his white shirt.

"I'm not sure, sir," replied Berndt, turning back to Mueller. "*Reichsführer* Himmler ordered his arrest. Something about the theft of some gold."

"Really?" said Mueller, a tone of surprise in his voice. Berndt instantly realized he had put his foot in it this time. He knew that Mueller was ambitious and had been wanting to get something on Himmler for some time. On the other hand, Himmler still held the power of life and death over virtually every person in the *Reich*. The absurdity of this struggle for power within a regime doomed to extinction was apparent to everyone except the participants. In any case, Berndt sensed that it would be unwise to get caught in the middle. Such a thing could prove fatal.

A faint smile appeared on Mueller's lips. "Let me know what you find out," he said.

"Yes, sir," answered Berndt. Mueller retreated through the open door and closed it behind him, leaving Berndt and Koerbler to begin the interrogation. The first session lasted almost half an hour. In spite of the extensive soundproofing, Nordhoff's screams could be heard outside the room. The questioning wasn't going well because the questioners didn't have enough background information to ask the right questions. They decided to break it off until Himmler arrived.

The two men stood off to the side and lit cigarettes. Their conversation turned to the availability of fresh meat in the city. The casualness of it all was disgusting to Nordhoff. Here were two men who could switch from torture to innocent conversation as easily as changing shirts. Any fear Nordhoff may have felt had been replaced by contempt.

Faintly at first, then more distinctly, Nordhoff heard screams coming from somewhere else in the *Gestapo* basement. It sounded like a woman. Knowing he wasn't the only tenant on this particular night didn't comfort him much. Somewhere in the back of his mind, though, a question began to form. A feeling of horror came over him as he raised his head and asked, "Who is that?"

The two men looked at him, puzzled. Screams were so common in this place, neither had noticed them until Nordhoff spoke up. "Who is that?" Nordhoff asked again. A look of increasing comprehension spread across Berndt's face, followed by a sardonic sneer.

"Why, that's your wife," said Berndt.

Oh, my God, thought Nordhoff. *No! No, not Frieda!*

"We left a man at your apartment and he picked her up when she returned," said Berndt, obviously enjoying Nordhoff's reaction, "Don't fret. We do some of our best work on women." Berndt began to laugh.

"Not my wife!" sputtered Nordhoff, his swollen lips starting to bleed from the effort. "She doesn't know anything, She doesn't ... she ..." His voice trailed off. *Those bastards!* he thought. They were lying. It was obvious. Frieda couldn't have been arrested when she returned, because she hadn't left! A sense of victory swelled within him. They were guessing, clutching at straws. They knew nothing. The look of renewal Nordhoff's face was unmistakable. The two interrogators decided to resume their work. They were masters at their craft, and Nordhoff knew he had to steel himself against the next onslaught.

The second session was well underway when Himmler arrived. He set himself up in Mueller's office and sent for Berndt. "Have you learned anything yet?" he asked.

"No, *Herr Reichsführer*," said Berndt hesitantly. Success had its rewards, but failure was not understood, and never tolerated. "Begging your pardon, but we're really not sure what we should be asking."

"Very well," said Himmler with a sigh, as he removed his glasses and began massaging the bridge of his nose between the thumb and first two fingers of his right hand. "Nordhoff was responsible for having two hundred forty bars of gold shipped from Dachau to the Tegernsee." Himmler replaced his glasses. He was careful not to mention that the gold was to have been sent to his villa in Gmund. "The gold never arrived," he continued. "I am certain that Nordhoff knows what happened to it."

"If he knows anything at all, *Herr Reichsführer*, you can be assured we will get it out of him." Himmler only nodded and leaned back in the swivel chair. It looked as if it was going to be a long night and he was tired already.

As Berndt returned to the basement, Mueller was in another room congratulating himself for having the foresight to bug his own office. *Shipping gold to the Tegernsee?* he thought. *Himmler has a villa there in Gmund. Marvelous! How simply marvelous! Let him try explaining this one to the Führer!*

The interrogation continued on through the night. Toward morning an exhausted Berndt staggered into Mueller's office and awakened Himmler. "It's no use, *Herr Reichsführer*," he said. "He knows nothing."

Himmler stared at him blankly, not immediately aware of his surroundings. He had dozed off while studying the personnel file of Karl Schweizer, the *SS* officer reported to have picked up the gold shipment. Berndt's assessment of the situation was very disturbing. This was not the answer Himmler had wanted to hear. "Are you sure?" he asked.

"Yes, I am sure," replied Berndt. "I have used every method I know. If he knew anything, he would have told me."

Himmler was nervously tapping his teeth again. He considered having Berndt redouble his efforts, but he knew it was useless. "Shall I release the prisoner?" asked Berndt.

The *Reichsführer* gave Berndt a piercing look. The coldness of his eyes slowly returned. "No!" he answered emphatically. "He bungled the job and he will pay for it. You know what to do."

Berndt gave an understanding nod and left the room. Himmler began absent-mindedly to leaf through Karl Schweizer's personnel file.

In the basement Berndt gestured for Koerbler to unshackle Nordhoff. "*Herr* Nordhoff," said Berndt apologetically, "it seems we have made a very great mistake. I hope you will forgive us for the severity of our methods, but I also hope you understand the seriousness of losing such a large amount of gold. If you will just gather up your coat and other personal belongings over there, we will see that you get prompt medical attention, and then you will be free to go."

A feeling of triumph swept over Nordhoff as he lurched to his feet. He had won, damn it! He had won! The pain was almost unbearable as he shuffled along, but Nordhoff didn't care. He had won! Even his nephew was the object of some charitable thoughts. Perhaps he had misjudged Schweizer. Maybe this was going to turn out right after all.

As Nordhoff passed Berndt, he didn't hear the *Gestapo* agent remove his pistol from its holster. The last thought Nordhoff ever had was one of smug satisfaction at having outwitted them. He never heard the explosion as the bullet shattered the back of his skull and destroyed his brain. Berndt stared impassively at the body on the floor. He felt neither revulsion nor pity. He was merely doing his job. .

Upstairs, Himmler had just flipped the file on Schweizer closed when something caught his eye. Quickly, he reopened it. Yes, there it was. *Mutter: Helga Schweizer geb. Nordhoff.* His mother's maiden name was Nordhoff! Himmler was stunned. Nordhoff *was* involved! He was the only solid lead to the whereabouts of the gold. Just then the door opened and Berndt entered the room. Himmler started to rise from his chair. "Did you ..."

"Yes, he's dead," said Berndt. Himmler slumped back into the chair. His eyes fell and a deep frown appeared on his face. *Now what?* he thought. Himmler had a very bad peptic ulcer and right now his stomach was on fire. He picked up the file on Schweizer and stared at it. After several moments, he tossed it across the desk to Berndt.

"It appears you didn't do your job very well. The mother of the man who picked up the gold is named Nordhoff."

The color drained from Berndt's face. "But, *Herr Reichsführer*, I ..."

"Never mind!" said Himmler sharply. "It's too late for excuses. Alert all *Gestapo* offices and all *SS* units. Tell them *Untersturmführer* Karl Schweizer is to be apprehended and detained. I want him alive, do you understand?"

"Yes, *Herr Reichsführer.*"

39

"Don't bungle this assignment, Berndt. You won't have another chance if you do." Himmler pounded his fist on the desk for emphasis. "Find that gold!"

6

CINCINNATI March 9. 1979

Spring had come early to Cincinnati. Considering that the Midwest had just staggered through one of the worst winters on record, the warmer weather should have been a welcome relief, but it wasn't. In spite of all the years of flood control projects by the Army Corps of Engineers, the Ohio River still overflowed its banks in the spring, particularly after a hard winter, and this had been a hard one. It had lingered on like an unwelcome house guest. And as if the melting snow wasn't enough, there was always the rain, slow and steady.

Karl Schweizer contemplated all this as he sat behind the wheel of his Ford LTD listening to the quiet drone of the engine and the gentle splashing of rain on the car. The sky had been overcast for four days, and the gray half-light gave everything a washed-out appearance. Schweizer's face was expressionless as he stared straight ahead. Only his eyes showed any awareness of the scene before him as they slowly followed a solitary female figure making her way down the street, clutching an umbrella against the rain. As she disappeared into the mist of the fogged-up side window, Schweizer instinctively reached up and cleared a spot with his left hand. He watched the woman as she shook the water from her umbrella before entering the lobby of the Hillside Medical Tower, an unremarkable example of modern architecture done in sepulcher white. Schweizer couldn't help feeling a kinship with this stranger, and wondered what affliction had brought her to their common destination.

Schweizer had arrived ten minutes early for his appointment, but now was ten minutes late. *Well,* he thought as he killed the engine, *waiting won't make it go away.* As he sprinted across the street, the urgency of getting out of the rain distracted him, and for a few brief moments he was able to forget the reasons that brought him here.

In the lobby he found the building directory next to the elevator. It was a cheap black board with white plastic letters. As he scanned down the list of names he noted that some letters were missing and others were of non-uniform size. As a data processing professional, he found this lack of neatness somewhat irritating. Finally, he found the name he was looking for:

"Franklin P. Hendriks, PHD

41

Clinical Psychologist"

Schweizer took the elevator to the fifth floor. The lobby had been deserted and he was the only one on the elevator. It seemed more like Sunday than Friday. As he approached the psychologist's office door, a young woman came out of another office, so he just kept walking. He felt a bit embarrassed about seeing a "shrink." When the hallway was empty again Schweizer stopped in front of the door. His hands felt wet. He closed his eyes and said a silent prayer, then took a deep breath and entered.

He was relieved to see no one was in the waiting room except the receptionist. *Rather cute,* he thought. She had blue eyes and her chestnut-red hair was done in a Dorothy Hamill cut. Her nose was a little pointed, but it didn't detract from her appearance.

"May I help you, sir?" she asked pleasantly. Her smile had a phony look to it. Schweizer was reminded of his college days and the girls he would pass on, campus. They would trudge along with such a serious demeanor, sometimes approaching a scowl, but break into a bright smile and a cheery hello as they passed one of the male students. The receptionist was like that. Her mouth was smiling, but not her eyes. Perhaps she resented having to put down her romance magazine.

"Karl Schweizer. I'm here to see Dr. Hendriks ... Sorry I'm late."

"That's all right, Mr. Schweizer, the doctor's last patient ran a little over." The word "patient" made Schweizer even more uneasy. The implication was that he was sick, an implication that he didn't like at all. "Just a minute," she continued, "I'll see if the doctor is ready for you."

She returned in a few moments and ushered Schweizer into Hendriks' office. Dr. Hendriks was as unremarkable as the building he chose to have his office in. He was quite thin, as was his hair, and had a rather pallid complexion. The glasses seemed like an attempt to look intelligent, but it didn't quite work. Schweizer surveyed the room quickly. "Comfortable" was the best word he could think of to describe it. The wood paneling reminded him of his den at home. There was the obligatory potted plant, and of course the inevitable certificates and diplomas on the wall. Schweizer wondered if they were to impress the visitor or to shore up the doctor's own self-confidence.

The doctor was just finishing writing a few notes in a manila folder, and only looked up briefly when Schweizer entered the room. Finally, he closed the folder, rose from his desk, and extended his hand in greeting. "Mr. Schweizer! I'm sorry I kept you waiting. Please be seated and make yourself comfortable!"

What a phony, thought Schweizer. His receptionist certainly must have told him that Schweizer had just arrived.

"Well, I'm the one who was late," said Schweizer, a little irritated at having to apologize a second time.

"It doesn't matter," the doctor said, dismissing the apology with a shrug.

Schweizer glanced curiously about the room. "Where's the, uh ..."

"The couch?" said the doctor, finishing Schweizer's question for him. "I'm afraid that's a little old-fashioned. Some professionals still use it, but I prefer a more informal approach." He gestured toward two vinyl covered easy chairs facing each other with a circular glass coffee table between them. "Would you like to sit over there? Perhaps you would feel more relaxed."

The easy chairs did seem inviting compared to the one Schweizer was now sitting in. "Don't mind if I do," said Schweizer, as he relocated to the other side of the room.

Dr. Hendriks picked up a steno pad and turned on his tape recorder before joining Schweizer. The two men eyed each other tentatively, like two wrestlers sizing up their opponents, looking for an opening. "Are you comfortable?" asked the doctor.

"Yes."

"Good. First, I'd like to get some background information on you."

"All right," said Schweizer, "but there's something I would like to ask you first."

"What's that?"

"Well, if you are recording this, why do you need to take notes?"

Hendriks chuckled. "You know, that's the first time anyone has ever asked me that question. Actually, the recorder is to get down the entire session, and the note pad is to prompt myself with any questions I might think of when you are talking."

"Oh, I see," said Schweizer. He wondered why he hadn't figured that out himself.

"Okay, are you ready?"

"Shoot."

"How old are you?"

"About 55."

The doctor looked up, a little puzzled. "Well, uh, when were you born?"

"I don't know," answered Schweizer with a shrug.

"You don't know?"

"No, Doctor, I don't!" answered Schweizer emphatically. He didn't feel very cooperative. *Maybe he would make the doctor work for his answers,* he thought.

The doctor tried once more. "Do you know where you were

43

born?"

"I don't remember."

Hendriks scratched his chin with the eraser of his pencil as he pondered the situation. "Do you always have trouble remembering things?" he finally asked.

Schweizer shifted uneasily in the chair and let out a sigh. "Dr. Hendriks, my life began in 1945 at about the age of twenty. I have no memory of anything prior to that."

The doctor's eyebrows went up. "Go on, he urged.

"I received a severe head wound just before the war ended," said Schweizer, "and I was in a coma for six weeks, they say, and suffered a loss of memory because of brain damage."

Hendriks was scribbling rapidly on his pad when Schweizer concluded. When he finished writing he began to read back the question he had just written. "You say you received a head wound during the war."

"That's right."

"From a bullet, artillery shell, or what?"

"None of the above."

"I'm sorry?" said the doctor, a bit perplexed.

"Just a little joke, Dr. Hendriks," replied Schweizer. "Does it really matter? It was from a bombing, but I don't know what it was that hit me."

"Are there any other symptoms of brain trauma, such as loss of motor skills?"

"I can't think of any."

"Did you have to go through a relearning process after you were discharged from the hospital?"

"What do you mean?"

"Did you have to learn to tie your shoes again, or relearn vocabulary, or things like that?"

Schweizer looked away for a few moments and thought about the question. "No," he finally replied, "it was nothing like that."

"What was it like?"

Schweizer seemed to be struggling with the answer, trying to find the right words. "It's like meeting someone you know at a party, but not only do you not remember their name, you don't even remember that you should remember their name. There's just something familiar about them.

"Getting back to my first question, what about learning ability?"

"Nah, I don't have any trouble learning. I've always been pretty smart."

Silence fell over the room for a few moments, except for the sound of the pencil scratching as Dr. Hendriks continued to write. "You know, Mr. Schweizer, this is very remarkable."

"What do you mean?" asked Schweizer.

"Don't you think it's kind of unusual to have brain damage so extensive that it resulted in permanent memory loss, yet had no detrimental effect on other body functions, no learning disabilities? Why, you appear to be in perfect health."

"Well. I don't know about that," said Schweizer.

"When was the last time you had a physical?"

"About three months ago. I have one every year."

"Have you ever discussed your problem with the examining physician?"

When he had first sat down, Schweizer had begun to relax. Now, he wished he were somewhere else. The line of questioning had stirred up some very deep emotions. "No," he finally answered. "Just what are you driving at, Dr. Hendriks?"

The doctor ignored the question. "Mr. Schweizer, would you be willing to take a couple of quick tests?"

"What kind of tests?"

"Oh, nothing elaborate. It would only take a few minutes."

"Sure. Why not," said Schweizer wearily.

"This first one is quite simple," said Hendriks as he began to write several strings of digits on his note pad. Schweizer leaned a little forward to see what the doctor was writing.

"No fair cheating," said Hendriks with a laugh as he turned the pad away from Schweizer's view. It only took a few moments to get all the numbers written down, but Schweizer was beginning to feel more and more impatient.

"Okay, are you ready?" asked the doctor.

"Sure."

"All right, I'm going to read off a string of numbers and I want you to repeat them back to me in the same order in which I read them. Got that?"

"Uh, huh."

"We'll start with three digits first, then four and so forth, until we reach a level that you can't do."

Hendriks proceeded with the test: three digits, then four, then five, then six, then seven. On eight Schweizer was unable to repeat them in the correct order, so they tried it again with the same result.

"I guess seven is your limit," said Hendriks. "Let's try it backwards this time."

When they had finished that part of the test, Hendriks began to write down some more notes.

"Well, how did I do?" asked Schweizer.

He had always liked to take tests, because he was one of those who always did well on them. It also gave him a lot of ego satisfaction.

Hendriks looked up from his note pad. "When we did the digits forward, you were able to do seven. In reverse, you were able to do five. Five and four are considered good scores."

"So?"

"So, let's give you the second test."

Dr. Hendriks got up and went to his filing cabinet. He returned with a stack of nine cards and another note pad and a pencil.

"This is called the Bender-Gestalt test," said Hendriks as he handed the pad and pencil to Schweizer before returning to his own seat. "I'll show you each of these cards for five seconds and then I want you to draw what you saw from memory. Okay?"

Schweizer agreed and they began the test. The first card had a diamond with a circle attached. The second had two squiggly lines that intersected. Schweizer was becoming quite bored with it all. In a few minutes they were through and Hendriks had looked over all the drawings.

"So, what does all this prove?" asked Schweizer.

"Well, perhaps it doesn't prove anything to you, Mr. Schweizer, but it suggests to me that you don't have any brain damage at all. Your cognitive abilities are very much above average."

"Aw, c'mon Doc," said Schweizer in a mocking tone. "I told you I have this permanent amnesia. Isn't that proof?"

"Mr. Schweizer, the thought occurs to me ... well, first let me explain something about amnesia. We call this dissociative amnesia. There are only three possibilities for a cause. The first possibility is organic retrograde amnesia due to some insult to the brain. The second possibility is that you are lying. The third is what we call a fugue state, a dissociative reaction, a kind of escape to protect the mind from recognition of some terrible event."

"So, which is it, doc? Am I a liar or just crazy?"

"I think we can rule out number two. There is no conceivable reason for you to lie about your loss of memory for these many years. There's a good chance that your condition is a combination of possibilities one and three. It's impossible at this late date to determine whether or not your brain suffered some trauma in the distant past, but let's say, just for argument's sake, that it did. You should have recovered your memory long ago if it were due to a brain injury. It may have started out that way, but your present condition likely lies with possibility number three ... a subconscious desire to not remember some terrible event. Sometimes when we are faced with emotional stress that's very severe the mind suppresses the painful memories and we say that person has amnesia. Almost a hundred percent of the time the mind heals itself, so to speak, and memory returns within a very short period of time. On the other hand when brain tissue is damaged or destroyed, the resultant memory loss is permanent because brain tissue cannot be regenerated. Now suppose, and this is just speculation, just suppose your amnesia is because of some horrible event, but because your conscious mind has believed in the brain damage theory all these years, your memory is just being suppressed and was never really lost."

"Don't be ridiculous!" retorted Schweizer. "I told you, I suffered brain damage!"

"Mr. Schweizer, these two tests are given to screen for possible brain damage, yet you scored better than average on both of them. Don't you find that remarkable?"

Schweizer went into his sulk routine that he used on his wife when he was losing an argument. Dr. Hendriks was not impressed.

"It's interesting that you exhibit hostility when the brain damage theory is challenged," said the doctor.

"Who's hostile!" demanded Schweizer.

Dr. Hendriks ignored the question and asked one of his own. "Would you be willing to be examined by a neurologist?"

The nervous tick that Schweizer got in his right eye whenever he was pressed was beginning to distort his face.

"What for?" he asked.

"To determine if there really is brain damage."

"Look, Doctor, I told you ..."

"Yes," interrupted Hendriks, "I heard what you said, but I know what I can see ... and I want to see proof there really is some dysfunction because of your injuries. This could help us to get to the root of your problem."

"My problem has nothing to do with my memory."

Schweizer was sullen now.

Hendriks was beginning to weary of the game Schweizer seemed to be playing. Looking down at a chart in a manila folder he had just opened, he asked, "Perhaps you'd like to tell me what your problem is then. I see you were referred by Dr. Greene. Family doctor?"

"Yes" Schweizer answered. He was a bit subdued now. "I'm only here because my wife said if I didn't get help she'd leave me. I've been having this nightmare pretty regularly, and it's really been getting on my nerves lately. Last week things finally came to a head." Schweizer paused. He appeared to be searching for the right words. "Look," he continued. "I really don't feel like talking about this."

"Afraid?"

"Hell, I don't know," whined Schweizer.

"We could talk about other things first," Hendriks said gently. "If you like, we can come back to this when you feel more comfortable."

"All right," answered Schweizer. He suddenly felt very tired.

"Where are you from?" asked Hendriks. "You don't sound like a Cincinnati native."

"I'm from Germany."

"Oh, really?" Hendriks was quite surprised. "You don't have a trace of a German accent.".

"I must be pretty good at languages, "replied Schweizer. "I even know a little French, but I don't know where I learned it."

"Getting back to your wartime injuries ..." began the doctor.

Schweizer reacted sharply. "Look, I thought we weren't going to talk about that."

"No, we weren't going to talk about your nightmares and your marital problems. It's interesting that you should connect them up."

"Well I don't remember anything about the bombing."

"That's all right. I was going to ask you which side you were on."

"I told you I was from Germany," replied Schweizer.

"I'm sorry. How stupid of me. Anyway, what were you in? Army? Air Force?"

"*SS.*"

"Pardon me?"

"I said I was in the *SS.*"

Hendriks paused for a few moments, a look of deep thought on his face. "How would you feel if I told you my family are Dutch Jews?"

"So?"

"Doesn't that bother you, considering your *SS* background?" asked Hendriks.

"Hey, listen," Schweizer replied, "I don't care about a man's religion, and I don't care much about politics, either."

"Just trying to get a feel for your background."

"I think I'd rather talk about my marital problems."

"Fine. Begin anywhere you would like."

Schweizer's mind went back to the fight he had had with his wife, Carole, the previous week. "It's that damned nightmare," said Schweizer.

"Describe it to me."

The dream never varied. Schweizer had had the dream many times over the years since the war, but now it was becoming more frequent, more terrifying. It had gotten to the point that Schweizer dreaded sleep like death itself.

The sweat glistened on Schweizer's forehead and upper lip. He was uncovered except for a portion of the sheet twisted around the lower part of his left leg. A groan, then a stream of frightful, unintelligible words escaped his lips. His feet jerked spasmodically, as if he were trying to run.

As he tossed and turned on the bed, his suffering was shared by Carole, his wife of twenty-four years. As she lay next to him, she stared unblinkingly at the ceiling and thought of all the other nights and how it was always the same. She felt a deep sense of frustration, because she knew she could do nothing to help him.

At forty-four, Carole was as petite as Schweizer was large in stature. The blush of youth had not yet given way to the ravages of time. Her hair was almost black with only a hint of gray, and her delicate cheek bones, translucent complexion and rosy cheeks gave one the impression of Snow White come to life. But now in the darkness of her bedroom she felt very old as she listened to what had become an almost nightly ritual.

Schweizer found himself walking in a strange place. The air was calm and cool like an early spring evening. A sense of urgency and foreboding filled his mind. He wanted badly to turn around and look, but he was unable to make himself do it. His surroundings were all in shadow and everything was sharply silhouetted against an orange sky. The sky was always orange in the dream, like sunset on a clear day, except that the color was the same in all directions, a kind of permanent twilight. So, he pressed on as the fear and panic began to tighten in his chest. Then, off in the distance he saw three specks dancing on the wind. They grew larger as they came toward him. For a moment his fear subsided, replaced by a detached curiosity as he gazed at the specks. He was frozen in time. Past, present and future ceased to exist. As they drew nearer they seemed to shimmer in the light, like three great golden eagles. At last he saw them clearly and the golden color went away. They were three black crows, larger than any he had ever seen. Higher and higher they rose on flapping wings, and then they would glide, circling and reeling and playing tag with one another against the brilliant orange sky. Closer, ever closer, they came. They danced and played on the air currents, but inexorably they came. Schweizer's mind flooded with the urge to run. The command rushed by electrical impulses at the speed of light through the miles of nerve tissue from his brain to his feet. Too late! His feet were encased in thick, clinging mud. Each step was a struggle. Flight was impossible. Still they came. The panic he felt was unbearable. Now he heard their cries and felt the rush of air from their flapping wings. Soon, the noise was deafening. The birds must have sensed his fear, for now they were bearing straight for him. The roar was like a hundred waterfalls. The three crows were now so close he could see their eyes, deep black holes with fiery red dots in the center. He felt the heat and smelled the stench of their breath. Nausea swept through his body. He wanted to throw up, but couldn't. The sensation of evil was overpowering.

Just as they were upon him, a great dark shadow loomed suddenly before him. A black, brooding mountain rose straight out of the ground and seemed to touch the sky. He crouched and cried out in fear. His hair stood on end. Suddenly, a loud crack filled the air like a clap of thunder and shook the ground. Slowly, the mountain began to split and crumble, and huge boulders dislodged themselves and hurtled gracefully toward him in slow motion. Then the entire mountain buckled and collapsed, burying him in the rubble. He felt his flesh being torn from his body. The crows circled and on each he saw the evil, grinning face of death. Then all was darkness and there was no one to hear him scream.

Schweizer was sitting up in bed. His eyes were wide with terror and his whole body shook uncontrollably. The urge to hide or flee to the ends of the earth was overpowering. Slowly, the fantasy of the dream faded into the reality of his bedroom. Carole sat up and turned on the light. "It was the dream again, wasn't it?" she asked softly.

"Yeah," he replied with a heavy sigh as his shoulders slumped forward. Schweizer felt very weary and used up. Carole slipped her arms around him and held him close to her and rocked him gently. Tears had appeared in the corners of her eyes and were beginning to course down her cheeks. They sat there for several minutes. Neither spoke.

Finally, Schweizer swung his feet over the edge of the bed and picked his robe up off the chair. "I've got to get something to relax me," he announced.

"Why don't you lie down, Karl?" Carole suggested. "I'll get you something from the medicine chest"

"What I need, *Schatz*, isn't found in a medicine chest" he said as he headed for the den. Carole's voice rose as fast as she did from the bed. "Honey, you know the doctor said you should cut out the drinking ..."

"What the hell does he know about anything?"

"At least he ...," she called after him, but he was gone. "Oh, why do I even bother!" she said to herself in disgust.

The emotions Schweizer experienced after each occurrence of the nightmare were a little fear, and a great deal of anger. The problem was that he didn't know what he was afraid of or where to direct his anger. So he drank. Alcohol was not a problem, yet, but he knew that it could become one. He wasn't sure that he really cared.

Schweizer was almost at the bottom of the stairs when something caught his attention. He stopped and strained to hear. Several seconds passed. He heard it again. Ever so quietly, he crept to the bottom of the stairs. The sound was coming from the living room. Schweizer slowed his breathing. It was so quiet, he could hear his heart beating.

From the living room came what sounded like a long sigh whispering and a smacking noise. Schweizer gripped the door frame and peered around into the darkness. As he shifted his body weight his robe rustled softly. He was sure anyone within a hundred feet could hear him moving.

On the sofa was a dark shape. No, two dark shapes. One was his seventeen-year-old daughter, Carolyn. *It must be one o'clock in the morning,* Schweizer thought. It was too late to be up on a school night and it particularly bothered him that her boyfriend was with her. He could hear them whispering, but couldn't understand the words.

"C'mon, Carolyn, you love me, don't you?"

"Oh, Rick, you know I do," she said pleadingly, "but I can't."

"Sure you can, if you love me."

Schweizer could see they were kissing and his mouth twisted into a frown. As a father, he felt he should break it up, but the memory of his college days and the times he had groped around in the dark with Carole caused the frown to disappear. As he turned to go, Schweizer heard a sudden, sharp intake of breath and then a low moan. He stood transfixed in the doorway, neither able to enter or to leave.

"You do love me, don't you, Rick?" whispered Carolyn.

"You know I do, Babe," he answered.

Schweizer heard more whispering, then the rustling of clothing as they both changed positions. Then he heard a sharp intake of breath again. Schweizer realized now it had gone beyond simple hugging and kissing. He flipped on the light.

The first thing he saw was Carolyn's startled face over Rick's shoulder. Rick jumped to his feet and Carolyn began to hastily button her blouse. At first, Schweizer was stunned, but then he was furious.

"You lousy creep!" Schweizer yelled as he strode toward them. "I'm going to break your goddamned neck!"

Carolyn jumped between Rick and her father. "No, Daddy, don't!"

Rick, his face white from shock, jumped behind the sofa. Schweizer slowly advanced toward him, his face an angry red.

"I don't want any trouble, now," said Rick as his eyes darted around the room looking for any route of escape.

"Well, that's exactly what you're going to get," was the reply.

"What's going on here?" demanded Carole. She had heard the

shouting and had come downstairs to investigate. She stood in the doorway and surveyed the entire scene.

"Look at your daughter!" cried Schweizer. "Look at her! This creep was ... was ..." He couldn't make himself say it.

Carole saw that Carolyn was still buttoning up her blouse. She was more disappointed than outraged.

"Don't get excited," said Carole. "We can discuss this calmly."

"Don't get excited?" he shot back. "What the hell kind of a mother are you?"

With Schweizer's attention diverted, Rick began edging toward the door.

"Hold it right there, creep, I'm not through with you yet!"

Rick looked pleadingly at Carole. "Mrs. Schweizer, please ..."

"Why don't we talk about this in the morning," offered Carole, "after everyone has had a chance to cool down."

Schweizer was incredulous. "Can't you ... don't you ..." he sputtered. "Oh, to hell with it! You know all the answers!"

Schweizer spun on his heel and left the room.

Carole nodded to Rick and said quietly, "I think you had better go home now."

He didn't need to be asked twice.

In the den, Schweizer went straight to the liquor cabinet. Behind the louvered doors was a miniature fridge where he kept ice cubes, six-ounce cans of orange juice, and other mixers. He was in no mood for a mixed drink, so he just dropped two ice cubes into a glass and poured three fingers of Canadian Club over them. As he slowly swished the liquor and ice around in the glass, he tried to think about what a mess his life had become lately, but his mind was just a jumble of random thoughts.

The den was his favorite place. The oak-paneled walls gave him a sense of warmth and security. It was real oak, none of that cheap stuff. One wall was lined with books, another had a fireplace, and the other two had leaded glass windows with stained glass around their outer edges. In front of one window was a small desk and chair, and in the center of the room, facing the fireplace, was a leather upholstered sofa. The den was a kind of trophy room, too. Above the fireplace was a 16 x 20 family portrait and on the other walls were plaques and pictures he had accumulated over the years.

Schweizer's favorite picture was of him and his airplane, a 1970 Piper Cherokee Arrow, white with blue and gold trim. He had even gotten the FAA to give him a special registration number: N425KC. The four-two-five stood for his wedding anniversary, April 25th, and the KC stood for Karl and Carole.

The Schweizers lived in Mariemont, an exclusive neighborhood, but close to the Lunken Airport. Some nights, when he really wanted to be alone, Schweizer would take the Arrow up and cruise around for anywhere from a few minutes to a couple of hours.

Just then Carole came into the room. "I think we had better have a talk, Karl."

Schweizer said nothing, but walked over to the window and stood with his back to her. He found it annoying that she had violated the privacy of his den. She knew he came here when he wanted to be alone. But Carole was not put off by his silence, because she had seen this little act before.

"Something has to be done if we're to have any peace in this family," she said. "You're making nervous wrecks out of both Carolyn and me with your moods and fits of temper."

Of course she was right. Schweizer had undergone a radical personality change in the past year. For some reason he had begun to shout when he didn't have his way and to nitpick at everything Carole did. If she didn't say something just right, Schweizer would play dumb as if he didn't understand what she meant. Carole couldn't begin to count the times she had said, "You know what I mean." She knew it had something to do with the nightmare, because each time he had it he would become a little meaner, a little more coarse in his behavior.

Schweizer's thoughts returned to his daughter and the scene he had witnessed in the living room, and his temperature began to rise. *He had a right to be angry,* he thought. What was so unusual about wanting to punch out some punk kid he had caught screwing his daughter? Carole understood Schweizer's anger, but she was worried that he might eventually become violent. Schweizer wanted to say something, but didn't. He just took another drink and began studying the blue spruce that grew at the corner of their Tudor-style house.

"You're not going to find any answers at the bottom of a whiskey bottle!" said his wife angrily.

Schweizer was rapidly losing control. "Aw, shove it up your ass, Carole!"

The retort stunned her. It was totally out of character for Schweizer to use such crude language. "No one's going to talk to me like that!" Carole shouted as she took one step and slapped the half-empty glass from his hand.

Schweizer's reaction was sudden and decisive. He struck her full on the mouth with the back of his left hand, knocking her backwards over the arm of the sofa. Carole collapsed in a heap on the floor and broke into sobs. Blood was running from both her nose and her mouth.

"Mother!" cried Carolyn as she rushed into the room.

Carolyn sat on the floor and cradled her mother in her arms. They just rocked back and forth and cried. The horror of what he had done hit Schweizer with full force and he felt a deep sense of loss for the sweet relationship he had always shared with his wife. In all the years they had been married, he had never laid a hand on her in anger.

"I've had all I can take, Karl," said Carole between sobs. "There's nothing I can do for you anymore. If you don't get help, and I mean professional help, then I'm leaving and I won't look back."

Schweizer said nothing, but just looked at the floor. He had been unwilling to face his problem squarely, but now he was being forced to make a decision. He turned and headed for the liquor cabinet for a refill. He'd think about it tomorrow.

Dr. Hendriks had been listening very intently. He sat tapping his left thumb with his pencil as he contemplated the story Schweizer had just related.

"Tell me something, Mr. Schweizer," said Hendriks. "Has this anti-social behavior been apparent in your other relationships?"

"What do you mean?"

"Have other people noticed this change in your personality? Do you have trouble getting along with people you work with?"

"Yeah, they think I'm a real sonofabitch around there."

"Hmmm. By the way, just what do you do, anyway?"

"I'm the financial vice-president of Amalgamated Department Stores."

Hendriks was impressed. Amalgamated was one of the largest chains in the country, with home offices located in Cincinnati.

"And before that?"

"Well, I started out as a junior accountant. Then when the big computers came out I was a programmer. After that I was programming manager, then data processing manager, and now this. I've been with Amalgamated for twenty-one years."

"I'm more convinced than ever that you never received any brain damage, Mr. Schweizer. Someone with severe brain damage could never possess the skills necessary to function in a data processing environment. I suspect your problem lies in the past you have been suppressing for all these years. I think you should have that neurological exam, because once you are convinced that your memory is there, it will be much easier to dig it out."

"Perhaps you're right," said Schweizer. He wasn't going to commit himself to anything just yet.

Hendriks looked at his watch and frowned. "Oh, dear," he said, "looks like I ran over again." He quickly wrote in his note pad. "This is the name and address of Dr. Craig Richards. Give him a call and then come back and see me."

"Maybe I will," said Schweizer.

When he got back to his office, Schweizer sat for a long time staring at the piece of paper that Dr. Hendriks had given him. Schweizer used to wonder about his past. Now he wasn't sure he wanted to know about it at all. Maybe he was afraid of it. Then he thought of Carole and Carolyn, and all the happy times over the years. He knew it was time to bite the bullet. He picked up the phone and began to dial the number on the sheet of paper.

7

The neurological exam wasn't at all what Schweizer had imagined. Actually, he wasn't quite sure just what he had expected. He had entertained some vague idea of exotic machines with a multitude of wires attached to various parts of his body, and when they didn't materialize he felt somehow cheated. When Schweizer had his last physical in November, a medical assistant did all the tests and the doctor only talked to him for about three minutes. Dr. Craig Richards was handling the neurological exam himself.

"Now I want you to stand up and close your eyes," said Dr. Richards. "Okay, now put your arms straight out to the side and balance on your right foot."

"Is this a physical, or am I trying out for the Olympics?" asked Schweizer.

"Everything has its purpose, Mr. Schweizer," said the doctor with a smile. Schweizer had a smart remark for just about everything, but Dr. Richards was not one to be intimidated. His "bedside manner" was at its best. "Okay, now balance on your left foot. Very good. You can put your foot down now."

Schweizer opened his eyes and looked at the doctor. "Is this going to take much longer?" he asked.

Dr. Richards was writing notes on a form. "We're almost through," he said without looking up. As the doctor continued to write, Schweizer noted how youthful Craig Richards was in appearance. Schweizer figured he must be at least 30, but he didn't look much over 25. He had the trim look of an athlete, with dark wavy hair. Probably a big man with the student nurses.

"This time I want you to put your arms out just like last time," said the doctor as he put down his pencil, "but now I want you to point your index fingers. Okay, close your eyes and in one smooth motion touch your fingertips together. Very good." The doctor began to write again. "Go ahead and strip down to your shorts."

The doctor gave Schweizer a quick examination of all his vital signs, pausing several times to write on the chart. Then he spent what Schweizer considered an unusually long time checking Schweizer's eyes. "What's so important about the eyes?" asked Schweizer.

"You've probably heard the saying, 'the eyes are the windows of the soul.' Well, the eyes are also the windows of the brain. You'd be surprised how much the eyes can tell us about your general health."

"Is that so?"

"Mm-hmm. Okay, lie down on the table and close your eyes. I'm going to rub the bottoms of your feet with a cotton ball and a pin. You tell me which is which."

"All right," said Schweizer.

The doctor alternated from one foot to the other, mixing up the sequence of cotton ball and pin. Schweizer chose the right one every time. "You can sit up now, "said Dr. Richards, who then sat down and wrote a few more notes. "How did you get the scar on your side?" he asked when he finished writing.

Schweizer looked down at the ugly scar tissue on his right rib cage. Whenever he thought about it, he felt a burning sensation, a sort of phantom pain.

"I really don't know, doctor," he said. "I've just always had it."

The doctor had a thoughtful look on his face. Dr. Hendriks hadn't told him of Schweizer's amnesia.

"You can get dressed now," he said, as he began to write more notes.

"Is that it?" asked Schweizer. "Aren't you going to hook me up to a machine or something?"

"Nope," the doctor said. "No need to."

"How come?"

Dr. Richards put down his pencil and looked Schweizer squarely in the eye. "Neurologically speaking, Mr. Schweizer, you're in perfect health."

Schweizer felt somehow empty. He had always had a comfortable feeling about his past, a feeling of resignation. Now he felt as though he had been stripped naked in the middle of a crowded room. Someone had put the key into the long-neglected door to his past, and the thought of what might lie on the other side filled Schweizer with panic.

"You must be mistaken," Schweizer said weakly.

"I'm afraid not, Mr. Schweizer. You could stand to lose fifteen pounds, but otherwise you're in perfect health."

"But they told me I had brain damage," Schweizer protested.

"Not a chance," said Dr. Richards firmly. "There's nothing wrong with your brain, Mr. Schweizer. As far as your mind is concerned ... well, that's between you and Dr. Hendriks."

Schweizer sat staring at the floor, his hands gripping the edge of the examining table. A quote he heard Paul Harvey use on the radio kept running through his mind: "There's no use worrying. Nothing's going to turn out right anyway."

8

Schweizer was doing his best to appear unconcerned as Dr. Hendriks read through the neurological report. He might have succeeded, if he hadn't kept shifting around in his chair. It wasn't a very comfortable chair, though, and Schweizer was hoping that his discomfort wouldn't be misinterpreted.

The report was only two pages and Schweizer noticed that Dr. Hendriks was reading through it for the third time.

"Uh, say, Doc, how many times are you going to read that thing?" asked Schweizer, irritated. The question had caught Hendriks off guard and he appeared to be genuinely surprised as he looked up.

"What do you mean?"

"I mean, don't you think you should have read that before I got here? After all, it's only two pages."

Hendriks was blushing and felt angry with himself that he was showing his own feelings. "Surely you don't think you're my only patient, do you?"

Schweizer frowned and looked away. He instinctively knew that he couldn't win an argument with Dr. Hendriks.

"Well, what does it say?" he asked.

Hendriks had already regained his composure. "I think you know what it says."

"Hey, if I knew what it said, I wouldn't be here," said Schweizer angrily. The lie wasn't very convincing.

Dr. Hendriks sat with his fingertips joined in the form of a triangle. The triangle rested against his lips as he peered intently at Schweizer.

"Frankly, Mr. Schweizer," he said, choosing his words carefully, "I'm really not sure why you *are* here. You seem to be afraid to regain your memory. In fact, you seem to be actively resisting it."

His eyes downcast, Schweizer slumped in his chair. "I guess you're right," said Schweizer, his voice subdued. "I *am* afraid of the past. I've had a very orderly existence until recently. I'm used to taking charge of my life, not having my life take charge of me."

"Can't you see, Mr. Schweizer, that this is how you can take charge of your life again?"

"How so?"

"When you find your past and confront it, you can take charge and control your life, rather than let the unknown control you through your subconscious."

"Do you really think so?"

"Of course!" Dr. Hendriks paused to let it sink in. "I'm reminded of a line from the old Pogo comic strip . 'We have met the enemy and he is us.'"

"So you're saying I'm my own worst enemy."

"In this case, yes."

"Well, Dr. Hendriks, what do you suggest I do?"

"All right, let's start at the very beginning. What's the earliest thing you can remember?"

"That would be the hospital in Augsburg."

"Go on."

"Everything is pretty vague. I don't know how long I was there. I had been in a coma for some time. It's all so disjointed."

"Just relax and close your eyes. Try to form a mental picture of what you remember, then tell me what you see."

Schweizer closed his eyes. Slowly, the images began to form, the images of that spring of 1945.

Berndt always found hospitals depressing. They reminded him that human life is frail, which caused him to think of his own eventual demise. He had been raised a Catholic, but the dozen years he had served in the *Gestapo* had left him devoid of any religion. He was content to take life as it came, but somewhere in the back of his mind he had doubts. *What if,* he would wonder, *what if? Maybe there really was a hereafter.*

The comatose patient lying on the hospital bed made him uneasy, too. The name on the chart said, "Karl Schweizer," but it could have been anybody. Schweizer's head was swathed in bandages. Only his right eye, nose and mouth were showing.

Why did I have to answer that damn phone? thought Berndt. *Maybe if I hadn't someone else would be here instead of me.* Berndt looked at his watch. It was almost four o'clock. Dinner would be brought in soon. At least the food was good. He couldn't say the same for his chair. In three weeks he had become intimately acquainted with this chair. Berndt had tried every position known to man, but it was impossible to sit in it comfortably.

Just then, the door opened with a bump. It was *Fräulein* Hildegard Forster pushing a cart with the dinner trays on it.

"And how is the patient today, *Herr* Berndt?" she asked cheerily.

"He died ..."

"What!"

"... of sheer boredom."

"Oh, you're just joking," she said with a slight giggle.

"Oh, you mean him," said Berndt, feigning surprise. "I thought you were asking about me."

Berndt pulled a cigarette from his shirt pocket and began tapping it against the back of his hand to pack the tobacco down. He wondered how, in spite of the war, they still managed to get American cigarettes. *Probably taken off prisoners*, he thought.

"Now, *Herr* Berndt," said *Fräulein* Forster in her motherly voice, "you know you can't smoke in the hospital."

Berndt stopped tapping the cigarette and gave the nurse a menacing look. Her mouth opened, but no words formed. Berndt's eyes locked with hers as he put the cigarette between his lips. The nurse looked away nervously.

"Well, that's what the rules say," she said weakly, before she turned and fled through the open door.

Berndt struck a match and held it to the end of the cigarette. He inhaled deeply and blew a cloud of smoke toward the ceiling. Only then did he allow himself a faint smile. *It never hurts to remind them who makes the rules in this country*, he thought.

The cigarette had a stale taste and Berndt put it out after only a few puffs. He pulled the package out of his pocket and looked at it. Berndt preferred American cigarettes, and the wrapper said "Lucky Strike." He decided they were either someone's pre-war stock or black market counterfeits. In either case, they just didn't cut it as far as he was concerned.

A feeling of uneasiness came over Berndt. Perhaps he had been too brusque with the nurse. He tried to think of home and how things had been before the war. Somehow, he just couldn't make the uneasiness go away. It was as if something were cueing his subconscious. Slowly, he turned his head to look at Schweizer. Amongst the bandages an eye was staring at Berndt. Schweizer was looking back.

"You shouldn't have been so rude to her," said Schweizer.

Berndt jumped to his feet, startled by the voice, and rushed from the room. He found a phone and hurriedly dialed the number he had written on a book of matches.

"Hello, Koerbler?" he said. "He's awake ... yes, that's right. Get over here as fast as you can." Berndt hung up and hurried back to the room.

In the room Schweizer was moving about as if trying to get up. Berndt pulled a chair up to the bed and turned it around and sat on it backwards, his arms resting on the back of the chair.

"How are you feeling, Schweizer?" he asked. Schweizer just looked at Berndt blankly and said nothing. Berndt tried again. "Do you understand me?"

"Yes, I understand you."

"Good! Now then, what happened to it?"

"Where am I?"

"You're in a hospital. Now what about the shipment you picked up at Dachau on March 17th?"

"What happened? How did I get here?"

Berndt was beginning to get impatient. "Listen, Schweizer ..."

"Schweizer?"

"Yes, that's your name isn't it?"

"I ... I don't know."

"Don't play stupid with me, Schweizer. This isn't Berlin and we're not in the *Gestapo* cellar, but I can be just as tough."

Berndt could hear a lot of commotion in the hallway. *It must be Koerbler*, he thought.

"Did you say *Gestapo?*"

The door opened, but Berndt did not turn around.

"Yes, *Gestapo*, Schweizer, and you know we always find out what we want to know."

"Excuse me, gentlemen," said a voice in English.

Berndt jumped to his feet and spun around. In the doorway was an American army captain, holding a .45 automatic. Instinctively, Berndt went for the pistol he always carried in his coat. It was a foolish gesture. Before Berndt could get his weapon out, the American captain raised his gun and fired.

The explosion was deafening in the enclosed room. The heavy slug shattered Berndt's right wrist before entering his chest, causing him to drop his pistol to the floor. The force of the bullet slammed him against the wall. Berndt's mouth hung open and his eyes were wide with surprise as he looked down at the blood flowing from the hole in his chest. A feeling of drunkenness came over him and all the strength went out of his knees. Slowly, he slumped to the floor. Then there was only blackness.

"Stupid bastard," said Captain Chamberlain as he walked over to where Berndt lay. He reached down and felt for Berndt's pulse. "Hey, Murphy!" he called out into the hall. "Get a doctor in here. This *kraut's* still alive."

In a few moments, a corporal appeared at the door with a doctor. He also had Koerbler. "Captain, here s another one."

Koerbler pushed his way into the room. "You shot him?" he said in English.

"You speak English?" asked Chamberlain.

"You shot him? Why?" demanded Koerbler.

"He left me no choice, pardner," said Chamberlain. "He went for his gun. Do you know him?"

"He is my associate."

Chamberlain turned his attention to Schweizer. Pointing at Koerbler he asked, "Do you know this guy?" Schweizer didn't respond.

"I don't think he speaks English," said Koerbler.

"Yeah, maybe so," said Chamberlain. "You guys *Gestapo*, huh?" Koerbler did not answer. "What are you doing here?" Still no answer. "Maybe the guy on the bed knows what's going on. Hey, Murphy! Go get the interpreter."

"Sure thing, Captain," replied Murphy.

Chamberlain looked back at Schweizer. He had lapsed into unconsciousness.

"Do you remember the names of any of these men?" asked Hendriks.

Schweizer appeared to be deep in thought. "No" he said, "I don't remember any names, but I have the impression they were government agents, maybe *Gestapo*."

"Why do you suppose they were questioning a hospital patient?"

"I have no idea."

"Had you committed a crime?"

Schweizer shrugged. "Almost anything was a crime back then."

"Yes, but don't you find it unusual that they were waiting in your room, waiting for you to wake up?"

"Perhaps."

"What I'm getting at," said Hendriks, "is that maybe these men could tell you something significant about your past, something that might cue your memory."

Schweizer laughed derisively. "Right! May I use your phone? I'll call them right now."

Dr. Hendriks had a patient, fatherly look on his face.

"Mr. Schweizer," he said evenly, "I studied in Germany for one year as an undergraduate. It's pretty hard to get lost in that country. Everyone is required to register with the police when they move into a town or move out. I shouldn't think it would be too difficult to find these men, if they are still alive."

"I don't even know their names," said Schweizer.

"Um-mm, that is a problem," said Hendriks. "I'll have to give that some thought. Well, anyway, what else do you remember from the hospital?"

"Not much. Just that it became a prison facility. The medical personnel remained, but several American sentries were posted. Sometime in June, I don't remember when, I was transferred to a prisoner-of-war camp."

"Oh? Where was that?"

"Fürstenfeldbruck. It's somewhere between Augsburg and Munich."

"Can you remember anything about the camp?"

"Sure," said Schweizer. "It was a hell of a place." Schweizer had a far-away look in his eyes. "It was just a lot of tents with a barbed wire fence around it. The guards were combat veterans, and, man, how they hated us. At first we lived out in the open. They took everything we had and left us with just a spoon. No food or water for nearly a week. We used the spoons to catch raindrops. After awhile we were loaded into trucks and shipped to a camp at Heilbronn. *SS* were kept separate from the *Wehrmacht* soldiers. Then the interrogations began."

"How long were you there?"

A smile crept across Schweizer's face. "Not very long," he said. "I escaped."

"Tell me about it," said Hendriks.

The images in Schweizer's mind were very vivid. As he thought back to those days, a feeling of contentment came over him.

Schweizer didn't look much like an *SS* officer when he was discharged from the hospital. His uniform had been scrounged up from someplace. It had no hat or rank insignia, and it didn't fit too well. Attached to his jacket pocket with a piece of wire was a shipping tag with his name, rank, and the letters "*SS.*"

After his short stay at Fürstenfeldbruck he was picked up by an Army 6x6 truck and driven to his new home at Heilbronn. The others in the truck wouldn't speak to him. It was rumored that the *SS* were being singled out for harsh treatment, and no one wanted to risk guilt by association.

It was almost noon when the truck arrived at the compound. Schweizer could see some of the prisoners lining up for lunch. They were a shabby looking lot, and one was left to wonder how an army of men such as these had conquered most of Europe.

Inside the compound, Schweizer and the others jumped down from the truck and fell in in a loose formation. An MP went down the row checking off each man's shipping tag against a list he was carrying on a clipboard. When he was finished, he turned to a frail-looking individual and said, "Okay, Max, give 'em the lowdown in their own lingo."

The interpreter stepped forward and looked the men over. *"Deutsche Soldaten, ich heisse Max Frohm,"* he began. "There are only a few rules here. First, the war is over, so there is no need to escape. We are processing prisoners daily to be sent home. However, if you attempt to escape, you will be dealt with severely. Second, all prisoners are required to work. That includes work outside the compound as well as inside." The interpreter proceeded to outline work rules and schedules. Schweizer didn't listen very carefully. His attention was on the mess tent and the hunger that was gnawing at his gut.

Finally, the lecture was over and the new arrivals began to mingle with the other *SS* prisoners. Most of them had a sullen look about them as they looked Schweizer over. One of the men stepped forward and extended his hand. "Pay the *Amis* no mind," he said. "I am Manfred von Mauthausen, the senior officer. Are you an officer or enlisted?"

"*Untersturmführer* Karl Schweizer," was the reply.

"You will, of course, excuse me if I don't welcome you," said Mauthausen, indicating the camp with a sweeping gesture, "but this isn't the sort of place one welcomes a compatriot to."

Schweizer nodded in agreement. It wasn't first class accommodations, but at least there was fresh air and sunshine. He would make do. Just then a truck pulled up and the prisoners began to line up.

"It looks like our turn to eat," said Mauthausen. "Reichert here will show you where to stow your gear, then come join us."

Schweizer looked down at his "gear", a barracks bag containing another makeshift uniform, one change of underwear, two pairs of socks and a spoon. It wasn't much, but for all he knew, it was everything he had in the world.

At the mess truck, Schweizer got his ration of food, a thin soup, and joined the others sitting on the ground to eat. He didn't feel much like talking and apparently neither did the others, but he knew they were all looking at him. One of the men handed out the bread. One large portion was given to each group and it was meticulously divided so that each man got an equal share. The man who cut up the bread got the last piece.

"Where is your home?" asked Mauthausen. It was obvious that he was probing for something, but Schweizer wasn't sure what. In any case, he felt embarrassed by the question, because he didn't know the answer.

"Is it so important?" responded Schweizer. Thrust, parry. Two could play that game.

"Not really," said Mauthausen. "I taught linguistics at Freiburg before the war and I can't place your accent."

Siegfried Buehner joined in the game. "What unit did you serve with?" he asked.

Schweizer set his spoon down and looked at the others. Everyone had stopped eating and was staring at him. The air was heavy with hostility, but Schweizer ignored it. He picked up his spoon and resumed eating." Why are you asking all these questions?" he asked.

"Why are you avoiding the answers?" parried Mauthausen.

Schweizer continued chewing for several moments while he collected his thoughts. "Because I don't know the answers," he finally said. "I have no memory."

"You what?" exclaimed the man opposite Schweizer.

"That's a good one," called out another man from the end of the table. "I think I'll use that story myself." Everybody laughed.

Suddenly, Schweizer felt overwhelmed by his emotions. Tears were forming in his eyes as he stood up.

"All right!" he said, pointing to the bandages that still covered part of his head. "You see this? The doctors had to rebuild my skull. I was buried under tons of rubble and I was in a coma for six weeks. They say I will never remember anything. Do you hear? Not anything! So you can take your questions ..." Schweizer stopped in mid-sentence. Someone had taken hold of his arm, Schweizer turned to see who it was.

"I'm Friedrich Kalt," the man said. "I am sure I speak for everyone when I say, please forgive us for being so harsh. The Americans have not treated us well, and we would not be surprised to find them trying to plant a spy among us. So we are sorry for being so hard on you."

"Yes, that's right," someone said. Several others murmured their agreement.

Schweizer sat down and resumed eating. He didn't look up again until he had finished.

As Karl was walking toward the garbage canst he was joined by Friedrich Kalt. "It is most unfortunate about your injuries," said Kalt. "Will you ever regain your memory?"

"The doctor said there was a slight chance, but not to get my hopes up," said Schweizer.

"I see," said Kalt. "You know, from the moment you arrived I have had the feeling that we have met somewhere before. Is that possible?"

"I suppose anything is possible," said Schweizer. "But, no, you don't look familiar to me at all."

"Perhaps I'm mistaken," said Kalt. "Maybe when your bandages are completely removed and I can get a better look."

"Maybe," said Schweizer. "Maybe not."

"Where did you come from?"

"What do you mean?"

"I mean, were you in another camp?"

"I was in a hospital."

"How did you get here? Did you come directly from hospital?"

"I was at Fürstenfeldbruck."

"There's a camp there?"

"I wouldn't call it a camp. If this is hell, I wouldn't know what to call that. There was no wire. They just surrounded us with tanks. No buildings. No tents. We were just out in the open. At night they kept the lights of the tanks on. Smoking was not allowed. One night someone tried to light a cigarette and the guards opened fire. Two or three men were hit. I don't know who I hated worse, the guards or the man who lit the match."

"It isn't much better here." Kalt put his hand on Schweizer's arm as if to restrain him. Schweizer turned and looked at Kalt. "What are your future plans?" Kalt continued.

Schweizer looked at the ground and kicked a few loose rocks around. "I don't know," he said slowly.

"Just get out of here, I guess, and try to put my life back together."

"That may not be as soon as you think," said Kalt.

"Why not?" asked Schweizer.

"Prisoners are being sent to France and England, and are being used as laborers to rebuild the cities," said Kalt.

"Perhaps that's as it should be."

A look of irritation spread across Kalt's face. "No, no," he said. "You don't understand. Who's going to rebuild *our* cities? How long will it take to rebuild theirs? We could be forced to work for years! And those are just the *Wehrmacht* soldiers. Besides, it's against the Geneva Convention."

"Well, we're here," said Schweizer, "and they have the guns. If they say work, I suppose we will have to work."

Schweizer turned away and started walking back to the SS tents. Kalt decided to get in a parting shot. "You won't do much work if you're dead," he said.

Schweizer turned and faced Kalt. "What do you mean, dead?"

"You see how they treat us, don't you?" asked Kalt.

Schweizer half laughed and shook his head. "I don't think being last in line for meals is much to worry about."

"That's not the point," said Kalt. "Haven't you heard the talk about war crimes trials?"

"No," said Schweizer. "Have you committed any?"

Kalt's face turned red.

"That's not for me to say, Schweizer. *They* will decide what is a war crime, whom to try, and what the punishment shall be. They are already after the SS. Do you want a rope around your neck?"

The thought of a rope around his neck gave Schweizer a vague feeling of uneasiness. "No, of course not," he said.

"The question now," said Kalt, "is, have *you* committed any war crimes?"

"I really wouldn't know," said Schweizer nervously. I don't remember."

"Ah, that's my point exactly," said Kalt, pounding his right fist into his left hand. "The only safe place to be is anywhere our captors are not."

"You mean escape," said Schweizer.

"Precisely."

"How are you going to do it?" asked Schweizer.

"Do you want to come along?" countered Kalt.

"I don't know. I'll have to think about it."

"I tell you what, Schweizer. Meet me after supper and we will talk."

"All right," said Schweizer.

"Until then, think about what I have said and consider your options." Kalt walked away feeling very confident. There *were* no options.

After supper Kalt sought out Schweizer again.

"So, what do you think, Schweizer? Do you want to stay? Or take your chances with me?"

"How far would we get like this?" asked Schweizer. "These uniforms are the only clothing we have. We will be picked up immediately, or worse, shot. I hear we aren't even being called prisoners of war, but disarmed enemy forces, so they can ignore the Geneva Convention. The Americans are still at war with us even though the war is over."

"For every guard there are thousands of prisoners and more arriving every day. They can't watch us all, all of the time. I have made contact with people, people who can get us civilian clothing. This is not a real camp. No barracks. Just some barbed wire." Kalt paused a few moments for emphasis. "Schweizer, if we stay we will die."

"I will have to think about it."

"Don't think too long. I'm leaving in a few days."

It didn't require much thought for Schweizer to make a decision, and a few days later Kalt and Schweizer were strolling over a mountain pass into Switzerland.

Dr. Hendriks had become so involved in listening to Schweizer's tale, he had stopped taking notes. Schweizer paused and leaned back in his chair, a troubled look on his face. Several moments passed in silence. The only sound was the two men breathing and the quiet whirr of the tape recorder.

"Is this difficult to talk about?" asked Hendriks.

Schweizer looked up and the troubled look fell away.

"No, he said. I was Just wondering how my life would have been had I not gone with him."

"Where did you go?" asked Hendriks.

"We went to Switzerland," said Schweizer. "Getting away was so easy, I don't know why more didn't do it."

"Then what happened?" asked Hendriks.

"Kalt had friends in Switzerland," said Schweizer. "He helped me get a job in a hotel, but it was nothing. After four years I was sick of it."

Dr. Hendriks looked at his watch. "Our time is up," he said "but I feel we shouldn't stop. Can you stay a few minutes longer?"

"I suppose so," said Schweizer as he stood up and stretched. "Are you going to charge me time and a half for overtime?"

"No," said Hendriks, laughing. "Just a minute while I put a fresh tape in the machine."

Schweizer walked over to the window and looked out. In the distance he could see the trees of Ault Park. The memory of the romps he had had with Carolyn as she was growing up gave him a very mellow feeling.

Meanwhile, Hendriks reloaded the recorder and returned to his seat. Looking at his notes he said, "Okay, it's four years later and you are sick of your job. Then what?"

Schweizer didn't answer at first. He had a faraway look in his eyes. Finally, he returned to his chair. "I applied for admission to the University of Cincinnati, got a student visa and came to America," he said.

"Why Cincinnati?"

"Why not? I heard it was a good school and that there was a German community here."

"Sounds reasonable," said Hendriks.

"When I was a senior, I met my wife. She was a freshman. Two years later we got married. Then I became a permanent resident, and became a citizen."

Dr. Hendriks sat tapping his pencil against his forehead. "I would like to recommend a course of action, Mr. Schweizer. It just might be the solution to your problem."

"What's that?"

"What you should have done thirty-four years ago. Confront your past."

"How do I do that?"

"Find those men from the hospital. Find any family you might have in Germany. I'm surprised you didn't think of this yourself."

Schweizer had a look of dismay. "Do you have any idea how much that could cost?" he asked.

"How much is your marriage worth?" countered Hendriks.

"Good point," said Schweizer. "But I don't even know where to begin. Any suggestions on finding those agents?"

"You were taken prisoner by the Army. Obviously, so were they. They may have even been in the same camp as you."

"Could have been. There were tens of thousands of prisoners at Heilbronn."

"Exactly. Contact the Army. There must be a record somewhere."

"And if I find them ...?"

"No one can predict what will happen. Find out everything you can. If your memory returns, great! If not ... well, at least you tried. Anything positive you do will help. Remember that." Hendriks looked at his watch again. "Now, if you will excuse me, I have another patient. Let me know what you decide to do."

The two men stood and shook hands.

"Doctor" said Schweizer, "it's been a long time since I felt this good about myself. I know I'll succeed."

"I'm sure you will, Karl," said Hendriks as he led Schweizer to the door. "Good luck."

Schweizer had a definite bounce in his step as he returned to his car. The ever-present knot in his stomach was beginning to loosen.

9

Schweizer sat leaning over his desk, his left hand resting against his forehead like an eyeshade. The only sound was the gentle tapping of his mechanical pencil on the notepad that lay in front of him.

He had felt so relaxed and at peace with himself when he had left Dr. Hendriks, but now he felt the same old tension and irritability. The pad on his desk was for writing down a plan of action, but he had been staring at it for almost twenty minutes, unable to make a decision.

Schweizer thought of the ultimatum by his wife. He thought of the counsel he had received from Dr. Hendriks. Schweizer wanted to save his marriage, but he was afraid ... afraid of what dark secrets may lay hidden in his past. He found himself wishing that things were as they had once been.

The calendar on his desk lay open to Saturday, March 17th. Schweizer reached to flip the page to the correct date when a strange feeling came over him. He stared at the calendar for several moments before the feeling passed. It was almost an automatic reflex as Schweizer reached for the intercom switch.

"Miss Jensen?" he said.

"Yes Mr. Schweizer?"

"Would you get Mr. Thompson on the phone, please?"

"Right away, sir."

Schweizer leaned back in his chair and gazed out the Window. A few blocks south was the Carew Tower, the tallest building in Cincinnati. It wasn't the Empire State Building, but it would do for a town this size. A little farther on was Riverfront Stadium. Schweizer wondered if the Reds were going to put it together this season. Losing Pete Rose had been quite a blow. Across the river he could see Newport, Kentucky, the location of porno theaters, hookers, and sleazy bars. Quite a contrast to Cincinnati.

Schweizer thought of how beautiful Cincinnati was in the early spring. He thought of his relationship with Thomas J. Thompson, the company president. Schweizer was the president's protégé. Each time Thompson had been promoted, Schweizer had moved up, too. It had long been taken for granted that Schweizer would eventually become president. At least it had been until recently. Schweizer then thought of all the things that were familiar or gave meaning to his life, and of how close he was to losing them.

"Mr. Schweizer," said Miss Jensen over the intercom, "Mr.

Thompson is on line two."

Schweizer picked up the phone, but hesitated for several seconds. Finally, he took a deep breath and punched the button with the flashing light.

"T.J.?"

"Yes, Karl! How are you?"

"Fine, thanks."

"Great! Glad to hear it!"

Schweizer's eyes rolled toward the ceiling. Thompson was really pouring it on. He was irrepressible. In all the years Schweizer had known him, Thompson had always been a glad-hander, always pressing the flesh, giving egos a boost, and knew all the latest jokes, some of which would make a sailor blush.

"T.J.?"

"Yes?"

"You know how you've been pressuring me to take a vacation?"

"Well, I wouldn't exactly ..."

"Oh, come on, T.J., don't patronize me."

"I'm sorry, Karl," said Thompson. "You need someone to listen and here I'm playing the politician."

"I've been to see a doctor and he wants me to get away for awhile. I don't know what's been going on in my head. I don't like myself very much lately. I can't understand why my moods can change so suddenly. When I came back from the doctor I felt great, and now ... damn, I feel rotten."

"I wish I could say I understand," said Thompson. "But I *am* trying."

"I know that and I appreciate it," said Schweizer, subdued. "Anyway, I've decided to follow my doctor's advice."

"I'm glad to hear that, Karl. In a couple of weeks you'll be your old self again."

"I wish that were true," said Schweizer. "Actually I thought I might want to be gone a little bit longer."

"How long do you need?"

"Three to six months."

Thompson almost dropped the phone. "It's that bad huh?"

"Yes, T.J., it's that bad."

"Karl, I would not even consider a request like that from someone else. But you've been with us for more than twenty years and you've done a good job for us. I think we can help you out."

"You know I wouldn't even ask if it weren't necessary" said Schweizer.

"I know that, Karl. And don't worry about your paycheck. You'll

71

keep getting it every payday."

"You don't have to do that," Schweizer protested. "I've got savings."

"Consider it a sabbatical or an investment. Whatever. Don't worry about it!"

"Thanks, T.J."

"By the way, where are you going?"

"Nowhere right now," Schweizer answered. "I have to make some plans first."

"Well, keep in touch," said Thompson, "and don't worry about a thing."

"Thanks, T.J."

Schweizer hung up the phone and began filling his briefcase. He had a vague feeling that he would never see this office again.

10

It was just blind chance that Schweizer ran into Chris Denton, a former neighbor, while wandering through the stacks at the university library. Chris was a retired National Guard colonel, working on a course in medieval history. Schweizer was looking for clues on how to find the men who had interrogated him at the hospital.

"Today is your lucky day," said Chris, when Schweizer had finished telling his story. "All you have to do is contact the Department of the Army at the Pentagon. At the Center for Military History they can tell you which unit captured the town you were hospitalized in, who the officers were in the unit, and just about anything else you might want to know."

"How does that help me find the *Gestapo* agents?" Schweizer asked.

"You could check personnel for any of the officers in that unit who might still be serving. If they are retired, there's the military records center in St. Louis. Someone might remember those guys. They also have records of POW camps. And you might also want to visit the National Archives."

Schweizer thanked his friend and went home to pack. He still didn't have a plan of action, but at least now he knew where to start.

Schweizer taxied onto the runway and advanced the Cherokee's throttle to full power. At 75 knots he pulled back on the wheel, added a little trim, and in a few seconds the vibration of tires on pavement was replaced by the smoothness of flight. Schweizer was glad that his quest was finally underway. Flying had come naturally to him and he loved it.

The weather had deteriorated faster than had been forecast. Conditions had changed gradually at first from clear skies at Cincinnati to a few wispy clouds by the time Schweizer had reached the Clarksburg VOR. But then the sky changed abruptly to overcast. An invisible barrier created by the Appalachians was holding back the clouds.

Distant memories of the instruction he had received on weather flying at ground school floated into Schweizer's consciousness. It irritated him that he was now going to have to make an instrument landing. When he had been briefed at the flight service station before departure, he had been told it would be clearing before his estimated arrival time. Now he was only about fifty miles out and Washington was reporting 800 broken, 1500 overcast and 12 miles visibility in a steady rain.

Flying VFR on top created a deception of its own. Up here the sky was clear and blue, the sun was shining and the wind was only a gentle breeze. Below stretched an immense carpet of fluffy white clouds. Its beauty belied the fact that unseen danger lurked within: vertigo, wind shears and other turbulence, and hidden obstructions. Schweizer remembered something his instrument flight instructor had once said about weather flying: "It's better to be down here wishing you were up there, than to be up there wishing you were down here."

The blanket of whiteness below had a textured appearance. It looked so inviting. Schweizer thought of how it would be to lie down and pull a cloud over himself. It reminded him of a quilt his mother had tucked him in with when he was a little boy. His mother ... a sudden shiver shook his body. Schweizer had never before remembered anything from his forgotten past, and now two miles above the Virginia countryside his mind was flooded with the image of an attractive young woman with brown hair pulled back in a bun and gentle brown eyes, leaning over him and tucking a soft white quilt around his shoulders. She was wearing a blue dress with small white polka dots. It was only instinct, but he knew it was his mother. A great warmth surged through Schweizer and he smiled.

The image began to fade. Schweizer sought to cling to the memory and wrap himself within it. But as quickly as it came, it was gone, leaving Schweizer with a feeling of loneliness like he had never felt before.

The awareness of where he was allowed Schweizer to push the pain from his mind and concentrate on the task at hand. He opened his flight case and withdrew his book of approach plates. He quickly located the one for Washington National and, removing it from the binder, slipped it under the clip on the wheel. Schweizer had never flown into Washington before, so he would need to make a quick study of the approach plate during his descent. He throttled back to 19 inches of manifold pressure and trimmed the nose up enough to set up a glide of 750 feet per minute at 120 knots. It was a long way down. He had been cruising at 12,500 and the tops were reported at 4000 feet. Schweizer began to read the approach plate, trying to get a mental picture of the landing procedure.

"What the hell kind of approach is this?" he wondered out loud. "Radar vectors will be provided to the Potomac River." The approach plate for Washington National indicated that an instrument approach was to be made to the Potomac River and then to follow the river to the airport. It was not your usual landing pattern, but since aircraft were restricted from flying over the White House and it lay directly in the normal glide path, some bureaucrat in the FAA had devised this little piece of insanity.

The top of the overcast was approaching fast, so Schweizer thought he had better call up Washington National before entering the soup. He dialed in the prescribed frequency and then keyed his mike. "Washington National, Cherokee four-two-five-kilo-charlie with you on one-two-zero-point-niner."

"Aircraft calling Washington National, say again your call sign."

"This is Cherokee four-two-five-kilo-charlie about fifteen miles west. I'm transponder equipped and I'd like vectors to the ILS."

"Cherokee four-two-five-kilo-charlie, squawk two-five-seven-seven and ident." Schweizer dialed in the requested transponder code and pushed the green ident button. causing it to light up. "Cherokee four-two-five-kilo-charlie, radar contact, twelve miles west of the field and say your altitude."

"Four thousand eight hundred and descending."

"Cherokee four-two-five-kilo-eharlie, reduce your speed to ninety knots and maintain at or above two thousand feet. Turn to heading zero-seven-zero."

At that instant the Cherokee entered the overcast and the friendly skies turned into a road full of chuckholes. Schweizer turned off the auto pilot and focused his attention on the instruments. Flying was fun, but instrument landings were sometimes sweaty and always serious business. It was only about ten minutes to touchdown, but he knew it would seem much longer, and that it only took a second to kill you.

Carole had long since quit flying with Schweizer. Even the slightest turbulence gave her motion sickness. Schweizer wondered what she would think about this as the airplane alternated between updrafts and down drafts, causing the needle on the vertical speed indicator to peg in both directions.

As suddenly as he had entered, Schweizer was out of the clouds and into the rain. Once again that feeling of *déjà vu* settled over him as the landscape below took on the appearance of farm fields separated by rows of trees. He had the unmistakable impression of having been there before. Then the feeling slowly faded away. Instead of trees and fields, there were streets and buildings.

In another few minutes the Cherokee's wheels gently bumped onto the pavement of runway one-eight. Another death-defying feat, Schweizer joked to himself. As he taxied to the ramp he checked the time. It was only 11:30. Maybe he could get the information he needed before the day was over.

11

WASHINGTON, D.C.

Schweizer was removing his suitcase from the luggage compartment of the Cherokee when a blue van stopped next to the plane. "Do you need a ride to the terminal?" called out the driver.

Schweizer picked up his suitcase and walked over to the van. "I need to pick up a car rental."

"Sure thing," said the driver, a pimply-faced kid, about nineteen.

During the short ride to the terminal Schweizer began to wish he had walked instead. The driver had a body odor problem that seemed to contaminate everything around him. His hair had a look reminiscent of the "greasy kid stuff" days and his face had an oily appearance beneath the mask of red, pus-filled bumps.

At the Hertz counter the reservation Schweizer had phoned ahead was ready, and the girl behind the counter gave him directions on a Washington D.C. map to get to the Quality Inn on New Jersey Avenue. As Schweizer went to get the car, a 1979 Thunderbird, he noticed a sign that read:
"Reserved for
Supreme Court Justices
Members of Congress
Diplomats"

It reminded him of a line from *Animal Farm*. Something about all animals being equal, but some being more equal than others. Apparently, the same was true in the land of the free and the home of the brave.

The drive into the city was only about ten minutes. Schweizer took Interstate 395 to D Street and then to New Jersey Avenue. He was afforded a good view of the Capitol before plunging into a tunnel that went under the mall.

After checking in at the hotel, Schweizer decided to skip lunch since the Washington day was well underway. The fact that his hotel and car were costing over a hundred dollars per day also served as inspiration to complete his research as quickly as possible. A phone call to the U.S. Army Center of Military History revealed that it was located in Room 6A 034 of the Forrestal Building rather than the Pentagon as Schweizer had expected. He wrote the address and room number on a piece of hotel stationery, then checked the map he had gotten at the Hertz counter and found the Forrestal Building to be only a few blocks away, so he decided to walk.

The Forrestal Building, located just south of the Smithsonian Institute, was a typical example of the uninspired modern architecture that had taken the country by something less than storm, and keeps sprouting up around the country like weeds after a summer rain. It was tall and narrow. Schweizer wondered what the late Secretary of Defense would have thought of it.

The Center of Military History was in the west end of the sixth floor. After getting off the elevator, Schweizer pulled a piece of paper from his pocket and looked at the number he had written down when he had called earlier from the hotel. Room 6A 034 was huge and filled with file cabinets. A sign-in register was just inside the door. Schweizer was signing in when a middle-aged woman approached and said: "Is there anything I can help you find? I'm the archivist."

Schweizer looked up at the woman. She was not unattractive, but her lack of makeup, the drab colors of her clothes, and her straight, limp hair gave her the stereotyped appearance of the old maid librarian.

"I'm looking for information about the closing days of World War II, primarily prisoner-of-war camps in Europe and the disposition of prisoners," said Schweizer.

"American, French, German, or Italian?"

"Excuse me?" said Schweizer, puzzled.

"Do you want to know about American prisoners or French prisoners or ...?"

"German."

"I believe the records of prisoner-of-war camps are at the National Archives."

"Oh, I see," said Schweizer, disappointed.

"Exactly what is it you wanted to find out?" asked the archivist.

Schweizer had begun drifting toward the door. "I just wanted to see if I could find out what happened to prisoners taken in a particular town," he said.

The archivist smiled and said: "Come with me. I think we have a book that can help you." The archivist led the way to a stack of bookshelves.

"You have quite a facility here," said Schweizer.

"We employ about eighty or ninety people. We are currently working on the Vietnam War."

"Do you have much on World War II?"

"Yes, indeed," said the woman, pointing at a set of books. "This series is the U.S. Army in World War II. It consists of about eighty volumes, and covers virtually every aspect of the war." She located a volume and pulled it from the shelf. "This is called *The Last Offensive,* and covers from the Battle of the Bulge to the end of the European war."

Schweizer looked at the book in amazement. It was easily 500 pages and covered a period of only about four months. He thanked the archivist for her help and took the book to a reading table.

To Schweizer's delight, he found the history in chronological order. It didn't ramble, as some history texts do. Casually, he thumbed through the table of contents, intrigued by some of the chapter headings and subheadings: "Operation Lumberjack," "A Bridgehead to Nowhere."

Following the table of contents was a list of maps and illustrations. One name seemed to leap off the page: "Hammelburg."

Where had he heard that name? Had he been there before? Schweizer leaned back and closed his eyes, trying to clear his mind of all extraneous thoughts.

Suddenly, he burst out laughing, causing the other people in the room to look at him. Hammelburg was the name of the town near the prisoner-of-war camp in the television show, "Hogan's Heroes." Schweizer smiled and shook his head as he flipped to the index in the back and looked up "prisoners." For more than thirty minutes he read every reference on prisoners-of-war, but could find nothing of value to his search.

Next Schweizer looked up Augsburg in the index. He had always wondered about the incident at the hospital and how the American army could have entered so quietly. He found only one reference to Augsburg, and it read in part:

"As the 3rd Division approached the city on 27 April, word came from an adjacent unit that two civilians had arrived to arrange surrender ... Within Augsburg the combat commander, Generalmajor Franz Fehn, intended to fight ... small underground groups ... spread the word that the authorities had already capitulated and that everybody should display white flags. A civilian patrol reached one of the American columns to lead a battalion commander and a small group to a bunker shared by General Fehn and civilian functionaries of the city. Given five minutes to surrender, General Fehn marched dutifully out to view a city already fluttering with white flags."

Schweizer leaned back in his chair and shoved his hands into his pockets, a frown on his face. Now he knew why the *Gestapo* agent had been surprised in his room, but so what? He didn't know who the man was or where to find him or who to turn to for help. A feeling of depression was beginning to settle over Schweizer when he heard a voice say: "Did you find what you were looking for?" It was the archivist.

"No," said Schweizer, looking up at the woman. She seemed eager to help, but Schweizer didn't feel much like asking. "I found the town, but no information about prisoners taken there."

"What town was it?"

"Augsburg."

"Oh, that would have been very late in the war," she said.

"Yes, it was," said Schweizer. "It was the end of April."

"I'm afraid you won't have much luck if you are looking for a particular prisoner. There were literally millions of prisoners taken in the last weeks of the war."

"The man I'm looking for was in the *Gestapo*," said Schweizer. "He was arrested in a hospital in Augsburg."

The archivist had a quizzical look on her face. "How would you know that?" she asked.

"I was a patient in that hospital," said Schweizer. He was grinning, but didn't know why.

The archivist opened her mouth as if to say, "Oh," and began to nod her head up and down. "You need to read the operational reports of the unit that captured Augsburg," she said. "Just a minute, I'll be right back."

A short time later the woman returned with another green book that looked much like the one Schweizer had been reading. She was looking through the book as she approached the reading table. "According to the chronology," she said, "the city of Augsburg was captured by the 7th and 15th Regiments of the 3rd Infantry Division on April 28, 1945."

"That's great!" said Schweizer, triumphantly. "Can you get me the operational reports for those units?"

"Oh, we don't have them. Those are at the National Archives."

"Oh, and where's that?" asked Schweizer, undeterred.

"It's just up the street, at Eighth and Pennsylvania. It's just a short walk."

Schweizer thanked her and headed for the door. Things were looking up already.

The National Archives Building was more in keeping with the traditional architecture of the early planners of Washington. Its neoclassic design, enriched by Corinthian columns, was very impressive, Schweizer thought as he mounted the steps to the entrance, but it did remind him of many post office buildings he had seen.

In the lobby was an information desk with an officer sitting behind it reading a magazine. As Schweizer approached, the officer put down his magazine and looked up.

"May I help you, sir?" he asked.

"I hope so," said Schweizer, feeling a bit uneasy. "I was just over at the Army Center of Military History and they referred me to the Archives."

"Have you ever been here before?" asked the officer.

"No, I haven't."

"Then you will need a researcher identification card," said the officer. "Just go to room 201 and they'll help you." Schweizer turned to go. "Oh, one other thing," said the officer, handing a booklet to Schweizer, "this brochure might help you. It's a guide on how to use the Archives."

Schweizer thanked him and then went to find room 201. He wondered if there would be a lot of red tape and bureaucratic nonsense just to find out a little information. He hadn't needed a card at the Army Center of Military History. Why did he need one here?

The researcher identification card application wasn't complicated at all. It only asked for Schweizer's name and address, and the purpose of his research. The card was issued immediately and Schweizer was referred to a consultant.

The consultant was a younger man, who Schweizer guessed to be about thirty. His dress was conservative, in contrast to his rather long hair. He introduced himself as Ron Miller of the Modern Military Branch.

"I note on your application you are interested in World War II," said Miller. Schweizer nodded. "Is there any aspect of the war that you are primarily interested in?" asked Miller.

Schweizer had another feeling of *déjà vu*. He was reminded of the time he lost his bank credit card on a vacation trip to Las Vegas. First he had called his bank and told someone of the loss. Then he was referred to the bankcard customer service, then to the lost card department, and finally to an investigator. Each time he had to tell his story from the beginning. Once again Schweizer told the object of his research: "I'm looking for information on the disposition of German prisoners at the close of the war. I'm particularly interested in prisoners taken in Augsburg, Germany."

"Augsburg was captured in the final days of the war," said Miller. "Many prisoners were merely classified, discharged and sent home."

"What about *SS*?" asked Schweizer.

"Oh, well, that's a different matter entirely. *SS*, *Gestapo*, and anyone suspected of war crimes were held for further investigation."

That's encouraging, thought Schweizer. "What happened to the *SS* captured in Augsburg?"

Miller had a puzzled look on his face. "*SS*? I don't believe there were any *SS* troops in Augsburg," he said.

"Well, more specifically, *Gestapo*," said Schweizer. "They were part of the *SS*, weren't they?"

"Of course," said Miller, slightly embarrassed. "Any town the size of Augsburg would have had a *Gestapo* office. You'll need to research the operational reports of the unit that captured Augsburg."

"And that would be the 7th and 15th regiments of the 3rd Infantry Division," volunteered Schweizer.

Miller smiled. "I see you've been researching already."

Schweizer nodded. "I was over at the Army Center of Military History."

"Just a minute," said Miller, getting up from the table. "I'll see where those operational reports are located."

Miller returned in a couple of minutes and sat down.

"The records you want are at the Washington National Records Center in Suitland, Maryland," he said.

Schweizer looked surprised. "I was told those records were in the archives."

"And of course they are," said Miller. "That's our General Archives Division. It's only eight miles from here and there's a free shuttle that leaves the Pennsylvania Avenue entrance four times daily."

"I have a car," said Schweizer. "How do I get there?"

"Take Pennsylvania Avenue about seven miles east to Silverhill Road, turn right ... there's a Buick dealer on the corner ... and go about a mile to Suitland road. It's the second or third light. Turn right and go past the Suitland compound. You'll see a radar tower that looks like a golf ball in the sky. Turn left just before you get to two cemeteries, one on either side of the road. You'll come to a red brick building. It looks like one story, but it's really two. One is underground." Schweizer hurriedly wrote the directions down in his pocket notebook. "If you are interested in published histories, you might want to write to the U.S. Army History Research Collection, Carlisle Barracks, Carlisle, Pennsylvania. I've written the address down for you." Miller handed Schweizer a piece of paper. Schweizer looked at it briefly before shoving it into his pocket.

"Which one has the more detailed information?" asked Schweizer.

"Suitland has the original documents," said Miller. "But you might want to try both."

"Thanks for your help," said Schweizer, getting up from the table.

"When you get to Suitland, go to room 105," said Miller.

"Room 105?"

"Yes. To reach it, turn right after entering the building and proceed along the corridor. You can't miss it."

Schweizer looked at his watch. It was almost 3 PM and his stomach was reminding him that he hadn't eaten since breakfast. Maybe he would get lucky. He could always eat dinner later.

Half an hour later, Schweizer was sitting in the public research room of the National Records Center, a stack of binders in front of him. It took over an hour to read through the records of the 7th Regiment for April 27th through the 30th. No luck.

It was almost 5 PM when Schweizer found what he was looking for. He re-read it several times to be sure he was not mistaken. The document was a typewritten report of a detail sent to secure the town hospital facilities. It read:

"28 APR 45 1635 HRS-By order of Lt. Col. George Fredericks my detail entered and secured control of German hospital on Ulmerstrasse. Doctor in charge was Werner Kempke, who, along w/hosp. staff, offered complete cooperation. Found a number of German military personnel masquerading as civilian patients and turned them over to provost marshal for classification and disposition. Encountered resistance from Gestapo agent in one of the rooms. Said agent seriously wounded and another Gestapo agent placed under arrest. Left Sgt. Milliken & detail of three men in charge.
Merritt R. Chamberlain
Capt. USAR O-1600903"

Schweizer was writing down the name and service number when a girl approached and said, "I'm sorry, sir, but we will be closing in five minutes."

"Uh, thanks," said Schweizer absentmindedly. The girl turned and walked away. "Hey! Wait a minute!" Schweizer called after her.

The girl stopped and turned around. "Yes?"

Schweizer got up from the table clutching the paper on which he had just written the name. "How would I go about finding a man who served in World War II?" he asked.

The girl looked puzzled for a moment. "You'd probably have to contact the military records center in St. Louis," she said.

Schweizer's feeling of success faded like a hooker's phony smile. The whole thing was beginning to look like the world's biggest runaround. "There is one other possibility," said the girl, noting Schweizer's look of disappointment.

"What's that?"

"If he was an officer, there's always the chance he is still on active duty," she said. Schweizer's expression began to brighten. "You might try contacting Army Personnel at the Pentagon."

Schweizer thanked her and gathered up his things. It wasn't much to go on, but he didn't want to fly to St. Louis until he had exhausted all possible sources in Washington. Schweizer looked at his watch. It was too late to continue researching. Perhaps tomorrow his efforts would be more fruitful.

The lobby of the Pentagon was like a small shopping mall. There were gift shops, a flower shop and a bank of pay phones off to one side. The entrance itself was a set of doors manned by a security guard. Schweizer approached the guard on duty, gave his name, and stated his business. The security guard looked up from the list on his clipboard. "I'm sorry, Mr. Schweizer, but your name is not on my list. Is Army personnel expecting you?"

Schweizer grimaced. "No, I'm just here on the spur of the moment."

The security guard's demeanor shifted from polite solicitude to don't-bother-me-I'm-busy. "Sir, if you have legitimate business in the Pentagon, you should phone ahead for clearance," he said curtly. "Then your name would be on our roster and ..."

"Excuse me," interrupted Schweizer. He was trying to remain polite. "I've come all the way from Cincinnati and I would like to talk to the people in Army personnel. Could you call them for me? It would probably save time."

The guard's expression did not change. "When you have the proper authorization, sir, I'll be happy to help you."

The guard turned away and tried to appear busy. Schweizer looked around, feeling embarrassed by the rejection. After a few other visitors had been cleared, the guard looked up at Schweizer again. "Sir, there's a public phone just over there," said the guard, pointing at the pay phones. "I'm sure if you call Army personnel, they will be happy to help you."

Schweizer wanted to say something crude, but didn't. He spun around instead, and headed for the pay phones. A few minutes later he was back at the entrance and the security guard was just hanging up the phone. Schweizer was fuming. He hated getting the runaround.

"Army personnel will send someone down to escort you," said the guard. "Please sign in here and wear this at all times while you are in the building. Please remember to return it before you leave." He handed Schweizer a large plastic badge on a chain marked, "VISITOR," which Schweizer slipped over his head and around his neck.

A few minutes later a young black woman appeared to escort Schweizer to Army personnel. She was cheerful and friendly, a sharp contrast to the security guard. "My name is Amy," she said as they walked along one of the many corridors. "What can we help you with?"

"I'm looking for someone who served in the Army during World War II," said Schweizer.

"Oh," said Amy thoughtfully, "I doubt that we can be of much help. The records of veterans are stored in St. Louis and there's also the problem of the Privacy Act."

"I understand," said Schweizer. "I'm just trying the long shot that he might still be in the Army."

At the personnel office, Amy left Schweizer in a chair next to her desk. She took the name and serial number Schweizer had found on the report and entered it on a computer terminal in the next room. Five minutes later she returned with a smile on her face. "Your biorhythms must all be positive today, Mr. Schweizer. Not only is General Chamberlain still in the Army, but he's assigned to Ft. Meade. I called him and he has agreed to see you."

Amy looked quite pleased with herself and Schweizer was more than a little surprised. "Where's Ft. Meade?" he asked.

"Come over here and I'll show you on the map," said Amy. A few minutes later Schweizer was in his car and on his way. The incident with the security guard was already forgotten.

General Chamberlain sat looking across his desk at Schweizer. He had a very thoughtful, curious look on his face. "Have we met somewhere, Mr. Schweizer?" he asked.

"I was hoping you could tell me that, General," said Schweizer. "I was in a German hospital in Augsburg at the close of the war. Apparently you were there, too."

Chamberlain's look turned to puzzlement. He had been to Augsburg, it was true, but he was sure he had not been hospitalized. "I'm sorry, but it just doesn't ring a bell. I was never in a hospital."

"No, you don't understand. You weren't *in* it, you *captured* it."

A smile crept across Chamberlain's face as his mind conjured up images of the past. "Oh, yes," he said slowly, "I remember that. Yes, it was in April of '45, wasn't it?"

"That's right," said Schweizer eagerly. "There was a man shot in the hospital that day. Do you remember that?"

"Yes, I certainly do," said Chamberlain, pausing for emphasis. "I shot him." Chamberlain's expression became quizzical. "How do you know all this?"

"I was there," said Schweizer.

"Where?"

"In the bed!" said Schweizer, a bit too triumphantly. Chamberlain leaned back in his chair and swiveled toward the window. "I don't see where all this is leading, Mr. Schweizer. Perhaps you could ..."

"What was his name?"

"Who?"

"The man you shot."

"I never knew," said Chamberlain. "And even if I did, I wouldn't remember it after all these years."

Schweizer was beginning to feel frustrated and desperate again. He asked, "Do you know what happened to him? It's very important."

Chamberlain scratched his chin and looked down at his desk. His visitor seemed sincere and he didn't want to brush him off. "Well," he said slowly, "if he wasn't planted in a hole in the ground, he would have been hospitalized and then processed as a prisoner-of-war. Other than that, I have no idea what became of him."

Schweizer looked downcast. This had been his most promising lead and now he didn't know what to do. He rose and extended his hand to the general. "I appreciate you taking the time to see me, General," he said, unable to hide his disappointment. "If you happen to remember ..."

"You know, he did have a partner," said Chamberlain.

"Yes, I know. Do you know what happened to him?"

"Yes. I recall we turned him over to Max. That was the last I ever saw of him."

Schweizer sat down and pulled out his notebook. The name sounded vaguely familiar. "Max? Max who?" he asked.

"Max Frohm. He was our interrogator, detached from the OSS."

"Do you have any idea where this man is, this Max Frohm?" asked Schweizer as he wrote notes.

"Not really. However, the OSS was the forerunner of the CIA. Maybe he stayed with intelligence. Why don't you inquire at the CIA? They're over in Langley, Virginia."

Schweizer thanked General Chamberlain and hurried to his car. It was lunchtime, but food would have to wait. If he were lucky, he could finish his business by the end of the day.

The drive to CIA headquarters was interesting. Langley, Virginia, wasn't on any maps that Schweizer looked at, probably for security reasons. Fortunately for Schweizer, it was one of the worst kept secrets in Washington. Directions were fairly simple: take the parkway up the Potomac and exit at the sign marked "CIA." Twenty minutes later, after signing in at the front gate, Schweizer parked in a stall marked "Visitor."

The CIA building was very impressive. Situated in a densely

wooded area and surrounded by a high fence, it had about seven levels above ground and no telling how many below. Judging by the size of the parking lot and the number of cars, Schweizer estimated several thousand employees must be working for the CIA.

The receptionist across the lobby from the entrance had been alerted by the security guard at the front gate and she was waiting to receive Schweizer. Schweizer was careful not to step on the CIA emblem inlaid in the terrazzo floor as he approached the reception desk.

"Good afternoon, sir," said the girl, smiling. "Welcome to the Central Intelligence Agency. Is there anything I can help you with?"

Schweizer was impressed with the girl. She was attractive, well groomed, and didn't come across as a phony like so many other receptionists he had met. He wondered if she were involved in intelligence work, too, or just sat behind the reception desk every day. "My name is Karl Schweizer," he said. "I'm trying to locate someone who may have been, or possibly still is, employed by the CIA."

The girl's face took on a thoughtful look. "Normally that kind of information is not given out, sir," she said. "But what's the name? Perhaps I can help you anyway."

"The man I'm looking for was with the OSS during World War II," said Schweizer. "It occurred to me that he may have stayed on with the CIA after the war."

"Hmmm. Maybe I'll have you talk to our Public Information Officer," she said slowly. "Yes, I think he can help you."

The girl picked up the phone and dialed a number. A phone rang in the Security office and was answered by John Canfield.

"Hello, this is Wendy Turner in reception," said the girl. "I have a gentleman here who needs some help."

"Sure," said Canfield and hung up.

In the lobby Canfield offered his hand to Schweizer and said, "Welcome to the CIA. How can I be of service to you?"

"Hi. My name is Karl Schweizer. I'm looking for someone who used to be in the OSS. I was hoping you could help."

"OSS? That was a long time ago," said Canfield. "Wendy, give Mr. Schweizer a visitor's pass and I'll take him to personnel."

Wendy pulled a plastic badge from her desk drawer and recorded the number in the visitor's log. Emblazoned across the pass in red block letters was, "MUST BE ACCOMPANIED."

Canfield led the way to a set of double doors marked "AUTHORIZED PERSONNEL ONLY." Through the doors was a wide hallway with offices on either side. As they passed along the corridor, only a few people seemed to notice their passage. Several turns later they came to a glassed in foyer with the word "PERSONNEL" stenciled on the glass next to the door. As they entered the secretary smiled, but said nothing when she noticed Schweizer's visitor pass. Canfield crossed the foyer to a white door. A buzzing sound came from the latch and Canfield pushed the door open. Through the door Schweizer could see what appeared to be a small office with a desk and two chairs, one on each side. Schweizer thought it must be an interview room.

Canfield smiled and nodded for Schweizer to go in. Schweizer looked at Canfield and then at the secretary, who was also smiling. Something didn't seem quite right, but Schweizer just shrugged and entered the room. "If you'll just wait here, I'll have a personnel officer help you," said Canfield.

Schweizer sat down and looked around. Behind him he heard the door click shut. The room was devoid of any decor other than the desk and chairs. There wasn't even a magazine to help him pass the time. The more he thought about it, the more Schweizer thought the word "interrogation" better suited the room.

A few minutes later, the door buzzed again and a young woman entered. She was well-dressed and was carrying a plastic notebook. "Hi!" she said cheerily as she sat down opposite Schweizer. "I'm Connie Davis, personnel specialist. I understand you're looking for a former employee of the agency."

"Well, I can't say for sure," said Schweizer. "The man I'm looking for was in the OSS during the war and I thought he might have been in the CIA, too."

"I see," said Connie. She opened the plastic notebook. Inside was a yellow legal pad on one side and under a clip on the other side was the card he had filled out at the reception desk. Connie wrote a few notes before continuing. "Were you in the OSS?" she asked.

"No," said Schweizer, feeling a bit nervous.

"Were you in the army, then?" asked Connie.

Schweizer was beginning to perspire. He felt like there was a see-through mirror into his soul. "No."

Connie Davis wrote a few more notes, then asked: "What's the name of the person you're looking for?"

"Max Frohm," said Schweizer.

"How do you spell it?"

"F-R-O-H-M."

"Now the important question," said Connie, looking directly into Schweizer's eyes. "Why are you looking for this man?"

"Well, I, uh, it's, uh, well, actually it's kind of personal," said Schweizer, feeling chagrined.

"Couldn't you be more specific?" she asked. Schweizer just shook his head and looked down at the desk. He couldn't bring himself to tell her all the personal things he had told Dr. Hendriks.

The young woman flipped the notebook closed and stood up. "This isn't much to go on," she said, "but I'll see what I can do." The door buzzed again and she left.

Canfield was sitting on the edge of the secretary's desk plying his charms, but to no avail. He had made absolutely no progress in the six months he had known her. "How did it go?" he asked Connie.

"It's pretty thin," she replied, "and everything he did say was rather evasive."

"Who's he looking for?" asked Canfield.

"Max Frohm. Ring any bells?"

Canfield shook his head and slid off the secretary's desk. "See you later, Jan," he said to the secretary. He followed Connie through a door into the main personnel office. It was a huge room with several rows of desks.

Connie led the way to a glassed-in office. She sat down at a desk, opened the notebook and turned it around for Canfield to read.

"What do you think?" she asked after he had gone over everything.

"Obviously we're going to have to put it on the computer," he said. "And we may as well check Schweizer out while we're at it. Did you notice the spelling of his first name? K instead of C."

"Mmmm, yes," said Connie. "European?"

"Germany, Switzerland, Austria ... take your pick," said Canfield.

"You don't think they would be so obvious, do you?" asked Connie.

Canfield shrugged his shoulders. "You never know," he said. "I once heard of a guy caught smuggling gold. It was just lying right there on the front seat of his car. The customs officer had already waved him on and he would have gotten away with it if the sunlight hadn't reflected off of the gold."

"You seem to have a story for everything," said Connie, smiling.

"Yeah, I know a few," said Canfield. "Did I ever tell you the one about the three nuns?"

"Never mind," chided Connie. "Your reputation has preceded you."

"That bad, huh?" said Canfield, feigning chagrin. Connie gave him a knowing smile.

"Tell you what," she said, "you do a work-up on Schweizer, check NCIC and SSA, and I'll see what I can find on Max Frohm."

"Sounds good. See you in a while."

Connie watched Canfield as he left. He had been pursuing her for several months, and though she found him attractive, he had a reputation as a womanizer.

The computer terminal in Connie's office gave her access to all the online personnel files of the agency. Some terminals were locked out to certain files, but Connie was cleared for all personnel files. She sat down at the terminal and logged onto the system with her password. A message appeared on the screen: "Good afternoon, Connie Davis. You are now logged on the Personnel Information System. Please remember to log off when you are through."

Connie first did a search of the current personnel file. She entered: "PRNS FROHM." The computer did a search of the file and in a few moments responded with a list of all Agency employees with a last name similar to Frohm, everything from Farr to Fuhriman. Connie went through the list several times, but wasn't able to find a listing for Max Frohm. Well, that's not surprising, Connie said to herself. If he had been in the OSS he's probably retired now.

The retired list found by the computer search was about three times longer and it took several minutes to visually search it since the names were not in alphabetical order. Only twelve names appeared on the screen at a time, one for each of the numbered PF keys on the side of the keyboard. Several pages into the list she found it:

"FROHM, MAXIMILLIAN 212-42-8986 4038 7/31/64 PF9." Connie recognized the department code 4038 as East Germany section, Soviet Bloc division of the Clandestine Services branch.

Connie pressed the PF9 key and waited. A few seconds later the computer responded: "PLEASE ENTER YOUR PASSWORD."

That's odd, thought Connie, *it's never asked me for a password before.* She entered her password and the machine responded: "INVALID PASSWORD-REENTER WITH CORRECT PASSWORD." Connie entered her password again. This time the message read: "SECURITY VIOLATION-THIS TERMINAL NOW DISABLED." Connie pushed the "clear" button. Nothing happened. She noticed the "input locked" light was on, so she tried the "reset" button. Nothing. She tried several keys. No response. Just then the phone rang. Connie picked up the phone and said, "Personnel. Connie Davis."

"Uh, yeah, this is Weston down in the Operations Center," said a male voice. "We got a message on the console that there's been a security violation on your terminal. You know anything about that?"

Connie hesitated. She felt embarrassed, as if she had been caught eavesdropping on a private conversation. "Well," she said slowly, "I was doing some research on the retired personnel file and the computer asked for a password, which I've never seen happen before, so I entered my password and everything just locked up."

After several seconds of silence on the other end of the line Weston finally said, "Here's what let's do. I'm going to bring your terminal back up, but don't do anything on it. I'll be right up and check it out. Okay?"

"All right," said Connie and hung up. She sat there staring at the phone, numbed by the disquieting feeling that she had somehow committed a serious breach of the Agency's security rules. *Perhaps it would be better if Mr. Schweizer were not around,* she thought. Connie picked up the phone and dialed the receptionist in the waiting area. "Hi, this is Connie. Would you please tell Mr. Schweizer that we are unable to locate any record of Mr. Frohm? And ask him to please sign out at the reception desk. Thanks."

Schweizer was less than thrilled by the news that his search had been in vain. He had been left waiting for several minutes and when he had tried the door it was locked. He knocked on it several times, but no one responded. Angry? That was too mild to describe how he felt.

Back at Connie Davis' office she was showing Brad Weston the steps she had taken in the search for Frohm's personnel file. When the computer asked for the password again, Weston said, "Could you let me sit down please? 1 want to try something."

"Sure," said Connie and got up from the terminal. Weston sat down and pressed the "interrupt" key. Then he entered: "OPCENTINQ," followed by his own password. The computer responded: "THIS IS A SECURE FILE-EYES ONLY DDI DDP." Weston leaned back in the chair and thought for a few moments. Then he turned to Connie and said accusingly, "I'm not even sure the President could see this file. Why were you trying to get into it?"

Connie bit her lower lip and her eyes darted around nervously as she tried to collect her thoughts. "Uh, well, you see, there was this man who was asking about Frohm and I was just researching it and ..."

"What man?" asked Weston.

Just then Canfield burst into the room. "Hey, I've got the info on Schweizer and it's pretty ... interesting ..." Canfield's voice trailed off when he saw Weston.

"You in on this, too?" asked Weston. "Who's Schweizer?"

"He's the man I told you about," said Connie.

"In on what?" demanded Canfield.

"Unauthorized access to secure files," said Weston.

"Now just a minute," said Canfield. "I happen to work for Security, and what do you mean 'unauthorized access'?"

Weston looked at the ID badge hanging from Canfield's shirt pocket. "I'm referring to Miss Davis here trying to access the personnel file on this Frohm guy. It's secure. Eyes only. Hot stuff. You know." Turning to Connie, Weston asked, "Who's Schweizer and where is he?"

"He's just some guy who walked in off the street and asked about Frohm," said Connie lamely. "And he's left already."

Weston shook his head and said: "Just walked in off the street and asked about a former employee whose file is classified eyes only? Oh, brother!" Then, turning to Canfield: "What's your part in this?"

"I've been researching Schweizer," said Canfield.

"Okay, what have you got?" asked Weston. Canfield went over to Connie's desk and spread out the computer report. "I checked NCIC. Nothing there, no criminal record. His social security number was issued 9/12/49. The application has the usual stuff, except he was born in Switzerland. Checked his alien registration number with INS. He was admitted on a student visa 8/1/49 and received naturalization papers 5/19/55. Seems he married a local girl and decided to stay. The FAA issued him a private pilot certificate in 1961, and that's about it. No other agencies have any information on him. I could have checked his driving record and credit history, but didn't think it was necessary. And, oh yes, he's a registered Republican."

Weston turned and looked out through the glass partition. "We may have a real problem," he said. "If this Schweizer's a sleeper, he's pretty deep. Thirty years, that's a long time." Weston turned back to the other two. "At any rate, this is too big for us to handle. The brass are over in D.C. at a National Security Council meeting. In the meantime we better find this guy. Where's he from?"

"Cincinnati," said Canfield.

"Probably registered in a hotel or motel in the area," said Weston. "Check it out through your department, will you Canfield? I'll follow up with the deputy director when he gets back."

"Okay, I'll get right on it," said Canfield.

"What about me?" asked Connie.

"Nothing for now," said Weston. "Just sit tight."

Schweizer felt depressed as he drove back to the city. The lead on Frohm had looked so promising. Now he would have to find another way. He looked at his watch. The National Archives were open late. Perhaps he would try there again.

12

Schweizer flopped down on the bed and kicked his shoes off. He looked around at the spartan furnishings in the room and thought of how he could be in anyone of a thousand hotels and not know where he was without going outside. Hotel rooms were always depressing, and the day's activities only intensified that feeling. The frustration of his encounter with the mindlessness of the federal bureaucracy had left him drained of all energy. His body cried out for sleep, but the grumbling from his stomach reminded him that he hadn't eaten since breakfast. He checked his watch. Only a little after eight. He thought he'd call Carole first, then go out for a hamburger or something.

Carole answered the phone on the third ring. "Hi, sweetheart," said Schweizer.

"Oh, hello," answered Carole, "thought it would probably be you. How did it go?"

"Aw, it was a big waste of time. If the people in this country could see how the bureaucrats are running this mess, there would be an armed revolt that would make the French Revolution look like a church service."

"I'm sorry."

"What are you sorry about?" said Schweizer sharply. "I'm the one with the problem."

"You don't have to get angry," said Carole. "I was just trying to show I cared."

Schweizer felt a little embarrassed. "You're right. I've just had a long, frustrating day and I'm ready to bite off anybody's head."

"What are you going to do now?" she asked.

"I don't know. Maybe I'll hang around here a day or two. Maybe I'll just fly home in the morning."

"Does that mean you're giving up?"

The question meant more than it seemed. Schweizer knew that if he quit so easily there wasn't much chance of saving their marriage. On the other hand, he didn't know what course of action to take. What he really wanted was to be left alone so he could plan his next move.

"No," he answered, "I'm not giving up, but I don't know what I'm going to do next, either."

"Oh," said Carole in a quiet voice, unable to hide her disappointment.

There was a long pause as each waited for the other to speak first. "I love you, Carole," said Schweizer.

"I'm glad."

Her response was noncommittal and Schweizer had hoped for more.

"Don't you love me?" he asked.

"I don't know," she said.

"What do you mean, you don't know?"

"I don't know how I feel."

"Carole ..."

"I'm sorry Karl. I just wish things were like they were before."

"Oh, I see," said Schweizer bitterly. His disappointment was turning into anger. "It's all right for me to make a commitment by running all over the country, but you'll just keep your options open."

"That's not what I meant, Karl."

"Yeah? Well, I'll see you when I get there. Good-bye."

Schweizer slammed the receiver down and slumped back on the bed with his arms folded and his jaw clenched tight. He was more hurt than angry. His world was collapsing around him and he felt powerless to stop it.

Several moments passed as he sat staring at the wall, then the phone rang. He was sure it was Carole, but he didn't want to talk to her. After about the twentieth ring he picked it up.

"Yeah? What do you want?"

"You Schweizer?" It was a male voice and Schweizer felt embarrassed for the rude way he had answered the phone.

"Yes, I'm Karl Schweizer. Who are you?"

The caller ignored the question. "I have the information you're looking for."

"What information?"

"Don't be stupid, Schweizer. Just meet me at the Lincoln Memorial."

"When?"

"As soon as you can get there."

"How will I know you?"

"I'll find you. What are you driving?"

"A '79 Thunderbird. It's midnight blue."

"What's the license number?"

"Just a minute," said Schweizer as he fished the car keys from his pocket. "It's MWJ 704. That's a Maryland number."

"Don't keep me waiting," said the caller, then hung up.

Schweizer hurriedly put his shoes on and then grabbed his jacket. He hadn't felt this excited since the day he bought his airplane. By the time he reached the elevator he had forgotten the harsh words with Carole and that he was still hungry.

The parking terrace beneath the hotel was deserted and in the dim light it took Schweizer a few seconds to get his bearings. As he walked to the car he felt in his pocket for the keys. He was almost to the Thunderbird when he realized he didn't have them. "Damn it!" he said out loud. Schweizer started to turn around when something hit him in the back. Before he realized what was happening he was sprawled over the trunk lid of the car next to the Thunderbird. His attacker was twisting Schweizer's right arm behind his back and had immobilized his left arm by simply leaning on it.

"I ... I don't have any money," said Schweizer. The man was breathing hard from the exertion and was pressing Schweizer's head against the trunk lid with his own.

"Don't want your money," the man grunted in Schweizer's ear.

"What do you want?" asked Schweizer. The man pushed sharply on Schweizer's right arm, causing him to cry out m pain.

"Do you know what this is?" the man asked as he pushed something in front of Schweizer's face. It was too close for him to focus on, but when he tried to pull his head back to get a better look the man twisted his arm a little harder.

"I can't see it," Schweizer cried out. "It's too close."

The man held the object a little further away from Schweizer's face. "That better?" he asked.

A hot flash shot through Schweizer's body. In the man's hand was a small caliber revolver, probably a .22, and Schweizer had seen enough spy movies to know the fat cylinder on the end of the barrel was a silencer. "That's ... that's a silencer, isn't it?" he stammered.

"That's right, turkey. So, if I have to blow you away nobody's gonna hear it, nobody's gonna help you. It's just you and me. You got that?"

"Y-yes."

"And don't try to turn around, because if you see my face you're gonna become a permanent resident. Understand?"

"Yes," grunted Schweizer.

"All right, you've been looking awfully hard for Max Frohm."

"Are you Frohm?"

"No. I just want to know why you want him and why you thought you could find him through the CIA."

"Are you CIA?" asked Schweizer.

The response was another sharp twist of the arm. "I'll ask the questions, you just answer them."

"All right."

"Now what about it?"

"I knew Frohm in the army during World War II," said Schweizer. "I just wanted to look him up."

Schweizer felt the pain in his right arm increase sharply as his assailant applied more pressure. "Not a very good story," the man said. Schweizer heard the click of the gun's hammer being drawn back.

"Wait!" said Schweizer. "I was a German POW and he was the interrogator. I was told he could help me."

"Who told you?"

"General Chamberlain at Ft. Meade."

"How can Frohm help you?"

"I was injured in a bombing and lost my memory. I was hoping Frohm might help me find some of the other prisoners who might help me learn about my past."

"At least you got the interrogator part right," the man said. "I'll have to check the rest."

Just then they could hear the sound of a car coming down the ramp. Schweizer felt the coldness of steel as his assailant pressed the muzzle of the pistol against the mastoid bone behind Schweizer's right ear. "I'm leaving now," the man said. "Don't turn around, or my face will be the last one you ever see."

Schweizer could hear the sound of retreating footsteps as the man ran for the stairway door. The door opened and slammed shut, but Schweizer didn't move. He didn't know if it was from fear or because his arm hurt so badly. The car coming down the ramp stopped next to Schweizer and the driver rolled down the window.

"Hey, buddy, are you all right?" the driver asked.

Schweizer stood up and began massaging some feeling back into his arm. Sweat was running down his face and his heart was racing.

"Yeah, I'm okay."

The car drove on, leaving Schweizer standing alone in the semi-darkness, bewildered by what had just happened. He decided to return to his room and have dinner sent up. Hotel food wasn't the greatest, but at least he was safer. Schweizer saw no point in going to the Lincoln Memorial. He was sure the man with the gun was the one who had called earlier. Maybe the search for his past wasn't worth it. It certainly wasn't worth getting shot.

Schweizer found himself running down a long dark tunnel, the sound of pursuing footsteps and heavy breathing close behind him. He saw a ladder just ahead, and clamored up it. At the top was a trap door. Schweizer pushed, but it wouldn't open. He could hear his pursuer coming up the ladder. He pushed once more and the door opened a crack. A bell began to ring. Slowly, the darkness faded and the ringing became louder.

Schweizer fumbled for the phone next to the bed and lifted the receiver. "Hello," he muttered.

"Time to get up," said a female voice.

"What?"

"This is your wakeup call, sir. It's 6:30."

"Thank you," said Schweizer and replaced the receiver. After a quick shower and shave Schweizer began packing his bag. He didn't see any reason for pursuing his search in Washington any longer. Perhaps it would be better to return home and develop a new plan.

At the registration counter in the lobby Schweizer set his luggage down and took out a credit card.

"I'm checking out of room 419."

The clerk began thumbing through a desk-top file and pulled out the registration card Schweizer had filled out two days earlier. A paper clip was on the edge of the card. The clerk turned the card over and removed a plain white envelope.

"Looks like you have a message here, Mr. Schweizer," said the clerk as he held out the envelope.

Schweizer hesitated, then reached for the message. The memory of the encounter in the parking terrace was too fresh. Schweizer pocketed the envelope and finished checking out. He would have time to read it on the way to the airport.

As the elevator door opened for his level of the parking terrace, Schweizer was gripped by a feeling of dread. He quickly walked to his car, paying more attention to his surroundings than he had the previous night. Schweizer reached in his pocket for the car keys and felt the envelope. He fished it out and tore it open. It read simply:

"In New Orleans is a bar called the Buccaneer. Ask for Simon and say you are looking for the Red Rooster. He can help you.
  Lincoln"

Schweizer wadded the note into a ball and jammed it into his pocket. Perhaps he wouldn't be going home so soon after all.

13

NEW ORLEANS

The flight to New Orleans was uneventful. The marginal weather that Schweizer had experienced on the flight from Cincinnati to Washington had dissipated, and the air was as smooth as a velvet cushion. He hoped that this was a good omen that the rest of his search would go as smoothly.

After checking into a motel near the airport, Schweizer caught a cab into town. The driver gave Schweizer a funny look when given the name of the bar, but the look went unnoticed as Schweizer settled back and pulled the crumpled note out of his pocket. He read and re-read the note several times. It all seemed so melodramatic. Who was Simon? Who was Lincoln? Obviously, Max Frohm was the Red Rooster, but why such a juvenile attempt to be like something out of a James Bond movie? Maybe it was all for real. At any rate Schweizer would soon find out what was going on ... or at least he hoped he would.

Schweizer had never been to New Orleans before and he was glad he had taken a cab instead of renting a car. As the cab wound through the city streets Schweizer became hopelessly lost. Before long the cab was driving through streets barely wide enough for one car. Schweizer recognized the area as the French Quarter from some long-forgotten movie he had once seen.

People seemed to be everywhere. *Probably a lot of tourists*, Schweizer thought. He noticed a sign advertising triple-X rated 16mm movies. Another place displayed pictures of mostly nude girls, and a barker was out front encouraging people to come in and see the show.

Schweizer noted the streets were all one-way. As narrow as they were, he thought it would probably be better if cars were banned altogether. Traffic was a mess and he noticed that pedestrians were making faster progress than the cab. It was mid-afternoon and part of the traffic jam was because of beer trucks restocking the bars for the evening business.

As the cab crept slowly down the street, something unusual caught Schweizer's eye. Two young men, body builder types, were standing on the sidewalk wearing only bikini briefs. They were tanned and good-looking, but the sight of them caused Schweizer to laugh out loud.

The cab stopped next to them and through the open door of the establishment Schweizer could see a male go-go dancer in a cage. Lights were flashing and the blare of music penetrated the closed windows of the cab. One of the young men did a bump and grind in Schweizer's direction and flashed a come-hither smile. Schweizer's smile changed to a smirk and he shook his head. The body builder shrugged and turned away.

"Well, mister?" said the cab driver.

"Well, what?"

"You owe me $12.85."

It took a couple of seconds to sink in before Schweizer leaned over to the window and looked at the sign over the barroom door. It read: "Buccaneer Lounge."

"Well, you gonna pay me, sweetheart?" asked the driver with a grin.

Schweizer's face felt hot as he fished a twenty dollar bill out of his wallet and handed it to the driver.

"Keep it," he said, getting out of the cab.

"Yeah, thanks," said the driver, pocketing the money. Then, as he put the car in gear, he said half-aloud, "Well, you never can tell."

Schweizer stood looking at the open doorway. He had never been in one of these places and he couldn't have felt more out of place if he had found himself in a ladies restroom. The two muscle boys were looking him over pretty thoroughly, and that only added to Schweizer's discomfort.

"You lookin' for action, mister?" asked one of the young men. "Or are you just here to make fun of the fags?"

Schweizer hung his head down and looked at the sidewalk. His first inclination was to just walk away, but then he remembered why he had come to New Orleans.

"Actually, boys, I'm looking for someone," he said.

"Anybody we know?"

"Uh, well, I was told to ask for Simon."

"Well, hey, yeah, Simon!" The two boys' faces lit up like three-year-olds on Christmas morning. "Sure, Simon's here. C'mon, we'll take you back."

Schweizer followed the two to the back of the bar. There in a dimly lit corner two middle-aged men were sitting in a booth. "Hey, Simon, there's someone here to see you."

The two men looked up at Schweizer. "What's your name?" asked one of them.

"I'm Karl Schweizer."

"Mmm, yes," said the man. "Would you gentlemen excuse me? This is private business."

The two boys and the other man said their good-byes and made their way to the front of the bar. Simon made a welcoming gesture with his hand. "Won't you be seated?"

Schweizer settled into the seat opposite Simon. His first impression was that Simon would look more at home in a board room than in a gay bar. He looked like a cross between Peter Graves and Cary Grant. His hair was silver, but his face looked youngish, about mid-thirties. He was freshly shaven, unusual for this time of day, and he wore his clothes like a fashion model. He wore a white shirt, open at the collar, and a choker gold necklace. On his right wrist was a gold chain bracelet, and on his left was a Rolex gold watch. Its crystal had a cut-glass appearance, obviously expensive. His hands looked soft and manicured. The most striking thing about him was his glasses. The lenses were tinted at the top and faded to clear at the bottom. They added an air of mystery, and on a woman Schweizer would have considered them quite sexy.

"Well, how do you like our fair city, Mr. Schweizer?"

"I haven't had a chance to see it yet... How do you know my name?"

"Oh, I've been expecting you... Have you never been here before?"

"No."

"That's really unfortunate. You must come during Mardi Gras. You'll never forget it."

"I really didn't come here to sightsee," said Schweizer.

"Well," said Simon, "a little small talk is good to break the ice, don't you think?"

Schweizer did not reply. He had removed the note from his pocket and was unfolding it on the table. "Just what is it you want, Mr. Schweizer?" asked Simon.

"I was told you could help me find the Red Rooster," said Schweizer as he pushed the note across the table.

Simon didn't look at the note, but a faint smile crossed his lips. "Ah, the Red Rooster. How long has it been since I heard that expression? At least ten years, I guess."

"I'm not really interested in the funny names," said Schweizer. The two men's eyes met for an instant and Schweizer thought he saw something dangerous, something dark and deadly. He retrieved the note and put it away. "I came here to find Max Frohm. Is that you?"

"You surprise me, Schweizer. Indeed you do. That was a very good guess." Schweizer's face brightened. "However, I am not he."

Schweizer frowned and looked at his hands which were now clasped on the table.

"You know, Schweizer, you're very fortunate to be alive right now," said Simon.

"You know about last night then."

"Oh, I know quite a bit about you, *Herr* Schweizer."

Schweizer felt all of his psychological defenses being stripped away. He felt as if Simon could look into his soul, but Schweizer could not see beyond Simon's smooth facade.

A smirk on his lips and a twinkle in his eye, Simon was obviously enjoying his superior position. Schweizer brought to bear his years of experience dealing with subordinates as he leaned across the table and said in a very firm voice, "Look, Simon, I don't give a damn what you know about me. I just want to know about Max Frohm."

Simon's eyes turned to ice. The two men were engaged in a psychological struggle, and neither seemed willing to give an inch. Abruptly, Simon leaned back and smiled disarmingly.

"You would make a formidable opponent," said Simon. "Actually, I know very little about you."

"Then why play games?"

Simon's brow was deeply furrowed. "You have upset a lot of people, Schweizer."

"But why?"

"In order to give you an answer, I would be required to reveal highly classified information," said Simon. "Perhaps Max can answer your questions, but I can't."

"When can I see him?" asked Schweizer eagerly.

"Not so fast, Schweizer. Max has left it up to me to determine if you are genuine."

"What do you mean, genuine?"

"Let's just say I am to decide whether or not you have a legitimate reason for seeing Max."

"And if you think I don't?"

"Then I would suggest you forget Max, go home to wherever you're from, but don't try to find him."

"And if I don't?"

Simon looked rather perturbed. He felt like he was dealing with a child who kept asking "why" to every answer given. "Mr. Schweizer, you don't seem to understand the caliber of people you're dealing with."

"CIA?" asked Schweizer. "Are you CIA?"

"I was," said Simon.

"Was? What happened?"

"Let's just say that they felt my sexual preferences made me vulnerable, a high security risk."

"Then how are you involved in all this?"

Simon laughed. "This is really quite funny," he said, "I'm supposed to be questioning you, but it seems the shoe is on the other foot."

"I don't think it's very funny."

"No, of course not," said Simon, now very serious.

"I've *got* to find Frohm," said Schweizer.

Simon leaned forward, his elbows on the table, and said in a low voice, "Why, Schweizer? Why do you want to find Max?"

"Do you want the full story or the condensed version?"

"I just want the true story."

"All right," said Schweizer, "I'll make this as short as possible. Near the end of World War II I was injured in a bombing. After several weeks in a coma I awoke with no memory. A *Gestapo* agent was in my room trying to interrogate me. I have only vague memories of that time. I never knew why they were questioning me. Anyway, when the American army captured the town, I ended up in a POW camp. So did the *Gestapo* agents. There were two of them, I think. I need to find these men, and I learned through the army that Max Frohm could help me find them."

"Excuse me for interrupting," said Simon, "but why do you need to find them?"

"Because they are the key to my past," said Schweizer. "I have been on the verge of a nervous breakdown, my marriage is coming apart, and I have been under a doctor's care. The doctor says if I can regain my memory it will be a lot easier to help me. So I am determined to find those men."

Simon appeared to be deep in thought.

"Well? What do you think?" asked Schweizer.

"I think it's the most bizarre story I have ever heard," said Simon.

"Bizarre?" exclaimed Schweizer.

"I guess ridiculous would be a better word. If it were up to me, I'd send you packing. But Max will decide. Wait here, I have to make a phone call."

Ten minutes later Simon returned to the booth and stood looking down at Schweizer.

"Well? What did he say?" asked Schweizer.

"He'll see you," said Simon. "I don't understand why. I advised against it, but he insisted."

"Fine," said Schweizer. "Now where is he? Is he here in New Orleans?"

"You can see him tomorrow at noon in Seattle."

"Seattle?"

"The mountain is not going to come to Mohammed, my friend. If you want to meet Max Frohm, it will have to be in Seattle."

"All right," said Schweizer, "give me the address."

"No address," said Simon. "Go to pier 57 on the waterfront.

There's a seafood restaurant there named 'The Galley.' It's a walkup fast food place. Take a copy of the *Times-Picayune* and tuck it under your arm. Max will contact you."

"Still playing games, I see," said Schweizer.

Simon let out a sigh. "Go to hell, Schweizer," he said and walked away.

An hour later Schweizer was in the air headed for Cincinnati. He had decided it would be better to park his plane and fly commercial. He didn't want to be late for his luncheon engagement.

14

SEATTLE

The view from the air when arriving at the Sea-Tac airport was breathtaking. Schweizer had elected to fly to Los Angeles first and then connect to Seattle on a Western DC-10. He was fortunate to get a window seat, but being on the left side, he only caught a fleeting glimpse of Mt. Rainier when the captain announced it. However, Schweizer did get a good view of Tacoma and Puget Sound. Most impressive, though, was the vast wooded areas. Schweizer made a mental note to consider moving here someday.

The drive into Seattle was further than for most cities Schweizer had flown to. That was because the Sea-Tac airport served both Seattle and Tacoma, and of necessity was located about midway between the two.

Schweizer picked up a city map at the rent-a-car counter. He noted that Seattle was well laid out and he easily located the waterfront area. Twenty minutes later he was exiting the interstate near the King Dome. In the distance he could see the top of the Space Needle, a relic from the world's fair.

After two wrong turns, one of them the wrong way on a one-way street, Schweizer found pier 57 and parked the car under what appeared to be an earlier generation's attempt at building a freeway. Quickly he crossed the street and headed for the fast-food restaurant about a block away.

The wind off the ocean was brisk and cold. Schweizer walked along with his shoulders hunched up. It was lunch time and he noted several joggers in shorts and tee-shirts, in sharp contrast to the crowd of people in heavy coats. *Bunch of health nuts*, he thought.

At pier 57 Schweizer pulled the copy of the *Times-Picayune* from his pocket and tucked it under his arm. He glanced around at the lunch-time crowd, wondering which one was Max Frohm. No one seemed to be paying any attention to Schweizer. One man, middle-aged and well dressed, seemed a likely looking prospect, but he hurried on down the street without looking back.

Schweizer looked at his watch. It was 12:05 PM. Maybe it was just a wild goose chase. The growl in his stomach reminded him that he hadn't eaten yet, so he decided he might as well have lunch. He got in line and started reading the menu above the counter.

"May I recommend the oysters, Mr. Schweizer?" said a male voice.

Schweizer turned and looked at the man next to him. He was short, about 5'6", and obviously past fifty. Covering the man's grey hair was a black and white checked cap. He was dressed in grey slacks, white shirt open at the neck, and a blue sweater. Unusual, considering the wind chill, and not at all the image Schweizer had expected. Frohm had a thin moustache and a twinkle in his eye that seemed to fade as Schweizer looked him over.

"You *are* Karl Schweizer, aren't you?" asked Frohm.

"Yes, but ..."

"I'm not what you expected," offered Frohm. "Is that it?"

Schweizer just shook his head and smiled. Inwardly, he was delighted. The shadow over his life was beginning to depart. It appeared he was finally going to find the key that might unlock his past.

"You have been a very difficult man to find," said Schweizer.

"Oh, not really," said Frohm. "How long have you been looking for me?"

"Three days," said Schweizer. *Is that all?* he thought. It seemed a lifetime ago that he had left Cincinnati for Washington.

"You see," said Frohm triumphantly, "I am not so hard to find."

"There's a lot of questions I'd like to ask you."

Frohm raised his hand like a policeman stopping traffic. "Please, Mr. Schweizer," he said with a chuckle, "everything in its proper time! First, let's eat."

"All right."

They ordered a bucket of steamed clams, oysters, and giant prawns. The french fries that accompanied the meal were actually unpeeled potatoes cut into quarters lengthwise and then deep-fried. They each got a glass of beer and took their meal to a table out on the pier where they could talk in private.

In spite of their ugly brown appearance, Schweizer found the potatoes to be quite tasty. And the oysters? Well, Schweizer had never had anything that tasted so delicious.

"Where do they get oysters like these?" asked Schweizer. "They're as big as a golf ball!"

"I understand they are harvested fresh everyday right out there," said Frohm, pointing at the waters of Puget Sound.

Schweizer looked out at the water. The wind had relented a bit and the water was not very choppy. He was unable to see the much of Puget Sound from where they sat. He heard the moan of a boat horn, and then a ferryboat, painted brilliant white, came into view plowing through the water in a southerly direction. The distant shore was a forest of trees painted in varying shades of dark green. A dim memory of walking barefoot through the trees next to a river floated across Schweizer's consciousness and then quickly disappeared.

"You have come a long way to see me, Mr. Schweizer," said Frohm. "I trust this is not just a social visit."

Schweizer sat staring at a half-eaten oyster. "No, of course not," he said. "What's this brown stuff in the oyster?"

"Oh, the usual thing that passes through the intestines of an animal."

Schweizer made a face and pushed the oysters away. "Come, come, now," said Frohm with a smile. "It's all in your mind, you know. Go ahead, it won't hurt you!"

"If it's all the same to you, I'll pass, thank you."

Frohm shrugged and pulled the container of oysters to his side of the table and began eating them. "Oysters are very good for you," said Frohm. "Some people believe they're an aphrodisiac. I'm not sure I really believe that, but, well, it doesn't hurt, if you know what I mean."

"Why all the mumbo jumbo, Frohm?" asked Schweizer. He felt like he was getting the runaround.

"What do you mean?" responded Frohm without looking up.

"Look, I was held at gunpoint in the basement of my hotel, sent to New Orleans, and now here. No one has offered one word of explanation. How come?"

Frohm finished the oysters and washed them down with the last swallow of beer. He sat for several moments staring at the empty glass, a serious look on his face. "It distresses me that you were held at gunpoint," said Frohm, "but it does not surprise me."

Schweizer looked attentive, but unconcerned. "You see," continued Frohm, "I spent twenty years in the Clandestine Operations branch before I retired from the CIA in 1964. No one, not even my family, knew I was with the CIA. My cover was working for the USIA. I was away a lot, but that was just part of the job. When you began making inquiries about me, it upset certain people. Not only the work I did, but even my connection with the agency was a closely guarded secret. You're lucky they didn't kill you."

"You don't really think ..."

"Oh, yes, Mr. Schweizer. Make no mistake about that. They would have, if it had been necessary."

Schweizer began to shiver, partly from the wind and partly from what he had just heard. He had thought these things only happened in movies. "What about Simon?" asked Schweizer.

"Simon is a good friend and that's all you need to know about him." Schweizer felt an unseen door being slammed in his face. "I wanted to meet you right away, but it was decided an intermediary should check you out first. I asked for Simon."

"Well, do I pass?" asked Schweizer.

"If you hadn't, you wouldn't be here," said Frohm as he gathered up the refuse from his meal. "Let's clean this mess up and then go for a walk. It's good for the digestion."

Frohm dropped the empty food containers in a trash barrel and strolled out to the end of the pier. The sound of water lapping against pilings was very soothing. "You're like a ghost from the past," said Frohm.

"In what way?" asked Schweizer.

"You were on my list of prisoners to interrogate, but before I could, you had disappeared. I never expected to come across you again."

Schweizer stopped walking. Taking Frohm by the elbow he asked, "What do you mean? You remember my name after all these years?"

"Well, considering the circumstances I could hardly ..." Frohm's voice trailed off when he saw the puzzled look on Schweizer's face. A flash of fear went through Frohm as he backed away from Schweizer. "You're not Schweizer. Who are you? What do you want?"

Schweizer was bewildered. "I don't understand," he said. "What are you talking about?"

Frohm didn't answer as he backed up to the railing of the pier. The two eyed each other, Frohm apprehensively and Schweizer uncertainly. "What do you want from me?" asked Frohm as he looked for some avenue of escape.

"I had hoped you could help me regain my memory," said Schweizer sarcastically. "I didn't know I was getting in with a bunch of screwballs."

It was Frohm's turn to look surprised. "Your memory?"

"Yeah, I was hoping you could give me the names of two prisoners, *Gestapo* agents."

"What is it you don't remember?"

Schweizer's eyes rolled upward. "If I knew what I had forgotten, then I wouldn't have forgotten it, would I?"

Frohm blushed. "I meant, what time in your life?" Schweizer pulled the hair back on the right side of his forehead. An ugly scar was clearly visible. "I got this in a bombing near the end of the war," said Schweizer. "I don't remember anything prior to waking up in the hospital."

Frohm's look of concern faded into a smile. Then he began to laugh. "What's so funny?" asked Schweizer.

"I'm sorry for the misunderstanding," said Frohm, more relaxed. "There are people who would like to see me dead, and for a moment there I thought you were an imposter."

"What gave you that idea?"

"It doesn't really matter. It's quite silly, actually. How would the names of these two prisoners help you regain your memory?"

"Well, I remember being questioned in the hospital. I thought perhaps if I could find these two, they might know something about my background, something that might cue my memory."

"Why have you waited all these years?" asked Frohm.

"They told me I would never remember," said Schweizer. "They said I had brain damage."

"Do you?'"

"No. I've been to a doctor and he says I should be able to remember, but I don't."

"But why now?"

Schweizer stood looking at his feet, hands in his pockets. "I've been to a psychologist," he said slowly. "I've been on the verge of a nervous breakdown ... my wife has threatened to leave me ... my life is a mess." Schweizer looked up at Frohm, a pleading look on his face. "The psychologist says the answers lie in my past. Won't you please help me?"

Frohm had a satisfied look on his face as he assessed the situation. "Yes, Schweizer, I can help you. I have all the notes from my interrogations."

"You do?" asked Schweizer, his face brightening.

"Yes. I had hoped to someday write a book. Come, I'll take you home with me."

"What about my rental car?" asked Schweizer.

"No problem," said Frohm. "I came into town on the bus. I'll ride with you."

Twenty minutes later Schweizer had crossed Lake Washington and was exiting the Interstate at Bellevue. "That's an interesting building," said Schweizer, pointing at a spire rising above the trees. "I find it quite attractive. What is it?"

"It's the new Mormon temple." Frohm frowned and shook his head. As they passed the site Schweizer could see construction equipment through the trees, evidence that the building was not yet complete. "It's all wrong," said Frohm. "The architecture doesn't fit the area. We fought it, but ... I hear they have a lot of money."

Schweizer nodded, but said nothing. He preferred to enjoy the ride and the scenery. It looked even better from the ground than it had from the air. A few minutes later they turned down a wooded lane and stopped in front of a ranch style home nestled among the trees.

"You live quite comfortably," said Schweizer. "How can you afford this on a government pension?"

"I teach languages at the university," said Frohm. "And I have modest tastes."

Inside the house Frohm led the way to a cluttered room that appeared to be a den or study. "Have a seat," said Frohm, motioning toward a student desk. It was the type that had a writing desk that attached to the side of the chair and curved around in front.

The room was very small, about 9' x 10', and two walls were lined with books, most of them in Russian and German. In the middle of the room was an old office desk, and Schweizer sat facing it, his own chair almost touching it. Frohm was going down the rows of books, looking for something. In the corner, next to Schweizer, was what appeared to be an exercise bicycle, but instead of a front wheel, it had a fan. "What's this?" asked Schweizer.

Frohm looked over his shoulder. "Oh, that?" Schweizer nodded. "I got that from a fallout shelter. If the power fails, you just peddle to keep the room ventilated. I haven't found a use for it yet, but I'm still thinking about it."

"Are you married?" asked Schweizer.

"Yes."

"Is your ..."

"I told her to go shopping today. We won't be disturbed." Frohm continued looking through the books. "Ah, here they are," he said triumphantly. He removed two cloth-bound volumes from behind a row of books. They were bluish-grey and had circular stains on the covers, apparently from coffee cups. Frohm sat down at his desk and blew the dust from the books.

Schweizer leaned forward, eager to discover what secrets the books might contain. He could see handwriting on lined pages. "Are those your interrogation notes?" asked Schweizer.

"Mmm, yes," said Frohm as he thumbed through the pages. "I'm trying to find the right dates. These aren't very well organized. I used both books."

Several moments passed as Frohm flipped through pages of the first book, sometimes stopping to read something half-aloud. Finally, he tossed the first book down and let out a sigh. "Not in that one," he said. Schweizer picked up the discarded book and began looking through it while Frohm started on the other one. It was not the most interesting thing Schweizer had read, but he could see the possibilities for writing a book.

About a third of the way through the book, Schweizer came upon a notation that caught his interest. It read:

"May 8, 1945-German High Command surrendered today-instructed to be on lookout for Georg Wetzel, SS - possible war criminal."

Schweizer had a vague impression of barbed wire and trees, but it quickly faded away.

"I think I have something here," said Frohm.

"What's that?" Schweizer tossed the book he had been looking at onto the desk and got up.

"Were you hospitalized in Augsburg?"

"Yes, that's right." Schweizer moved around the desk and looked over Frohm's shoulder.

"There were two *Gestapo* agents arrested in Augsburg in April, 1945. One of them had been wounded."

"That's it! That's it!" said Schweizer excitedly. "Who were they? Where are they from?"

"Be patient, Schweizer," said Frohm without looking up. "There's a lot of notes to look through. Do you mind if I smoke?" Schweizer nodded his assent and Frohm retrieved a pipe from the center drawer of his desk and began filling it from a green and red pouch of tobacco. "Why don't you sit down? This will take awhile longer."

Schweizer returned to his seat while Frohm lit his pipe and began reading the notebook. This time he turned the pages more slowly. Occasionally he would pause and use the pipe stem as a pointer as he read the faded pages.

Schweizer pulled his nail clippers out and began clipping his nails. They were already short, but clipping his nails was a nervous habit he had picked up many years before.

Slowly, Schweizer became aware that the only sound in the room was the clicking of his nail clippers. He looked across the desk at Frohm, who had now stopped turning pages and was gently nodding his head as if agreeing with what he was reading. Schweizer shifted in his seat and looked hard at Frohm. After several seconds Frohm's eyes became visible above the rims of his glasses.

"Does the name Klaus Dieter Berndt mean anything to you?" asked Frohm. Schweizer shook his head. "What about Hans Koerbler?" Schweizer shook his head again. "Well, my friend, those are the two men you must find."

"I take it the wounded man survived," said Schweizer.

Frohm nodded.

Schweizer had a pensive look on his face as he leaned on his forearms, with hands clasped in front of him. "It's funny," he said in a low tone. "I have looked so hard for those two names and now I don't know what to do with them. Any suggestions?"

"Possibly," said Frohm. "Berndt was from Munich and Koerbler was from a small village called Heidenheim. You could check with the local police, since citizens are required to register when moving to or from any town. You might also try the Library of Congress. I understand they have phone books from all over the world. Maybe you'll get lucky."

"Well, either way it looks like I'll be going to Europe. I've got a friend in Switzerland who might help me."

"Oh? Who is that?"

"His name is Kalt. We escaped from the POW camp together."

Frohm's eyebrows raised, almost imperceptibly, and his face took on an amused look. He looked directly at Schweizer and said, "You have a challenging adventure ahead of you. I wish you the best of luck. Let me write down these names for you."

Frohm quickly scribbled the names on a piece of paper and handed it across the desk. As Schweizer rose to leave Frohm stood up, walked around the desk and extended his hand. "I hope you find what you are looking for," he said.

Schweizer shook Frohm's hand and smiled. "Things are finally looking up. At least now I have some hope."

"Would it be an inconvenience to drop me off at the university?" asked Frohm. "My wife has the car."

"No problem," said Schweizer. "My flight doesn't leave until this evening."

15

MUNICH

The flight to Germany didn't start out as routinely as it ended. The Pan Am 747 departed New York's JFK airport in the evening. As the big jet climbed northward for Boston, New Foundland and the great circle route across the North Atlantic, the Pan Am captain chose a course with a spectacular view of Manhattan on the left. In an attempt to capture the bright city lights for his scrapbook, a tourist across the aisle from Schweizer took a picture with a flash. The unexpected brilliance inside the cabin caused a minor panic among those who didn't realize what had happened.

Schweizer just shook his head and frowned. *Serves him right, the idiot,* thought Schweizer. *All he'll get is a great shot of his flash reflection in the window.*

With little to do except read or sleep during the seven hours it would take to reach Frankfurt, Schweizer tried to sleep, since his arrival in Germany would be early morning Frankfurt time, and middle of the night by both New York time and his own biological clock. With a four-hour wait for a connecting flight to Munich, he wondered if it might not be quicker to take a train. But trains were noisy and bounced around a lot.

With the information he had gleaned from Max Frohm, Schweizer had visited the Library of Congress and researched their extensive collection of telephone books from around the world. He found several listings for Klaus Berndt, including one residing in Munich. Since he could find no listings for the right Koerbler, Schweizer decided to start with the Berndt in Munich because Frohm had indicated that Munich was Berndt's hometown. If that didn't pan out, he could then look up the other listings for Berndt. If he exhausted the Berndts, then Schweizer would try looking for Koerbler. Anyway, he was glad that he would have some local help.

Schweizer hadn't seen Friedrich Kalt in thirty years, but they had corresponded and exchanged Christmas cards irregularly. Kalt had even helped pay Schweizer's way through college. A warm feeling came over Schweizer as he remembered the telephone call he had made to Zurich earlier in the day.

"Hallo, hier ist Kalt." said the voice on the other end.

"Friedrich? Friedrich Kalt?" said Schweizer, *"Hier ist Karl Schweizer in Amerika."*

There was a moment of silence at the other end of the line. "Karl Schweizer? Is that really you?"

"In the flesh," said Schweizer.

"My god, man, how are you?" asked Kalt. "It's been such a long time. It's been, uh ..."

"Thirty years," volunteered Schweizer. "I wasn't sure you would remember me."

"*Ach, Mensch!*" said Kalt. "Who could forget someone such as you? What are you doing nowadays?"

"I'm on my way to Germany. My plane leaves tonight. I'll be in Munich tomorrow afternoon."

"That's good news, Karl. I hope you can come by and see me."

"Don't worry about that," said Schweizer. "If my business in Munich is unsuccessful, I'll definitely be going to Lausanne. I'm looking for a man named Klaus Dieter Berndt. If I'm lucky, he will be able to tell me things about my past."

"What do you mean, Karl?" asked Kalt.

"I've been to a doctor," said Schweizer. "He assures me that there is no physical reason for my loss of memory. We are hoping that Berndt can tell me information about my past that might stimulate my memory."

"I see," said Kalt. "But what does this Berndt fellow have to do with you?"

"He was a *Gestapo* agent."

"You never told me about any *Gestapo* agents," said Kalt.

"I didn't think it was important. He was in my hospital room when I woke up."

"What did he want?"

"That's what I hope to find out," replied Schweizer.

"If you want to learn of your past, why not just go to the German government?"

"I thought of that, but if the *Gestapo* wanted me, maybe the German government still does."

"Good thinking. It's best to leave some things in their grave. So, this man Berndt is in Lausanne then?"

"Well, I'm not sure," said Schweizer. "There is a Klaus Berndt in Lausanne, but I am going to try the Klaus Dieter Berndt in Munich first. Munich was his hometown."

"I see. How would you like it if I helped you in your search?"

"Thanks, Friedrich. I was hoping you would say that," said Schweizer. "Can you meet me in Munich tomorrow?"

"Let me check my schedule," said Kalt. After a brief pause, Kalt returned to the phone. "It's not possible for Monday, but Tuesday I will be there. Can you meet me at the *Hauptbahnhof*? My train will get in at 3:15 in the afternoon."

"Sure. That's fine."

"One more thing," said Kalt.

"What's that?"

"I'm very glad that you are coming."

Sleep didn't come easily for Schweizer sitting up in an airline seat. One of the stewardesses offered him a pillow and then roused him later to buckle his seat belt when the jet encountered turbulent weather somewhere over the Atlantic. Finally, he drifted off to sleep and began to dream.

Schweizer found himself on an airliner with no fuselage, only a frame. The other passengers were gaunt-looking, with hollow eyes and pale skin. Schweizer could feel the wind in his face, and below his feet he could see the ground. He knew he must remain seated, for if he left his seat, he would fall through the framework and be killed. The phantom plane flew lower and lower. At last the ground was so close, it was only a blur at his feet. Suddenly, Schweizer felt a sharp jolt and awoke struggling with his seat belt, overcome by the need to flee. He looked out the window and saw a small building flash by. A short distance away were rows of American military planes. The captain reversed thrust and Schweizer felt himself being pressed against the seat belt. Outside it was a dreary scene, overcast and small puddles of water on the ground. They had arrived at the Rhein-Main airport in Frankfurt.

Munich was not the land of beer-drinking Bavarians in *lederhosen* or buxom maidens wearing *dirndls* that Schweizer had expected. Instead he found a bustling metropolis artfully blending the old with the new. Schweizer was disappointed about the Alps, though. He had imagined the city to be ringed with scenic mountains, but found they were several miles to the south and could be seen only on very clear days.

It was well past noon when Schweizer checked into the *Hotel Vier Jahreszeiten*. He was tired, hungry and had a grubby feeling from not having bathed or shaved in more than 24 hours. He considered a nap, but decided against it. By the time he awakened, it would be late in the evening and he might miss his chance to visit Berndt today, and he didn't feel like waiting until tomorrow.

The hotel restaurant was not open for dinner yet, so after a bath and a shave he went to a *Gasthaus* down the street and ordered dinner. He found the *Kalbschnitzel und Karloffelsalat* much to his liking.

Restaurants in America advertised German cuisine, but it was always more of a promise than a reality. Schweizer ordered a stein of Löwenbräu with his meal. It was a treat to drink the real thing instead of the weak imitation sold back home.

After his meal, Schweizer stopped in a magazine shop and picked up a Munich city map and a map of the *Strassenbahn* routes. The address he had found for Klaus Dieter Berndt was not far, Hanigstrasse 161. Schweizer considered calling first, but rejected the idea, favoring instead a face-to-face meeting. Most people found it easier to hang up a phone than to slam a door in someone's face.

The public transportation was efficient and frequent, but many of the stops were in the middle of the street, since that was where the streetcar tracks were, a fact that Schweizer thought quite dangerous. Schweizer took the number 8 streetcar to within two blocks of the Berndt address. Hanigstrasse was a short street with only a few trees. None of the houses had what could reasonably be called a yard by American standards, though some of them had wooden fences and shrubbery.

Building number 161 was a two story affair with a stucco exterior, painted grey. The building itself was right against the sidewalk with a yard on the south side. Schweizer could see a row of garages behind the building, probably accessible from an alley. Next to the front door were four mailboxes, each with its own doorbell and a single intercom speaker. The name on number 4 read: BERNDT.

Schweizer looked at his watch. He had to calculate the time, because he hadn't reset his watch since leaving home. It was just after six in the evening, dinner time. In the waning light none of the windows appeared to be illuminated. Schweizer pressed the button for number 4 and stepped back to watch for a reaction.

A light came on in an upstairs window. A few seconds later the intercom speaker came to life. "Who is it?" asked a male voice.

"*Herr* Berndt?"

"Yes."

"Klaus Dieter Berndt?"

"Yes."

"My name is Karl Schweizer, *Herr* Berndt."

"Yes?"

"I have come all the way from America to see you, *Herr* Berndt," said Schweizer. "May I come up?"

The intercom fell silent, then Schweizer heard a barely audible click as it was turned off. Upstairs the light went off. Schweizer was perplexed. It was the quickest brush off he had ever been given. For several seconds he stood contemplating his next move. As he reached to press the button again, the door quietly opened and the head of a balding, white-haired man appeared . "What do you want?" he asked.

"Are you Klaus Berndt?"

"I am."

Schweizer felt ill at ease. He had come far and perhaps this was his man, but now he didn't know how to begin. The two men looked at each other. "The man I am looking for was a policeman during the war," said Schweizer.

A cold, hard look appeared in Berndt's eyes. "I am sorry. I cannot help you," he said as he withdrew his head into the doorway.

"Wait!" cried Schweizer. He lunged for the door and caught it just before it could click shut. Schweizer pushed the door open and looked into the darkened foyer. Standing at the foot of the stairs, looking defiant, was Berndt.

Just then a door opened and a middle-aged woman looked out. "Is anything wrong, *Herr* Berndt?" she asked.

The light from the doorway gave Schweizer his first good look at Berndt. He was dressed in rumpled dark pants, a dark sweater and a white shirt, buttoned at the throat. The collar was frayed and the shirt looked as if it hadn't seen the inside of a washing machine for a few weeks. "No, *Frau* Beck, nothing is wrong," said Berndt, motioning to the woman with his right hand. Schweizer's eyes were drawn to the hand. It was withered and deformed.

Frau Beck closed the door, leaving the two men semi-darkness. An old memory formed in Schweizer's mind. "You *are* the man," said Schweizer softly. "Your hand ... I was there when it happened. You *were* in the *Gestapo*."

"Schweizer ... Schweizer ... yes, now I remember," said Berndt.

"What do you remember?" asked Schweizer, his voice betraying excitement.

Berndt had a morose, far-away look in his eyes. Finally he looked up at Schweizer. "Why have you come back?" he asked. "Have you spent it all?"

"I ... I don't understand," said Schweizer. "Spent what?"

An angry look came over Berndt. He stepped forward and with his left hand, grown powerful from overdependence, he grasped Schweizer by the throat and slammed him against the wall. "No one, do you understand, not even my wife knows I was in the *Gestapo*! So go away! Go back to where you came from!" Schweizer heard the door open a crack and Berndt released his grip. "It's all right, *Frau* Beck," said Berndt. "My friend is just leaving."

The door closed quietly. "You must help me," insisted Schweizer in a hoarse whisper.

116

Berndt turned and mounted the stairs. "Good night, *Herr* Schweizer," he said.

"*Herr* Berndt ... please!" implored Schweizer.

Berndt paused for a few seconds and then over his shoulder he said: "If you come again, I'll kill you."

Dejected, Schweizer watched Berndt disappear through a door at the top of the stairs. He stood for several moments in the darkness, then walked out into the cool spring evening. He was too distraught to notice the car that slowed as it passed.

On the ride back to the hotel, Schweizer felt very low. As the streetcar bounced along, jet lag fatigue weighed heavily on his body. Schweizer thought that what he needed most was a few drinks and a lot of sleep. He didn't know what his next move was going to be, and right now he didn't even want to think about it.

Gradually the streets became brighter as the streetcar came closer to the city center. At the Sendlinger Tor Platz a striking young woman got on the streetcar. Schweizer figured she was in her mid-thirties. What attracted his attention was the suitcase she was carrying and the unhappy look on her face. She came and sat opposite Schweizer. He wondered if she were running away from something. Their, eyes met briefly and Schweizer managed a thin smile in spite of how depressed he was feeling. The woman looked down at her lap. "Are you a tourist?" asked Schweizer, surprised at his own boldness.

The woman looked up at Schweizer and tried to smile, but it looked more like a grimace. She shook her head and looked down at her lap again. In spite of the dim light of the streetcar, Schweizer could see that her eyes looked red. He wondered if she had been crying. "I couldn't help noticing your suitcase," said Schweizer, "so, naturally I thought you might be a tourist." The woman didn't look at him. "I'm from America, myself," he continued. "Are you from Munich?"

The young woman turned her head and looked out the window. The streetcar turned onto Maximillianstrasse. The hotel was only a few blocks away. Schweizer felt embarrassed that his attempts at conversation had been rebuffed. He had not meant to be forward. He just needed someone to talk to, to ease the anger and frustration he felt.

The streetcar rumbled to a halt in front of the hotel. The woman got up an instant before Schweizer did. She glanced nervously at him as she started for the exit. Schweizer knew she thought he was following her. He almost sat down again, but thought, *what the hell, let her think what she wants.*

As the woman stepped down from the streetcar, she saw Schweizer right behind her. The curb was some thirty feet away. She quickened her pace, looking furtively behind. She didn't see the car speeding towards her, but Schweizer did. He grabbed her by the elbow and jerked her back, turning her around. "Let go of me!" she yelled, pulling free. She heard the screech of tires on the pavement just before the car brushed her on the buttocks. The suitcase was knocked from her hand and bounced several feet along the pavement. The car slowed momentarily, then in a burst of speed disappeared around the corner.

Schweizer caught the woman by the elbows as she was pitched forward by the impact. Their faces were very close. Schweizer saw her eyes open wide as she realized what had happened. "I ... I ... I'm sorry," she stammered. "I thought ..."

"It's all right," said Schweizer. "Are you hurt?"

She stood fully erect, reached back and felt her bottom.

"No, I ..." she began, then burst into tears.

Schweizer slipped his arm around her shoulder. A crowd had begun to gather and someone had retrieved the suitcase. Schweizer thanked the man who had returned it, and then he helped the woman to the curb. "Are you staying here?" he asked.

"Yes," she said.

"What's your name?" he asked.

"Erika Koenig."

"My name is Karl Schweizer."

On the sidewalk they stopped, facing each other. Erika smiled. "Thank you," she said.

Schweizer looked at the ground for a few moments, searching for the right words. "I'm a stranger here," he said, "and I'm alone, and I thought maybe you were too, and I was wondering if you might want to have dinner with me."

Erika glanced around, as if looking for someone. She seemed to have something on her mind. Finally, she looked back at Schweizer and said: "All right. It doesn't make any difference now."

"Pardon me," said Schweizer. "I don't understand."

"It's nothing to do with you," said Erika. "I've just had a very bad experience today, that's all."

Schweizer nodded. "I can understand how you feel," he said.

Erika smiled and shook her head. "I have to check in," she said. "I'll be down in about fifteen minutes. Do you drink?"

"Occasionally," said Schweizer.

"Good," said Erika.

The evening was a moderate success in spite of the shaky beginning. Erika had seemed very distant at first, but she began to loosen up after dinner and several drinks. Schweizer learned she was thirty-six and had been divorced for five years. She also had two

118

children who lived with their father, a fact that Schweizer found unusual in spite of the women's lib movement.

In the beginning Schweizer had felt a twinge of guilt about trying to hustle Erika, but he managed to rationalize his actions by remembering how cool Carole had been when he had last seen her. By ten o'clock that night Schweizer was feeling pretty relaxed. He had even forgotten about the disastrous results of his meeting with Berndt. When Erika said she wanted to go back to the hotel, Schweizer had vague feelings of regret that the evening was already over.

The elevator hummed to a halt at the floor Erika's room was on. Schweizer stepped through the door with her. "Oh, are you on this floor, too?" she asked innocently.

Schweizer's face colored a bit. "No," he answered, "I thought I might walk you to your door."

Erika made a show of looking up and down the hall. "I don't seem to see any dangerous characters lurking in the hallway," she said teasingly. Schweizer began to blush furiously as beads of sweat formed on his brow. He was obviously in over his head and now was hoping only for a graceful withdrawal. Schweizer's discomfiture had become painfully apparent as Erika reached up and touched him on the cheek. "You would like to go to bed with me, wouldn't you?" she asked softly.

"The thought *had* crossed my mind," said Schweizer. Maybe there was hope for the situation after all.

"Poor baby," said Erika, "you've been married so long you've forgotten how to seduce a woman."

Schweizer had had enough. First the run-in with Berndt and now this. As he turned to go Erika grabbed his arm. "Karl, wait! I'm sorry. Please try to understand. I had a very great disappointment today, and I guess I just wanted to hurt somebody ... anybody."

"Sweetheart, you don't know what disappointment really is," said Schweizer bitterly, as he jerked his arm away. Erika hadn't expected her teasing to get this kind of a reaction. Schweizer had the "hurt little boy" look that his wife knew so well. Erika wasn't sure how to deal with it.

"Karl," said Erika softly, "won't you please forgive me?" Schweizer only shrugged. "I'd like it if you would walk me to my door," she added.

Just then the elevator door opened and two young women got off. They were chattering gaily in French and barely seemed to notice Schweizer and Erika as they passed. In a moment they were out of sight. The interruption had broken the tension, and Karl and Erika smiled at each other a little sheepishly.

"Shall we start over?" asked Erika.

"Why not?"

Erika reached in her purse for her key and handed it to Schweizer. He looked at the number on the key and then at the plastic sign on the wall opposite the elevator doors for directions. Erika took Schweizer's outstretched hand and gave it a squeeze. As they walked hand-in-hand to her door, neither spoke.

Schweizer unlocked the door and handed Erika the key.

"Thank you, Karl," she said. "You saved me from an otherwise dreary evening. It's no fun feeling sorry for yourself."

Schweizer looked longingly into her eyes. "Erika ..." he said as he took a tentative step toward her. Erika slipped easily into his arms and laid her head on his shoulder. A warm feeling spread through Schweizer's body as he held her close. All the hurt and frustration he had felt over the past several months faded into nothingness. After a few moments Erika looked up at him and a kind of unspoken communication passed between them. Schweizer maneuvered her through the open door and kicked it shut. In the darkness their lips met for the first time. He did not rush the kiss as some men are prone to do, but kissed her tenderly. Erika's lips parted to receive his probing tongue.

Twenty-four years of marriage had blunted Schweizer's sex drive. The act itself had become a routine now-and-then thing, one's marital duty, a release of tension. But now, as he held Erika and felt her respond to his caress, he felt once again like the young bull of his youth. He reached for the zipper of her dress. Erika's response was immediate and decisive. "No!" she said firmly and pushed away from him. "I don't like men to undress me."

"Aw, you're kidding ..."

"No, I just don't like it," said Erika as she flipped on the light. "I'll undress myself, if you don't mind."

"Oh, all right," said Schweizer with a shrug as he looked around the room. "Do you have a bathroom?"

"Yes, it's right through there," she said, pointing at the door, "but being so straight-laced, wouldn't you feel more comfortable undressing in the closet?"

"You're very funny," said Schweizer with a grin. He was finally beginning to appreciate her sense of humor now that he no longer had a chip on his shoulder. "If I did in the closet what I plan to do in the bathroom, the hotel would take back its welcome sign."

"Hurry back," said Erika sensuously. She was already beginning to undress when Schweizer closed the bathroom door.

When he finally returned, Erika looked up at him and tossed the magazine she had been reading onto the floor.

"Don't be bashful," she said and patted the bed. Schweizer came over and sat down. "What happened here?" she asked, fingering the scar on his rib cage.

"I was wounded in the war."

"Oh," was her only reaction. Erika pulled him to her and kissed him passionately. All the desire he had felt earlier returned in a rush.

His passion spent, Schweizer lay looking up at the ceiling, out of breath. Erika leaned up on her elbow and began drawing imaginary circles on Schweizer's chest with her index finger. She wore a very happy, satisfied smile. "I'm glad I met you," she said. "I only wish we had met sooner."

Schweizer did not respond. The alcohol and the exertion had taken their inevitable toll and he was snoring softly. Erika lay beside him for several minutes thinking of the evening they had spent together and of the circumstances that had brought them together in this strange city. After awhile she pulled the covers over Schweizer and like a loving mother tucked him in before turning out the light.

Along about dawn Schweizer awoke to find Erika kissing and caressing him. He didn't notice the tears that were wetting her cheeks. Surprisingly, he found himself equal to the task. He knew they would never believe this in Cincinnati. After making love for the third time, Schweizer fell into a deep sleep.

Brilliant sunlight flooded the room as the curtains were drawn back. The suddenness of it startled Schweizer awake. "What the hell's going on?" he demanded, shielding his eyes from the light.

The only response he heard was a giggle. Next to the window was a matronly appearing woman with a look of surprise on her face. Standing in the doorway was the source of the giggles, a plain-looking girl barely out of her teens. Behind her in the hall, Schweizer could see a cart with cleaning implements and fresh linen. Only then did he realize he was lying on top of the covers stark naked. He quickly threw the covers over himself.

"I'm sorry, sir," said the older woman. "We didn't know the room was still occupied. We only wanted to get it ready for the next occupant."

Schweizer looked quickly around the room. Erika's luggage was gone. "All right, all right," he said, motioning for them to leave. "Just give me a minute or two to get dressed."

"Yes, sir. Sorry, sir," said the maid as she retreated from the room. The young girl was still giggling. On the outside door handle Schweizer could see the "Do not disturb" sign had been turned around.

It now read: "Please clean this room immediately."

A vision of Erika with a teasing smile flashed into Schweizer's mind. "Damn her," muttered Schweizer to himself. He quickly dressed and went back to his own room to clean up. It was almost noon.

16

MUNICH

Though there was always the possibility of locating Koerbler, Schweizer still considered Berndt his best bet. Schweizer had not really had the opportunity of explaining his search to Berndt. Perhaps if Berndt could be assured of his sincerity and discretion, then perhaps the former *Gestapo* agent might be willing to shed some light on Schweizer's past. It was at least worth a try. Anyway, Schweizer didn't take the threat Berndt had made very seriously.

The streetcar ride to Berndt's neighborhood was a more pleasurable experience the second time. It was midday and the sun was shining brightly. The temperature was in the sixties and the first buds of spring had already begun to appear. Schweizer found the walk from the streetcar stop to Hanigstrasse very invigorating. He made a mental note to get more exercise when he got home to Cincinnati.

At the corner where Hanigstrasse began, Schweizer stopped abruptly. Two police cars and an ambulance were parked in front of Berndt's residence. A feeling of foreboding settled over Schweizer as he continued down the street.

Several people were standing around in front of the building. Some were talking to the police. Schweizer approached the apartment building, but stopped several yards away, unable to decide whether or not to inquire or just keep walking. Just then the front door opened and two shrouded figures were carried out on stretchers.

"Move along, please," said a policeman to Schweizer. He did not respond. He knew he couldn't leave without knowing whose bodies were on the stretchers.

"What happened?" asked Schweizer.

"An elderly couple were killed by a burglar," said the policeman.

"Who was it?" asked Schweizer.

"The name was Berndt," said the policeman. "Did you know them?"

Schweizer just looked at the bodies being loaded into the ambulance. "Could it have been a murder-suicide?" he asked.

The policeman gave Schweizer a curious look. "No," he said, "they were both tied up. Why do you ask?"

"Just curious," said Schweizer. "These things happen sometimes."

Standing next to the front door was *Frau* Beck, clutching a handkerchief and crying. She was being questioned by a policeman.

Schweizer decided to leave. The woman might recognize him and he didn't want to have to make any lengthy explanations. As he turned to go, his path was blocked by the same policeman who had spoken to him. "Just a minute, sir," said the officer. "You didn't answer my question."

Schweizer pulled his passport from his coat pocket and handed it to the policeman. "I'm just a tourist enjoying a walk in your city," said Schweizer.

"Oh, I'm sorry," said the officer, looking at the passport. "But your German is so good I never would have thought ..."

"It's all right," said Schweizer as he took back the passport. "Good day to you, sir." Schweizer walked briskly away. *What rotten luck,* he thought. *Now what?*

Schweizer had two hours to kill before Kalt's train was due to arrive. He spent part of the time window shopping on Kaufingerstrasse, but eventually found his way to a bar. It didn't take long to ease the pain.

By three o'clock Schweizer had consumed six mugs of beer and was feeling pretty mellow. The *Hauptbahnhof* was only a few blocks away, but Schweizer decided to take a cab. Walking the short distance was more adventure than he could handle, considering his current degree of sobriety.

In the train station, Schweizer found a schedule of arriving trains. The train from Zurich was due at 3:15 PM on track number nine. Schweizer located the gate with little difficulty. He looked at his watch ... 3:14. In the distance, some three hundred yards away, a train was approaching on track nine. Several moments later, the engine slid to a stop at the end of the track and doors began opening down the length of the train, disgorging several hundred passengers. Schweizer stood off to the side of the gate, wondering how he would recognize Kalt. Thirty years could make a big difference.

As they passed through the exit Schweizer searched the crowd looking for a familiar face. "Karl ... Karl Schweizer," someone called out behind him. Schweizer turned and saw a man dressed in a grey overcoat, carrying a suitcase. Without a doubt it was Kalt. He looked older and his hair, though thin on top, was a bit longer on the sides and now had turned salt and pepper grey, but it was definitely Friedrich Kalt. He rushed over to Schweizer and embraced him.

"Karl! How wonderful to see you!" said Kalt. "How was your trip?"

"Just fine, "said Schweizer, embarrassed by the smell of alcohol on his breath. "But how did you get past me?"

Kalt leaned away and took a good look at Schweizer. "It's a big crowd," he said. "I almost didn't see you. Anyway, did you have any luck?"

Schweizer's eyes were downcast. "Yes and no," he said. "I found Berndt ..."

"That's good news!" interrupted Kalt.

"... but he was murdered last night."

"My god!" said Kalt. "How is that possible?"

"I don't know. They said it was a burglar, killed both him and his wife."

"What a shame!" said Kalt, sounding sympathetic. "Did you get to speak to him at all?"

"Oh, yes," said Schweizer, "I talked to him all right, but he wouldn't tell me anything ... even threatened to kill me if I came back."

The crowd had dissipated, leaving the two men nearly alone by the track nine exit. Kalt had a very concerned expression on his face. "What are you going to do now?" he asked.

Schweizer shrugged his shoulders. "Go home, I guess."

"Oh, no, Karl, don't do that," said Kalt. "This is just a temporary setback. Besides, you spent a lot of money to get here. Enjoy it! Think of it as a vacation. In the meantime we can get our heads together and think of another plan."

"You 're probably right," said Schweizer.

"Of course I'm right," said Kalt. "Now where are you staying?"

"I'm at the *Vier Jahreszeiten*," said Schweizer.

"Oh, ho! A big spender! That's one of Munich's most expensive hotels."

"Is it? I leave such details to the travel agents," said Schweizer.

"I may as well check in there, too," said Kalt, picking up his suitcase and motioning toward the main entrance. "After you."

The two men were halfway across the lobby of the train station, when Schweizer spotted a familiar face. "Erika!" he called out. "Wait a minute. There's someone I'd like you to meet."

Erika was minus her suitcase, which Schweizer thought strange if she were going to catch a train. She smiled and took a halting step in their direction. Instantly the smile vanished and Erika's hand moved up in front of her mouth. She turned and began walking quickly away.

"What's wrong with her?" muttered Schweizer to himself. "Erika! Wait!"

Erika started to run and in seconds was out the main entrance. As Schweizer watched her disappear, he was bewildered by her reaction. *Was she embarrassed by their encounter of the previous night?* he wondered.

"Who was that?" asked Kalt.

"Just a girl I met last night," said Schweizer.

"Very attractive. I see you made a favorable impression on her." Kalt had a sly grin on his face.

"Well, I spent the night in her bed, if that's what you mean," said Schweizer. "I just can't understand why she would run away like that."

"She probably has a husband. Don't worry about it. It was just a one-night stand, wasn't it?"

Images of the previous evening were swimming in Schweizer's mind. He wanted to tell Kalt about Erika, about the warm and special feeling he had for her ... but he only said, "Yeah, I guess you're right again."

"Of course I'm right. Now let's go get some dinner and make some plans."

Bavarian cuisine was much to Kalt's liking. During the course of the meal, he had finished off a double portion of *Sauerbraten, Spätzle,* and *Rotkohl* along with a liter of beer. Throughout it all he had maintained a running commentary on what he had been doing for thirty years. Schweizer hardly spoke, but he was still not able to finish eating before Kalt did. What impressed Schweizer most, though, was the fact that Kalt looked fairly trim in spite of his robust appetite.

When Kalt had finished, he sat back and let out a loud belch. *Too much beer*, thought Schweizer. He looked up and noticed Kalt was eyeing the uneaten portion on his plate.

"What's wrong, Karl? Isn't the local food to your liking?"

"It's not that," said Schweizer. "The food is actually quite good." Schweizer picked up his fork and started eating again. Kalt had a definite look of disappointment on his face. "I keep thinking of Berndt," Schweizer continued. "Why would anyone want to kill him? He was my best lead."

"Don't despair," said Kalt, who had started on the basket of assorted bread and rolls. "Our next move will be to find your military service record. That should give us plenty of leads."

That suggestion caught Schweizer by surprise. "I thought you agreed we should stay away from that," he said.

Kalt finished spreading jam on his bread before answering. "That was before the death of *Herr* Berndt. Always tailor your actions to the current *and* anticipated circumstances. Did it occur to you that Berndt's untimely death may not have been coincidence?"

"No. Why do you ask?"

"No reason," said Kalt. "I'm just throwing out ideas. We should consider every possibility, no matter how remote or unreasonable it might sound."

"You can forget that one. No one knows why I'm here except you, my wife, my boss, and a guy named Max Frohm."

"Max Frohm? Who is he?"

The encounter in the hotel parking terrace, the flight to New Orleans and then to Seattle were very vivid memories. But Max Frohm? Schweizer dismissed the thought. "Frohm ... you remember him, don't you? He was an interrogator in the prisoner of war camp. I saw him recently in Seattle."

"Oh, yes." Kalt buttered another piece of bread. "I think we should look for your military service record, find out where you are from, and then see if we can find your family."

"Family?"

"Of course! Everyone has a family," said Kalt.

"It's funny, but I never really thought about having a family," said Schweizer. "I suppose you're right. We should look for relatives."

"Of course I'm right. I'll make inquiries about the location of old military records and we can be off in the morning. Agreed?"
Schweizer nodded. "Now that that's settled, let's have another glass of beer," said Kalt. *"Herr Ober! Noch ein Bier!"*

17

BERLIN

West Berlin was the most modern city Schweizer had ever seen. The city that had risen from the ruins was not the grand city envisioned by Hitler and Speer, but rather a conglomeration of glass, steel, brick, aluminum, and neon lights. What passed for modern architecture was for the most part only monuments to poor taste. Schweizer didn't think it felt very European.

Kalt's diligent inquiries had led them to the *Deutsche Dienststelle*, the repository for a wealth of official and historical information. As a precaution, it was decided that Schweizer would stay in the background and Kalt would do the talking. There was no point in getting involved in a possible war crimes investigation.

The records clerk who helped them looked like a refugee from the catacombs. He was average height, very thin, had a weak chin and wore glasses. His complexion was very sallow, which emphasized his five o'clock shadow. The overall impression was that of a sickly person.

"We are looking for military service records of men who served in World War II," said Kalt. "Could you point us in the right direction?"

"What exactly are you looking for?" asked the clerk. We have many records on file here."

Kalt looked at Schweizer before continuing. "Actually, we're hoping to find information on a former *SS* officer, a man named Karl Schweizer."

The clerk looked at Kalt, then at Schweizer. He looked roughly bored. "That may be a little difficult, "he said. "Schweizer is a rather common name. Do you have a service number or anything?"

"No," said Kalt, "only the name."

"May I ask your purpose in looking for these records?" asked the clerk.

"Certainly," said Kalt. "He is my cousin and we haven't seen him since the war."

The clerk looked skeptical. "Rather late to be looking for him, isn't it?"

"Better late than never, wouldn't you say?" said Kalt with a big smile.

"That's very true," said the clerk. "If you will wait, I will look for the correct microfilm."

Several minutes later the clerk returned, looking a bit mystified.

"What a strange coincidence," he said. "This microfilm has been signed out only twice in the several years we have had it. One of those times was just this morning. I have never seen that happen before."

"Life is full of coincidences, "said Kalt. "If we find what we are looking for, is it possible to get a copy?"

"Certainly."

In the taxi back to the airport Schweizer felt he could almost see images of documents dancing before his eyes. It had seemed like hours, turning the crank on the microfilm viewer and scanning each document. Actually, it had all been very easy and Schweizer wondered why he had never thought to do this before.

Meanwhile Kalt was examining the photocopy of Schweizer's service record. It was mostly routine stuff, a bureaucrat's view of one member of society. "Do you know your birth date?" asked Kalt.

"No, but I've always used June 16th, the day we left the camp."

"April 22, if you want to be correct."

"I don't think so," said Schweizer. "Every important document I have says June 16th."

"Does the name Pforzheim sound familiar?"

Schweizer looked out the window while he searched his memory. They were just passing the *Luftbrücken Denkmal*, the monument to the 1948 Berlin airlift, a curious structure vaguely resembling the tines of a fork. "No, I don't know what it is," said Schweizer.

The taxi was just entering Tempelhof airport, so Kalt put the paper away. "It's your home town," he said. "Instead of Munich, I think that should be our next stop."

18

PFORZHEIM

Pforzheim lay on the Enz River at the edge of the Black Forest. Noted for its jewelry industry, the city was nicknamed "*die Goldstadt*", the city of gold. Like Munich and Berlin, Pforzheim was a bombed city. Perhaps Phoenix would have been a more appropriate name. Like the bird of mythology, it had been destroyed by fire and rose again from the ashes. On February 23, 1945, the city was leveled by Allied bombers, killing most of the inhabitants and severely crippling the local economy. Some survivors believed the sole reason for the attack was to destroy the jewelry industry, thereby eliminating competition for the Swiss.

Schweizer and Kalt arrived by air at Stuttgart and rented a car for the drive to Pforzheim, only about 45 minutes away. It was late afternoon when the two men arrived. They registered at the Ruf Hotel opposite the train station and then, since the business day had not yet concluded, they went directly to the *Einwohnermeldeamt* in the *Rathaus* to see about locating members of the Schweizer family. It was there that Schweizer learned of the bombing and that the entire Schweizer family had perished.

"I'm sorry to be the conveyor of bad news," said the clerk. "Were there any other relatives, aunts or uncles. that may have been living in Pforzheim at that time?"

Schweizer had a helpless look on his face. "I don' know," he said.

"What was your mother's maiden name?" asked the clerk.

Schweizer referred to the photo copy of his service record. "It was Nordhoff," he said.

"Just a minute," said the clerk. He pulled an envelope marked "No-Nu" out of the file, removed the sheet of microfiche, and put it in the viewer. He moved the controls for a few moments. "Did you say Nordhoff?"

"Yes."

"I have a Frieda Nordhoff," said the clerk. "She has been a resident since 1947, and she is the widow of Wilhelm Nordhoff. Also, her maiden name was Geissler. Does that help?"

"No, I don't know anyone name Geissler," said Schweizer.

"Don't be too hasty," advised Kalt. "Perhaps her late husband was related to your mother."

Schweizer had a thoughtful look. It was disturbing that he had overlooked the obvious. It was a good thing that Kalt had come along. "I didn't think of that," he said. "I guess you're right again."

"Of course I'm right," said Kalt, smiling broadly at Schweizer. Then he said to the clerk, "Now, sir, do you have an address and a phone number for *Frau* Nordhoff?"

"No phone," said the clerk, "but the address is Zerennerstrasse 22."

"Thank you for your kindness," said Kalt solicitously. "Did you write that down, Karl?" Schweizer nodded and put his notebook away.

Pforzheim is situated on both sides of the valley through which the Enz River flows. Consequently, most streets run uphill from the center of town. The Nordhoff address was within walking distance of the *Rathaus*, so they decided to walk. Fortunately, it was within two blocks of the river, no big hills to climb.

The two men were out of breath by the time they reached their destination, a three story apartment building. It sat several feet back from the street. The front door was mostly opaque glass and there was the usual row of mailboxes, buttons, and intercom speaker. Schweizer pressed the button above the nameplate that read: NORDHOFF.

"Who is it?" asked a thin-sounding female voice.

"My name is Karl Schweizer, *Frau* Nordhoff. May I come up and see you?"

After a brief pause, the door release mechanism began to buzz. Schweizer pushed the door open and looked for the light switch. The light had an automatic shutoff circuit and the stairwell went dark just as they reached the third floor. Before Schweizer could press the doorbell, the door opened, revealing a short, white-haired woman well up in her seventies.

Frieda Nordhoff squinted hard as she looked at Schweizer. She didn't seem to notice Kalt. "Excuse me, *Frau* Nordhoff," said Schweizer, "but I was wondering if you might be related to my mother, Helga Schweizer. Her maiden name was Nordhoff."

"So, it *is* you," said *Frau* Nordhoff. "You've changed. But then 1 suppose we all have."

Schweizer smiled broadly and glanced at Kalt, who was also smiling. The search was finally beginning to bear fruit.

"Why have you come after so many years?" asked Frau Nordhoff.

"I, ah, was hoping to find my family," said Schweizer.

"You have the courage to face me after what you have done?" said *Frau* Nordhoff angrily. "Time has not erased it, nor will it ever!"

Schweizer looked at Kalt for help, but he only shrugged. "*Frau* Nordhoff ... uh, I, uh ... don't know how to begin, but, you see, I was hurt in the war and lost my memory. I don't remember you, my family or anything. I have come to you for help."

"Where were you that night when the *Gestapo* took my Wilhelm away?" demanded *Frau* Nordhoff, brushing aside Schweizer's explanation. She had turned very pale and her voice was quavering. "You never came. He waited for you. He trusted you. Then the *Gestapo* came." Her voice trailed off and she began to cry softly. "I never saw him again." *Frau* Nordhoff wiped the tears away. "What did you do with it?" she asked quietly.

"With what?" asked Schweizer, bewildered.

Frau Nordhoff had an incredulous look. "The gold ... the gold that you and Wilhelm stole."

Schweizer had a faraway look in his eyes. A vague impression of riding a truck in the rain came over him. He thought for a second he could smell fresh dirt. "I don't remember anything about gold," he said haltingly.

Frau Nordhoff seemed confused. "You don't? Then it must still be ... oh, my god!" She turned away.

Schweizer looked at Kalt and started to speak. Kalt raised a finger to his lips and shook his head. *Frau* Nordhoff turned back to them and said: "Get out! Go away! I don't want to see you again! "Then, as if noticing Kalt for the first time, "And take your friend with you!" She backed through the open door and slammed it shut.

"Very friendly family you have there," said Kalt with a grin.

"I don't understand it," said Schweizer. "This is so confusing."

"It's been a long day, Karl. Let's go back to the hotel. We can try again tomorrow."

The disappointing meeting with *Frau* Nordhoff had not dulled Kalt's appetite. He found the hotel's cuisine to be a gastronomical adventure. Black Forest game was the specialty, in addition to the usual German fare. Though Schweizer didn't feel very hungry, he ordered *Sauerbraten* and *Rotkohl*. Kalt asked the waiter to recommend something and ended up with *Hirschrucken*, a delicately flavored deer roast topped with sour cream. Kalt also knew his wines. He ordered a bottle of *Assmannhäuser Höllenberg*, a fine red Rhine wine.

Schweizer only picked at his food. The encounter with *Frau* Nordhoff had been very disturbing. He felt the way he did when meeting an old acquaintance whose name he had forgotten, It was on the tip of his tongue, but he couldn't quite remember it. Likewise, there was something just below the surface that Schweizer felt he should remember, but it just wouldn't come through.

Meanwhile, Kalt had cleared his plate in silence and followed the meal with several glasses of wine. "You must eat, Karl," he said. "The food here is delicious. And you haven't even touched the wine. Try it. It's superb!"

Schweizer managed a half smile. "I'm sorry, Friedrich. This whole thing has me baffled." He lifted his wineglass to his lips and drank. It *was* good. The wine was smooth, slightly pungent and deceptively strong. Schweizer thought it compared favorably with Burgundy.

He set his glass down and looked directly at Kalt. Kalt was looking at Schweizer's half-eaten meal. Schweizer looked down at his plate and back at Kalt. Then he pushed the plate across the table.

"Don't you want it?" asked Kalt.

"I'm not very hungry," said Schweizer. Kalt shrugged and picked up his fork. *This is funny*, thought Schweizer. *Every time I sit down to a meal, someone else wants to finish it.*

"I find this talk about gold very disturbing," said Schweizer. "If it's true, then I'm involved in some kind of criminal activity. And there was something Berndt said ..."

Kalt stopped in mid-bite. "What was that?" he asked.

"He asked me, 'Have you spent it all?'" said Schweizer. "It didn't make any sense until now."

Kalt chewed his food very slowly. He looked as though he wanted to say something, but was choosing his words carefully. "Is it your conclusion then, that you and your uncle were involved in a gold theft and that Berndt was on the case?"

"I suppose that's right," said Schweizer. "But if there was a theft ... I'm sure *Frau* Nordhoff knows where it is."

"Are you going to contact her again?" asked Kalt.

"I don't know. That's not why I came here. On the other hand, if the gold has anything to do with my past, I probably should find out more about it. I think I'll go see her again in the morning."

Towards midnight, Schweizer found himself unable to sleep. He decided to go for a walk. In the dimly lit corridor there seemed to be a pair of shoes next to every door, which brought a smile to Schweizer's face. Back home no one would leave their shoes outside the door to be shined. They would probably be stolen.

The night air was crisp and clear, and the stars could be seen in spite of the city lights. Schweizer walked the short distance to Leopoldplatz. There were not very many people about, unlike an American city of comparable size. Across the square was a restaurant that he had failed to notice earlier in the day. It was very modern looking and had the gilded image of an eagle on the front of the building, followed by the words, "Golden Adler" ... Gold Eagle. Schweizer had a strange feeling. Somewhere he had seen or heard a similar expression.

A few blocks further on, Schweizer came to a bridge over the Enz. He stopped and rested his forearms on the railing as he looked at the river. With almost no city noises to distract him he could hear the quiet sound of the swirling waters.

Item by item, Schweizer reviewed everything he had learned over the past several days. He had learned so much, but in summary he felt he was no closer to the facts about himself than when he had started. So many things had a familiar feel to them that he felt he couldn't rely on impressions or feelings anymore. Even the river had a familiar look about it.

A delivery truck turned the corner and crossed the bridge. The sound of the engine and the sight of the river made a connection in Schweizer's memory. Very clearly he saw himself standing on a bridge dropping a heavy object over the side and seeing the white foam from the splash as it hit the water.

Several moments passed as Schweizer concentrated, trying to remember, but it was no good. Finally, he turned around and started back to the hotel. In the morning he would get some answers, but now he needed sleep.

Breakfast at the Ruf Hotel was in sharp contrast to the previous evening's dinner: hard rolls, margarine, jam, assorted cheeses, wurst, and a cereal that looked like uncooked oatmeal with raisins in it. Schweizer had slept fitfully and rose early. When he saw what was on the breakfast menu, he wished he had slept in and waited for lunch.

When Kalt didn't come down for breakfast, Schweizer went up to awaken him. It took several knocks before a bleary-eyed Kalt appeared at the door wearing a bathrobe. "Good morning, Karl," he said. "What time is it?"

"Quarter past nine," replied Schweizer.

Kalt yawned and scratched his head. "I'm sorry, Karl. Too much wine last night. You wouldn't mind if I got some more sleep, would you?"

"I was going to see *Frau* Nordhoff this morning," said Schweizer. "I had hoped you would go with me."

"You handled it quite well last night," said Kalt. "You don't need me. But if you insist ..."

Schweizer was in the uncomfortable position of demanding something. He didn't want to offend Kalt by pressuring him. Under the circumstances, the best thing would be to go alone. "Looks like you're right again, "said Schweizer.

"Of course I'm right. And also very tired. If you would wake me for lunch, we could plan our next move."

Schweizer rang the doorbell for *Frau* Nordhoff several times and got no response. The door of the apartment building opened, and a fat woman with rosy cheeks came out carrying a shopping bag. She was wearing a heavy blue coat that looked more like a tent with buttons. The woman noticed whose bell Schweizer was ringing.

"*Entschuldigen Sie, bitte*" she said, "*Frau* Nordhoff is not at home."

"Do you know when she will return?"

"That is hard to say," the woman said. "She is in the hospital."

"That's too bad," Karl said. "When did she become ill?"

"Someone broke into her apartment and attacked her last night," said the woman. "It was terrible-just terrible."

Schweizer felt sick. First Berndt and now *Frau* Nordhoff. Who was doing these things? Could it be Kalt? No, he had arrived in Munich after the murder of Berndt. What about Erika? She had acted so strangely at their chance meeting in the train station. No, it couldn't be her, he decided. He didn't have a reason, just a gut feeling.

Then, too, there was the gold. Someone knew about it, and was probably willing to kill for it. Certainly it must be a substantial amount.

Schweizer thanked the woman for the information and started walking back to the hotel. Along the way he came to a small park. It was still two hours till noon, so Karl decided to relax on a park bench and do some thinking. He sat for several minutes staring down at the grass, oblivious to everyone and everything. Then a very commonplace thing caught his attention: the sound of footsteps.

Several other people had passed by him unnoticed, but there was a distinct pattern about these footsteps, a certain familiar rhythm. His mind was taken back to that night in Washington when a stranger had pressed a gun against his head. Just as they caught his attention, the footsteps stopped abruptly, then began again in the opposite direction at a quickened pace. Schweizer looked up in time to see a male figure disappear behind a bush at the corner of the park. On impulse he stood up and walked quickly to the corner. The street was deserted except for a young woman pushing a baby carriage.

When Schweizer arrived back at the hotel, he went directly to Kalt's room. He tried the door. It was open, so he went in. Kalt was lying under the covers, mouth open, and snoring like a sawmill. Schweizer pulled a chair up to the bed and sat there for several minutes listening to the serenade. Satisfied that Kalt was really sleeping, Schweizer gave the bed a sharp kick. Kalt quit snoring and started making a smacking sound. Schweizer kicked the bed again and said, "Wake up, Friedrich!"

Kalt opened his eyes and turned his head to look at Schweizer. "Is it lunch time?" he asked.

"No, it's not," said Schweizer. "But we have to talk."

Kalt stretched and yawned. The covers fell partly away and he pulled them back to cover himself. "What's the matter, Karl? Did *Frau* Nordhoff throw you out again?"

"She wasn't home," replied Schweizer. "She's in the hospital. Someone attacked her last night."

Kalt sat up abruptly. "Are you serious? Who did it? And why?"

"Who knows? Probably because of the gold ... of which I was so happily ignorant before last night." Schweizer felt a sudden chill. A few more pieces had just fallen into place. "If you and I didn't know about the gold before last night, then someone else knew about it all along. But who?"

"Karl, I think we should be on our way. If someone killed Berndt and then assaulted *Frau* Nordhoff because of the gold, then I don't think we should take chances with our own safety."

"You're right, of course," said Schweizer. "But I just can't come to grips with this. I started out to learn about my past. Now I am finding out things I'm not sure I want to know." Schweizer looked hard at Kalt. "How soon can you get packed? I want to get out of here as soon as possible."

"Right away," said Kalt, "but what about lunch?"

"Forget it. We'll get something on the way." Schweizer was up and had his hand on the door handle. "We're going to Hausach."

"Hausach? Where is that?" asked Kalt.

"I don't know. I just remember a direction sign with that name on it. And if I can remember the name of a town and not know where it is, then I think it's important enough to check it out."

Kalt swung his feet over the edge of the bed and reached for his pants. "You are probably right," said Kalt as he began to dress.

"Of course I'm right," said Schweizer, grinning. "Meet you down at the car in ten minutes."

Twenty minutes later, Schweizer and Kalt drove out of the train station parking lot, which served as the parking facility of the hotel. Schweizer was driving, and he followed the blue and white signs marked, *AUTOBAHN*. When they reached the *Autobahn*, Schweizer pulled over next to the sign that read, *EINFAHRT*. "Well, Friedrich, which way shall we go? Towards Karlsruhe or Stuttgart?"

"Stuttgart."

"Why Stuttgart?"

"No reason," said Kalt. "We can't sit here blocking traffic. Let's get on the *Autobahn* and find a rest area. Then we can look at the map."

"Suits me," said Schweizer and put the car in gear. A few minutes later they saw a sign that read: *"PARKPLATZ 1000 m."*

The rest area was at the top of a hill in a wooded area. Schweizer pulled in and shut the engine off. Rest areas in Germany always seemed to be in wooded areas, since the customary public sanitary facilities were the nearest bush or tree. A roll of toilet paper was a standard item in the glove box of most cars.

Schweizer had brought along a touring guide for Germany and a small stock of Michelin road maps he had purchased in a bookstore in Cincinnati. He looked through the index of towns in the touring guide, while Kalt began searching for Hausach in the number 206 road map. Neither of them noticed the dark blue Volkswagen that had entered the rest area just behind them and cruised slowly by, the driver scrutinizing them.

The Volkswagen continued on to the far end of the rest area. Then it did a strange thing just as Schweizer looked up. "Hey, Friedrich, look at that," he said. "That car drove right over the curb."

Kalt looked up in time to see the VW disappear down an incline into the trees. He stretched upward to get a better view. "Must be a shortcut to somewhere. It looks like a pretty well-worn path."

"That's odd," said Schweizer. "Back home the freeways are fenced off to prevent things like that. Oh, well ..."

Hausach was not listed in the index, so Schweizer began looking for it in map 205. He started at the top and scanned across and down using his index finger. He glanced over at Kalt, who, judging from the frown on his face, was not having much success.

Just then, a woman came out of the trees and walked across the cobble-stoned parking area toward a trash barrel. She was carrying a small sack in her hand. Schweizer called out to her, "Excuse me. Do you know where Hausach is?"

The woman continued to the trash barrel and deposited the sack, then she walked over to Schweizer. "Hausach?" she asked. Schweizer nodded and the woman shook her head. "I have never heard of it. Let me ask my husband."

She returned in a few moments and said, "He says that Hausach is on the main road south of Freudenstadt." Schweizer returned to his map and quickly located Freudenstadt in the Black Forest. He traced the main road with his finger and stopped at the name Hausach im Ginzigtal. "Here it is, Friedrich."

Kalt learned over to take a look. Just then bits of glass showered down on Kalt's head and he heard something whiz past his ear. At the same instant they both heard a loud pop. Schweizer looked at Kalt, who had a slightly stupid look on his face. Both looked at the small round hole in the windshield for an instant, then Schweizer yelled, "Get out of the car!"

Kalt had his door open and was half way out when he heard the popping sound again, followed by a thud as the bullet tore into the door just below the window. He threw himself down and crawled as quickly as he could to the back of the car, where Schweizer was waiting. Kalt was very pale and he was trembling. "I don't understand," he said in a hoarse voice.

"It's the gold," said Schweizer. "Whoever beat the information out of *Frau* Nordhoff wants to get rid of us." The sound of a car starting, followed by gears grinding, came from the trees at the end of the *Parkplatz*. Both men had the same thought ... the blue Volkswagen. They waited a few minutes after hearing the car drive away before venturing a look.

Schweizer stood up and looked around, then down at Kalt, who was cowering against the rear bumper. Other people in the rest area were staring in their direction. "Are you all right, Friedrich?"

"Yes, I think so. Just a few scrapes on my hands and knees."

Schweizer noticed a road service phone next to the traffic lanes. "Well, I guess I had better call the police."

"Do you think that is wise, Karl?"

"Do we have a choice? We can't go driving around in a car with two bullet holes in it. People are going to want to know why. As far as I'm concerned, it was just a psychopath getting a thrill. Is that how you see it?"

"Yes, yes," said Kalt eagerly. "No sense in saying more than is necessary." Schweizer walked over to the phone and placed the call.

A short time later three police cars were on the scene and several officers were searching the trees for evidence. Kalt and Schweizer stuck to their story of being the innocent victims of a psychopath with a gun. The officer in charge was skeptical. "According to your passports, one is Swiss and the other American. Tell me, why are you traveling together?" Apparently, he thought he had two international gangsters on his hands.

"Friedrich ... uh, *Herr* Kalt and I knew each other in Switzerland many years ago," said Schweizer. "I am on vacation and he is showing me around."

The policeman was persistent. "I understand you asked directions to Hausach. Why were you going there?"

Schweizer looked at Kalt. Neither had an answer. They never suspected the questioning would go this far. Schweizer decided to get off the defensive. "Now see here," he said. "Some lunatic shoots at us and you are questioning us like we committed a crime. Is this how visitors to Germany are usually treated?"

The officer was not prepared for the counterattack. He was searching for an appropriate response, when another officer came running up. "We have something," he said, out of breath. In his hand were two shell casings.

The first officer examined the shells carefully. "These are .223 cal., American made ... Remington. Probably an M-16 or AR-15. Very curious. I remember a case many years ago when an American soldier took his rifle into the forest and began shooting at cars. But those were .30 cal. There is an American base in Pforzheim." He put the shells in his pocket. "I would suggest you return to Pforzheim. We may need you further for the investigation."

"Are we in custody, then?" asked Kalt.

"No, you are free to go. We are merely asking for your cooperation."

Schweizer checked the time. It was 12:20. "We can be in Hausach in just over an hour. What do you think, Friedrich?"

Kalt hesitated. He wanted to be on his way, all right, but he was worried about the car. "I don't know, Karl. Should we get another car first?"

"This one runs," said Schweizer, sounding unconcerned. "If we finish our business in Hausach today, we can turn it in at Stuttgart tonight."

Kalt looked at the police officer, who was listening intently, before responding to Schweizer's suggestion. "My nerves are shot, Karl. Let's go back to the hotel where I can get some rest. All right?"

It was the sensible thing to do and Schweizer knew it. Still, he had no desire to be delayed by a police investigation. Also the gunfire had jarred loose some more bits of memory. He saw himself in a wooded area surrounded by men being shot. It was a sickening feeling. Schweizer emitted a sigh and nodded his head. "If that's what you want, Friedrich, we'll go back to the hotel."

The police officer smiled. "You have made a wise decision," he said. "Where will you be staying?"

"We were staying at the Ruf Hotel across from the train station," said Kalt. "I suppose we will go back there."

"Very good," said the officer. "When you are ready to go, just drive through the trees to the road below and turn right. It's the quickest way back into town. Otherwise, it's about ten kilometers to the next exit." The officer touched his right hand to his cap. *"Auf wiedersehen."*

Back at the car, Kalt and Schweizer cleaned up the bits of glass in silence. Finished, they got into the car and took the same route through the trees that the blue VW had taken earlier. About a mile down the road Kalt finally spoke. "We're going to Hausach, Karl."

"But I thought ..."

"It doesn't matter. That was for the policeman to hear. The worst possible thing for us now would be to be held up by the police. By the time they know we are gone, we will be out of their jurisdiction."

Schweizer had a satisfied look. "I just hope we can stay ahead of whoever has the gun," he said.

Twenty minutes later they had traversed Pforzheim and were on highway 294 to Freudenstadt. As they passed through the dense trees of the Black Forest, Schweizer was aware of his own familiarity with the area. Like a submarine after a long sea voyage, the long forgotten images from Schweizer's past were slowly rising to the surface. He was filled with a feeling of expectation.

19

HAUSACH

Like so many other villages, the skyline of Hausach was dominated by the church steeple. It was the first thing Kalt and Schweizer saw as they approached the village from the east, because their view was blocked by a grassy embankment, topped by railroad tracks. Just outside of town the road turned sharply to the south and passed through a narrow cut in the embankment, bridged by a railroad trestle. Mounted on the north side of the trestle was a convex mirror, found in so many places in Germany, to enable drivers to see and avoid oncoming cars through the sharp turn. The road itself could only accommodate one vehicle through the underpass. As they passed under the trestle, Schweizer had a very morbid feeling, like terminal claustrophobia. Through the trestle, the entire village came into view.

Judging from the size of it, Hausach must have had four, maybe five, thousand inhabitants. It was located in a narrow valley with the surrounding hills sloping gently upward toward the horizon.

Even without the steeple the church was the tallest building in Hausach. It appeared to be about three stories high and was very old. Built from brown stone, its black roof was in sharp contrast to most of the other buildings, which were steep and made of red tile. The more modern buildings looked very ordinary and were flat on top and looked quite out of place. Hausach, with its narrow streets and old houses, was a scene from the past.

Schweizer slowed the car and looked around. "Do you see anything familiar?" asked Kalt.

"Not exactly. It is, and then it isn't. I don't know, but something seems to be wrong. I just can't put my finger on it though."

On the southwest edge of town the terrain rose sharply. At the top of the rise was what looked like the ruins of an old castle. A stone tower was sticking up from the trees and what appeared to be a cemetery. The only way up was a footpath. Schweizer parked the car at the bottom. "Let's go for a walk, Friedrich."

Near the top, what had looked like a cemetery turned out to be a war memorial. A huge stone cross, about ten feet high, was flanked by six rectangular stones in an arc, three on each side. On each stone was mounted a bronze plaque, and facing the stones was a stone altar. Schweizer stopped to read the inscriptions while Kalt refreshed himself at the drinking fountain off to one side.

141

The plaques memorialized the local citizens who had lost their lives in the two great wars. The monument must have been fairly old. Though the plaques were not dated, the ones referring to the First World War were slightly different from those honoring the World War II dead. In his heart Schweizer hoped the monument would not have to be revised again at some future date.

Schweizer stood close to the monument and looked out over Hausach. The view did not seem any more familiar, but it gave him a good overall perspective. On the far side of the village were the railroad tracks and then the Kinzig River. His thirst quenched, Kalt joined Schweizer at the crest of the rise. "What do you think Karl?"

"I don't' know. I want to say, 'Yes, I know this place,' but I can't. I'm just not sure. The church looks familiar, but it does look like a lot of other churches."

The two men stood in silence for several minutes before Schweizer turned and started down the hill. Kalt followed slightly behind. At the car Schweizer rested his arms on top and looked at Kalt on the other side. "I guess it's just been a waste of time, Friedrich. We may as well go back to Stuttgart. Do you want to drive?"

"Okay, I'll drive. It's too bad. I know you must be terribly disappointed."

Schweizer shrugged and got into the car on the passenger side. He needed to relax and think things over.

They drove eastward through the narrow streets of Hausach, passing the church on their right. In a few moments they were out of the village and approaching the railroad trestle. Suddenly, Schweizer sat up straight and yelled, "Stop! Pull over!"

Kalt was so startled, he almost lost control of the car. When he had stopped, he asked: "What's wrong, Karl?"

"I didn't recognize it because we were going the wrong way," said Schweizer and got out of the car. "I want to look at something."

On the left side of the road, next to the embankment and the trestle, was a monument. Schweizer hurried over to read it. Kalt followed at a more leisurely pace.

Translated, the inscription read: "In memory of the citizens of Hausach who lost their lives defending this trestle from air attack on March 18, 1945, and five unknown German soldiers."

Tears welled lip in Schweizer's eyes as he read the plaque. "This is the place, Friedrich. It happened right here."

"Are you sure, Karl? Are you absolutely sure?"

"No," said Schweizer, "but I feel it. And it feels very, very real."

Kalt didn't know what else to say, so he remained silent. Schweizer just stood thinking, his eyes closed.

Approaching the trestle on the other side of the embankment was a motorcycle. Its approach went unnoticed, since the sound of its engine was muted by the high embankment. Then, with a sudden roar echoing under the trestle, the motorcycle flashed by just behind where Schweizer stood. Schweizer's body jerked involuntarily. He spun around and stumbled backward until he bumped into the monument. His eyes were on Kalt, but he did not see him.

The sudden sound had reached deep inside of Schweizer and touched something. His mind was filled with vivid images of events long past. Slowly, painfully, the door to that unused portion of his memory began to open.

Kalt was puzzled. First, his friend had looked pale, drained of color. Now his face was flushed and sweaty, and he was breathing rapidly. Kalt could only guess at the turmoil within the mind of Karl Schweizer.

In the distance Schweizer saw three large black birds. He knew he must either flee or perish. The nightmare that had tormented him in his sleep for so long had come to life. In an instant they were gone. Schweizer looked around. He saw his surroundings with different eyes. He looked back ... the birds had returned. They were closer now. He saw them more clearly. A shudder shook his body as he comprehended the birds. For they were not birds, but airplanes, and they were attacking!

The damaged circuits of Schweizer's memory had regenerated, and like a sophisticated' communications network, vast amounts of information were flooding his mind. In an. instant he experienced total recall of his past and just as suddenly, he could not remember what it had been like to not remember. Once more he was there, reliving again those long forgotten events.

20

DACHAU March 17, 1945

The trip from *Stalag VII-A* to Dachau took less than an hour. Nevertheless, Schweizer was worried. The scheduled time for picking up the gold was 10:30 AM and already it was past eleven as he turned down the main road at the Dachau camp. He feared that being late might prompt questions ... questions he would prefer not to answer. He need not have been concerned.

Wilhelm Weiter, the commandant, was eager to get rid of the gold and only made a cursory examination of Schweizer's papers. He didn't even accompany Schweizer, just sent along his adjutant, *Untersturmführer* Paul Dauer.

"Pleasant day for a trip," said Dauer, as they left Weiter's office. Schweizer did not respond. He was deep in thought about the task that lay before him. Dauer tried once again. "Did you volunteer for this or ..." He did not complete the sentence. No matter how he put it, it would come out wrong.

"I just do what I'm told and don't ask questions," said Schweizer. Dauer got the point.

"Do you want me to get some prisoners?" asked Dauer. "It's a lot of work for just two men."

"You mean you're not going to help?" asked Schweizer as he walked to the back of the truck. Dauer looked a bit nonplussed. *It was a good joke,* thought Schweizer. He needed a little humor to relieve the tension. "Don't worry," he said, flipping open the canvas flap on the truck. "I brought my own."

Dauer smiled and nodded his head up and down. He was glad he wasn't being asked to help.

The three guards climbed out, followed by the five prisoners. They didn't know where they were, nor did they particularly care. The atrocity committed by Wetzel back at the prison camp had left them all in a sullen mood. There had only been a couple of half-hearted attempts at conversation during the hour-long ride. But then the others never had much to say to Frank Hashimoto anyway.

The prisoners lined up in a loose formation and waited for instructions. Meanwhile, Dauer and Schweizer went inside to see that everything was ready. The driver just curled up and went to sleep, and the three youthful guards stood around trying not to look nervous.

Schweizer was not prepared for what awaited him. The one box of three gold bars was still open. The sight of so much gold was breathtaking. He stood for a few moments just gazing at it. It seemed to give off its own light.

"Beautiful, isn't it?" remarked Dauer. Schweizer grunted his agreement. "Bet you would like to have some of it, wouldn't you?"

Schweizer was nervous and began to sweat. He looked at Dauer suspiciously and said, "Why do you say that?"

Dauer shrugged. "Every man wants to be rich."

"I suppose that would include you, Dauer?" Schweizer had decided a good offense was the best defense.

"Well, I meant ..."

"Every man has his price, wouldn't you agree?"

"I didn't ..."

"Enough of this," said Schweizer, dismissing the conversation with a wave of his hand. "I am here on behalf of *Reichsführer* Himmler. Let's get on with it."

Dauer blushed and muttered a reply. He resented being bullied by this errand boy. He just wished he had the nerve to speak up and put him in his place.

"Put the lid back on this crate and I'll get my men," said Schweizer.

Schweizer returned a few minutes later with the five prisoners. "Lindner," he said, "you're in charge. Get these crates loaded into the truck."

"Okay, guys, let's load up," said Lindner.

Charlie Stagg tried lifting one of the crates by himself. Not expecting such heavy weight he dropped it to the floor. The box shattered and the gold bars tumbled out.

"So this is how much a human life is worth," said Lindner. When the other prisoners had seen the gold they were dazzled by the sight, but, unlike Lindner, they had forgotten the tragedy back at the camp. But then Mike Erickson had not been their closest friend.

Schweizer ignored Lindner's comment. He had had no part in the hanging at the camp. Nevertheless he didn't look forward to the killings that would have to be done before the day was over. "Get to work now. I want to be through in thirty minutes."

The work went slower than Schweizer had anticipated. In the end he had even put the three guards to work. Still, the job had taken nearly an hour to complete. It was after one o'clock before the truck rumbled out the front gate and headed south toward the Alps.

Schweizer was relieved to be underway. In the back of the truck four of the prisoners were beginning to worry. Frank Hashimoto didn't seem to be concerned all. Charlie Stagg voiced the concern the others were thinking. "Hey, guys, I don't like the looks of this."

"I don't either," said Tom Lutz.

"Why do you suppose the krauts are having us do this?" asked Stagg. "You don't think they consider us expendable, do you?"

"I don't know," said Kabello, "but I don't think we'll ever have a better chance to break out."

"What kind of talk is that?" snapped Hashimoto. "That will just cause us all a lot of trouble, so knock it off."

"Hey, listen to the Jap," sneered Lutz. "I always figured he was on their side."

"I am on the side of reason," argued Hashimoto. "The war is almost over. There is no point in trying to escape now. If we just sit tight, we'll all come through this okay."

"You're crazy! "said Stagg. "Do you think the Germans are going to show us all this gold and then let us live to tell about it?"

"Look at them," said Kabello, nodding toward the three young guards. "Taking their guns away would be like taking candy from a baby. What d'you say, guys?"

"Enough of this!" said Hashimoto, his eyes flashing. "I am the senior officer here. There will be no escape attempt!"

The oldest of the three guards rose halfway from his seat and spoke. *"Nicht reden! Ruhig bleiben!"* And to make his demand understood, he raised the muzzle of his MP-40 submachine gun and pointed it in the direction of the prisoners.

"Ain't you a little young to be playing with grownup toys?" Kabello asked the uncomprehending youth. "You might hurt yourself. Better go back to your friends in Kindergarten."

Kindergarten was one word the boy did understand and it angered him. He pulled the bolt back on his weapon.

"Hey, Tony, don't antagonize the kid," said Lutz in an earnest voice. "He might just spray us with that thing."

Kabello shook his head. "Nah, if he took a shot at us, he'd risk hitting the guys up front."

"Tony, he's just a kid ... and a German," responded Lutz.

"Yeah," added Stagg. "He might not be thinking of the guys up front."

Lindner spoke up in German. "Please ignore them. They are only joking." The boy sat down again, but kept a wary eye on Kabello.

"You still here?" Stagg asked Lindner.

"Yeah, we thought you got off at the last stop," Lutz added. Some of the guys laughed.

"If you're wondering why I haven't said much," volunteered Lindner, "it's because I've been thinking about Erickson, the gold, possible escape, and Major Hashimoto."

Hashimoto's ego swelled up a bit. It wasn't often he had been called major in the past few years and he appreciated it now. Life hadn't been easy since Pearl Harbor. Born in San Bernardino, California, to Nakashio and Aiko Hashimoto, Frank had wanted to be a soldier since childhood. He had gone to college, gotten a reserve commission and his military career was progressing as well as could be expected when it was derailed on December 7, 1941. He was thirty-two now and had been a major for four years. Promotions didn't come easy if your ancestors were Japanese.

"The thing that holds us together is discipline," Lindner continued. "With it we are a unit, directed at the same goal: resisting the Germans. Without it we are a mob of individuals, each at the mercy of the Nazis ... and you know how well disciplined they are. I would like to escape, too. But I'm a soldier, just as the rest of you are, and I feel we have a duty to respect the senior officer present, and that is what I intend to do."

Hashimoto reached over and slapped Lindner on the knee. "Thanks, kid. I won't forget it." The others fell silent, each reflecting on what Lindner had just said.

Up front, Schweizer was becoming increasingly nervous. In a few minutes they would be in Bad Tölz, the location of the *SS* officer training school. There had already been several delays at checkpoints along the way. Everybody wanted to see his papers. Schweizer had a feeling that they were expected by the way the sentries acted at the checkpoints. After seeing the papers they always referred to a paper on a clipboard. Fortunately, Bad Tölz was the last checkpoint and then it was only a few more miles to the Tegernsee. Equally fortuitous were the delays. The sun was getting low on the horizon and it would be easier to hide the gold under cover of darkness.

Half an hour later the truck took a fork in the road, bypassing Gmund, and followed the opposite shore of the Tegernsee. The sun was dipping toward the mountain peaks, and the late afternoon shadows were lengthening. Schweizer relaxed a little. Soon the gold would be hidden, but there was still the nasty business of disposing of the witnesses.

Their arrival at Nordhoff's summer home went virtually unnoticed. The house was set in a slight hollow, just a few hundred yards beyond the village, and when the truck was parked around behind the house, there were no visible indications of their presence.

Schweizer commandeered one of the submachine guns and put everyone, including the driver, to work unloading and stacking the gold behind the false wall in the cellar. Stealing the gold was one thing. Making a clean getaway was quite another. Time was not the important factor. Schweizer also had to make a call to Nordhoff, just as soon as he got back to Munich.

When the prisoners saw the delivery point for the gold, their earlier misgivings turned into genuine alarm. It was obvious now, even to Hashimoto, that if the gold had to be hidden behind a false wall, then their chances for survival were rapidly diminishing.

"I told you we should have jumped those kids," said Kabello. "They'll probably take us out and shoot us as soon as the job's done."

"He's right," said Lutz. "We blew our best chance."

Schweizer could tell by the anxious sound in the prisoners' voices that trouble was brewing. He stepped closer to the group and said: *"Lindner, Sagen Sie ihnen, nicht reden."*

"He says, no talking, guys," said Lindner.

The work progressed much faster than it had at Dachau. The four extra workers cut the time almost' half. When they were finished, the prisoners climbed back in the truck, tired and hungry. They hadn't eaten since early morning.

"Now what?" asked Stagg in the direction of Hashimoto.

"We wait," said the major.

"Haven't you caught on yet?" demanded Stagg angrily. "These guys are gonna shoot us!"

The truck lurched forward and headed back north, up from the valley where the village lay. "They could have shot us back there if they wanted," Hashimoto argued. "Why load us back in the truck?"

"You don't think the people in the village would have noticed?" said Lutz. "No witnesses."

They all slumped down in the back of the truck, each man keeping his thoughts to himself. Ten minutes later the truck slowed, made a turn, and then began to bounce around on what must have been a dirt road. A couple of minutes later it jerked to a stop.

The canvas flap was flipped open, revealing Schweizer, pistol in hand. *"Alle 'raus!"* he shouted.

"Looks like this is it, guys," said Lindner in a voice betraying weary resignation.

Lutz grabbed a handful of Hashimoto's shirt and sputtered, "You sonofabitch! I oughta kill you ... except he's gonna do it for me!" He jerked his hand away and jumped to the ground, leaving Hashimoto alone with his thoughts.

"Come on, tell them all to get out," Schweizer said to Lindner.

"He wants you to get down, Major. I'm sorry."

"Not as sorry as 1 am, kid," Hashimoto said as he climbed down. "I'm just too much of an optimist. Should have listened to you guys."

Schweizer herded the prisoners over by a tall fir tree, then returned to where the boys were standing, their weapons ready. The driver, Franz Eberts, didn't like what was going on, but he wasn't about to complain.

All of the prisoners were scared and Stagg was crying. He kept whimpering, "I don't want to die. I don't want to die."

"Are we just going to stand here and take it?" asked Lutz.

"You got any ideas?" Kabello retorted.

Hashimoto was in a daze. Lindner looked around at the trees. It was almost dark. Maybe he could make a run for it.

"Boys, this is a man's work," said Schweizer to the guards. "Give me your weapon," he then said to the oldest.

"Are you going to shoot them?" the boy asked. Schweizer took the MP-40 from the boy and nodded.

"Stand over there, boys," he said, motioning toward a clump of bushes with the muzzle of the gun. As they walked toward the bushes, Schweizer drew the bolt back on the submachine gun. When the guards turned around, he squeezed the trigger, dropping all three of them with one burst.

Franz Eberts, the driver, was abruptly jarred from his lethargy. He had been casually leaning against the fender of the truck watching the proceedings, but now he stood fully erect and his pipe fell from his mouth as he shouted, "My god, man! Have you lost your senses?"

Schweizer turned toward the driver and raised the gun a second time. Eberts started to run just as Schweizer fired. A bullet hit Eberts in the leg, knocking him to the ground. The driver howled in pain and struggled to get up again. Schweizer took careful aim and squeezed the trigger once more. Nothing happened. He slid the bolt back and forth several times. Meanwhile, Eberts was up and staggering toward the trees. Schweizer was swearing and pounding on the weapon.

"It's jammed!" shouted Hashimoto. "Let's take him!"

The five prisoners sprinted toward Schweizer, who had thrown the weapon to the ground. For a brief instant he was plagued by indecision ... pull his pistol, or try for one of the other MP-40s. Too late, he opted for the pistol. Before it had cleared the holster, he was gang-tackled by the five Americans.

"Get the driver!" yelled Lindner. "Don't let him get away!"

Stagg scooped up Schweizer's fallen pistol and headed into the trees. A few moments later the sound of two shots was heard. By the time Stagg returned, the other prisoners had wrestled Schweizer to his feet. He was very pale and his body was shaking. Stagg approached the group and raised the pistol.

Lindner stepped in front of Schweizer and said: "Wait a minute, Stagg."

"Get out of my way, Lindner. I'm going to kill him."

"Yeah, what's wrong with you? Gone nuts all of a sudden?" It was Kabello speaking. Lindner hoped he could reason with the men before it was too late.

"Listen, fellas," said Lindner, "we all want to get out of here, right?" There was a murmur of agreement. "This man's our ticket to Switzerland. We have a truck and guns, but he's got the uniform, the right papers and ID. And he knows the country. If you kill him, we might not make it."

"He's right," said Lutz.

"Yeah, put it away," said Kabello.

Stagg looked disgusted. "Okay, so we don't kill him," he said. "What do we do about the gold?"

"Leave it," said Lindner.

"Are you nuts?" said Kabello. "It must be worth at least a million bucks! We can't just leave it."

"We can, and we will," said Lindner. "We don't have time to load it and I doubt we could sneak it over the border."

"Who put you in charge?" demanded Kabello. "You made a pretty speech about following the senior officer. What about that?"

"Things are different now," said Lindner. He looked searchingly at Hashimoto, who was hanging back on the fringe of the group. "Will you put me in charge, Major?" Hashimoto lowered his eyes and nodded his head.

"That ain't good enough," said Kabello.

"All right," said Lindner. "I'll tell you how it is. We need the kraut and you need me. I'm the only one of us who speaks German. If you don't do it my way, then I'll try it on my own."

"He's right," said Hashimoto.

"Who asked you?" snapped Kabello. "I don't care what you say, Lindner. We're not leaving that gold."

The others murmured their agreement.

Lindner looked at the ground, trying to come up with a solution. Finally, he said, "How about if we go back and get one box apiece? We could bury them in the woods and come back for them later."

"Later?" Lutz was skeptical.

"After the war. If anything happens to the bulk of the gold, at least we'll have something. The important thing is to get to Switzerland ... alive."

"He's right," said Hashimoto. This time no one criticized him. They all knew it was the best compromise.

During the ride back to the cottage no one spoke. Schweizer was scared. He didn't understand what was happening and Lindner

150

ignored his questions. The incident of Stagg pointing the pistol at him was fresh in his memory.

It only took ten minutes to load the gold. Back in the woods they buried it and stripped the Germans. Only two uniforms fit, the driver's and the one belonging to the oldest boy. Lindner put on the driver's uniform and Lutz put on the other. Hashimoto, Stagg and Kabello took the submachine guns and got in the back of the truck. Lutz and Lindner sat up front with Schweizer in the middle. It was starting to rain as they drove out onto the main road.

Time was their greatest enemy. The shortest distance to Switzerland was through Austria, but it would take too long. The roads were winding and the terrain was mountainous. There was also the possibility of snow storms at the higher elevation. On the other hand, it would be quicker to get on the *Autobahn* in Munich and make a dash to the west, then south into Switzerland. It would also be more dangerous, since the *Autobahn* was restricted to priority military traffic. However, Lindner had read Schweizer's travel authorization and was relying on the fact that it was signed by Heinrich Himmler and would intimidate any inquisitive sentries they might encounter.

On the return trip to Munich, flakes of snow began to fall with the rain at the higher elevations. The decision to take the *Autobahn* instead of striking out for Switzerland appeared to have been the best choice. A low pressure system had blown in from France, bringing rain in the lowlands and snow in the mountains.

The rain, combined with the darkness, would facilitate the prisoners' escape. It didn't seem likely that much military traffic would be on the roads in the inclement weather. In fact, sentries at the various checkpoints were too eager to get in from the rain to give the travel papers more than a cursory inspection. At Schweizer's suggestion, they took a more circuitous route to Munich, avoiding Gmund and the Tegernsee. Schweizer wanted to get away from the Americans, but he realized it would be far more perilous to fall into the hands of the *Gestapo*.

Lutz did the driving while Lindner kept the pistol pressed against Schweizer's ribs. They weren't able to go more than 40 miles an hour because of limited visibility in the rain, and because of the blackout covers over the headlights. They did manage a constant speed on the *Autobahn*, though.

"What do you intend to do with me," asked Schweizer. Lindner ignored him. Schweizer tried again. "I can help you get out of Germany."

"Yeah, like you were going to help us back there in the forest."

"I was simply doing my duty."

Lindner laughed. "You're a thief ... and a murderer. Don't talk to me about duty."

"You're going to kill me."

"Maybe ... maybe not. That depends mostly on you. Cooperate and maybe we'll let you go at the border."

Lindner pressed the pistol more firmly into Schweizer's ribs for emphasis. Schweizer fell silent. The only sounds were the engine, the rain, and the rhythmic oscillation of the wipers.

At Merklingen, about ninety miles west of Munich, they came upon a barricade across the *Autobahn*. Standing in the rain in front of it was a lone German soldier, rifle slung over his shoulder and waving a lantern.

As the truck slowed, Lindner called to the men in the back: "Roadblock!"

"Do you want me to run it?" asked Lutz.

"I only see one sentry," replied Lindner. "Let's play it by ear."

Schweizer's pulse quickened. He felt that his capture was nearly at an end, but he was reminded of the seriousness of his predicament by the pistol being pressed against his ribs. This whole thing was foolhardy anyway, trying to traverse most of southern Germany in wartime. Perhaps he should reason with them, persuade them to surrender. He decided against it, though. It would be better to escape, rather than attract attention from a third party.

The truck stopped a few feet in front of the sentry. Lutz thought he must either have a lot of guts or was just plain stupid. A slip of the foot on the brake pedal and the soldier would be another casualty of the war.

The sentry walked around to the driver's side. "If there's any trouble, you get the first bullet," Lindner said softly to Schweizer. Schweizer just looked straight ahead.

"You cannot go further on the *Autobahn*," said the soldier in heavily accented German. Schweizer concluded he must be an *Auslander* probably recruited from one of the Balkan countries.

"What's the problem?" asked Lindner.

"The bridge is out at Mühlhausen, completely destroyed. What is your destination?"

"Stuttgart."

The soldier was young and a little green, but he thought it strange, nevertheless, that an officer sat silent while a private did all the talking. He had a mind to press the issue, but didn't. No sense in inviting trouble, he decided, a decision that saved his life. "You can take the road northeast to Geislingen and then go west. It's further, but the road is better. Otherwise, you can drive south into Merklingen and take the first main road to the right."

Merklingen was south of the *Autobahn,* and south was the direction to Switzerland. "We'll take Merklingen," said Lindner. He poked Schweizer hard in the ribs with the pistol.

"Yes. Merklingen is a good idea," said Schweizer. "Thank you. Let's be on our way."

Nothing happened. Lutz didn't know it was time to go and Lindner couldn't tell him in English without alerting the sentry. *"Lutz, weiterfahren,"* said Lindner. Lutz gave Lindner a quizzical look. *"Weiterfahren!"* Lindner said again, motioning strenuously in the direction of Merklingen.

The light came on in Lutz's head. *"Oh, ja,"* he said and smiled disarmingly at the sentry. Lutz put the truck in gear and started rolling. The sentry watched the truck disappear into the darkness. Something was definitely wrong. He walked over to the makeshift guard shack and picked up the phone.

"Ja?" said a sleepy voice.

The sentry thought the situation over quickly. It was late and it was raining. He was cold and his shift was almost over. "Kurt, is the coffee hot?" he asked.

"Is that all you wanted?"

The sentry looked in the direction the truck had taken and said, "Yes. I'll be coming in soon." The line went dead.

After Lutz rolled the window up, Lindner let out a sigh of relief. "That was close. For a minute I thought I'd have to kill him."

"You should have," said Lutz.

"How come?" asked Lindner, surprised.

"One less kraut for our guys to worry about. You know what I mean?"

Lindner knew what he meant, but cold-bloodedly killing a man just wasn't in his repertoire. "That's why you're not in charge, Lutz. Killing him would have only alerted the authorities to look for us. Just drive. I'll do the thinking."

Instead of taking the turn to the west in Merklingen, the truck continued straight through the town. Lindner only had a vague idea of where they were going. The big problem was a lack of maps. None were in the truck and Schweizer claimed ignorance of this part of Germany, which, of course, was a lie.

Off the *Autobahn* it was slow going. Avoiding the large towns would just slow their progress more, so Lindner decided to press on and hope for the best. It was just past midnight when they entered the town of Tübingen, about thirty miles south of Stuttgart.

Tübingen was a fairly large city, but showed no signs of life. If anyone noticed the passage of the truck and its passengers, it was not readily apparent. The route through the city was confusing and Lutz wasn't sure of his bearings when they reached the outskirts of town. The sign next to the road said simply: *"nach Rottenburg,"* which meant nothing to anybody except Schweizer, and he wasn't telling.

About a mile further on they came to a fork in the road. Lutz pulled over to the side of the road and stopped.

"Why are you stopping?" asked Lindner.

"Do you know where we are?"

"No."

"Well, neither do I," said Lutz. "I don't even know what direction we're headed in."

Lindner lowered his eyes and tried to think. It was decision time, but he didn't feel comfortable making a decision without adequate information. On the other hand, no decision was worse than a bad decision. They couldn't just wait for the sun to come up. "Take the right fork," said Lindner.

"Any particular reason?"

"Yeah."

"What's that?"

"It's better than sitting here," said Lindner.

Lutz put the truck in gear again and took the road to the right. The rain had let up at last.

Nearly a mile down the road a barricade blocked the approach to a bridge over the Neckar River. In large black letters on the barricade were the words: *"VORSICHT! LEBENSGEFAHR!"* A sentry was standing next to the sign.

"Looks like the bridge is out," said Lutz. "Our flyboys really get around."

"It doesn't say that the bridge is out," said Lindner. "Let's stop and ask the sentry." Lindner poked Schweizer in the ribs with the pistol. "This time you do the talking."

"What shall I say?" asked Schweizer.

"Tell them we're lost. We're heading south to, uh ... to the Bodensee."

As the sentry approached the truck a shaft of light suddenly appeared in the darkness. For an instant a second sentry was silhouetted in the doorway of a house about fifty feet from the road. He closed the door and started walking toward the truck. In the back of the truck Stagg shook Hashimoto and Kabello awake. "We're stopped," he whispered. "Someone's coming. Could be trouble."

"Only authorized vehicles may cross the bridge," the sentry said through the driver's window.

"Why is that?" asked Schweizer.

"The bridge has been weakened by air attacks. May I see your travel papers please?"

Oh, brother, thought Lindner, *this one does it by the numbers.* He poked Schweizer in the ribs again. "We are lost," said Schweizer. "Could you tell us the way to Bodensee?"

"Yes. But first I must see your travel papers."

The second sentry had wandered toward the back of the truck. Lindner was having a difficult time listening to the conversation and keeping an eye on the second sentry. Meanwhile, Schweizer handed over the travel orders.

The sentry took out a flashlight and read the papers very carefully. "These papers authorize you to travel from Dachau to the Tegernsee, not the Bodensee."

"An administrative error," said Lindner. "You will notice the papers are signed by *Reichsführer* Himmler. We are on his business."

The sentry realized something was wrong. Why was a private speaking so boldly in the presence of an officer? "Hans, check the back of the truck," he called out. Then, bringing his rifle to a ready position he said, "Everybody out!"

Instantly, Lindner raised the pistol and fired one shot into the center of the sentry's forehead, sending him crashing backwards to the ground. Alerted by the shot, the second sentry turned toward the truck cab. Just then, Stagg lifted the canvas and Kabello fired a burst from his MP-40, killing the man instantly.

Stagg stood looking down at the dead sentry. "It's funny," he said. "One minute you're alive, then the next minute ... BANG! ... you're dead. I suppose it's better that way, quick, so you don't have time to think about it."

"What are you, a philosopher?" asked Kabello.

"Get the uniforms off those bodies," yelled Lindner from the cab, "and then let's get out of here."

Stagg, Kabello and Hashimoto jumped to the ground and began stripping the two sentries. Suddenly, a burst of machine gun fire raked the cab of the truck. One slug ripped into Lutz' back and lodged against his left shoulder blade. As Schweizer and Lindner scrambled from the cab, a bullet hit Schweizer in the ribs on the right side.

Three men came running from the house, firing submachine guns. They had only had time to put their pants on. As Stagg started to stand up, he received a hard kick to his backside that sent him sprawling. He rolled over to see Hashimoto standing there firing at the Germans. Kabello was in a crouch, firing his MP-40. Just then, four bullets tore into Frank Hashimoto. Without a sound he did a half pirouette and crumpled to the pavement.

Stagg crawled over to Hashimoto. He was still alive. One of the slugs had hit him in the neck, piercing the jugular. Hashimoto's eyes had a wild look in them and he was moving his lips as if trying to speak.

"Frank! Frank!" cried Stagg. It was the first time he had ever called Hashimoto by his first name. A gasp escaped Hashimoto's lips and his body quivered slightly, then slowly the life faded from his eyes.

Instantly, Stagg had Hashimoto's MP-40 and was up and running toward the enemy position. The swiftness and boldness of Stagg's attack startled the Germans. They broke for the house. None of them made it. Even after they were down, Stagg kept firing until his gun was empty. Finally, he turned around and walked slowly back to the others.

Back at the truck, Lindner was assessing the situation. Hashimoto was dead, and Lutz and Schweizer were both wounded. The escape was turning into a fiasco. He looked at Stagg, standing over Hashimoto's body. 'Tm sorry, Frank," said Stagg in a quiet voice.

"Hey, you guys, gather round," yelled Lindner. Stagg and Kabello joined Lindner at the truck. Lutz was still in the cab, moaning. "Okay, we need to get rid of the bodies. We'll have to throw them into the river."

"What about Hashimoto?" asked Stagg. "We're not ..."

"He's past caring about it," said Kabello.

"We can't just leave him like that. He saved my life," said Stagg.

"So what?" said Kabello. "We'll put his name in for a medal."

Stagg raised the muzzle of his MP-40. "We don't leave anyone behind. We ain't goin' nowhere without Frank!"

Kabello had a look of dismay. "Hey, man, he's dead! We can't just lug a body around with us."

Stagg's teeth were clenched as he spoke. "You help get him into the truck, or we'll be lugging *two* bodies!"

"Stagg's right," said Lindner. "We can't leave him behind. There's no time to argue. Kabello, you help Stagg put Hashimoto in the back of the truck. Let's get Lutz and the kraut in there, too. And you'll have to drive, Tony. I want Stagg in the back with me."

"Why are you riding in the back?" asked Kabello. "It looks like I'm going to have to take the kraut's place," replied Lindner.

"What do you mean?"

"We'll do a lot better with an officer in charge. Privates don't get any respect. After I've got his uniform on, I'll rap on the cab, and then you can stop and let me up front."

Kabello nodded in the direction of Schweizer. "We gonna shoot the bastard?"

"We'll see."

"C'mon!" said Stagg. "Let's quit beatin' our gums and get this show on the road!"

Kabello put a German uniform on while Lindner and Stagg carried the first three bodies to the bridge and dropped them over the side. Meanwhile, Schweizer sat on the pavement leaning against the right front wheel. He was in a great deal of pain and despaired of coming through this ordeal alive. *So much gold,* he thought. *What a pity if he were not able to spend some of it.*

Several minutes later they were loaded up and ready to go. "Which way?" asked Kabello.

Lindner looked at the warning sign for a moment. "You ever hear the expression, 'We'll cross that bridge when we come to it'?"

"Yeah."

"Well, we've come this far ... let's cross that bridge."

The bridge was more damaged than they had anticipated. Stagg and Lindner walked in front of the truck with the sentry's flashlight, looking for dangerous spots. As long as the truck was moving they could hear a continuous scraping sound of metal on metal as the heavy truck made its way across the bridge.

"Wait a minute," said Stagg. "Do you hear something?" Both men listened.

"Shut the engine off," said Lindner. Behind them they heard a distinct clackety-clack sound and the sound of an engine. "Sounds like ... damn! It's a tank coming up the road! I'm going back to move that sign. Don't worry about the bridge, just get to the other side!"

Lindner sprinted back the direction they had come, an MP-40 slung over his shoulder. When he reached the sign, the sound of the tank was much closer. He turned it around and pushed it down. Just then, he heard a crack and felt a bullet whiz past his ear. It had come from the house! Lindner looked and saw another German soldier in the doorway. *He must have spread the alarm,* thought Lindner. *Damn! Should have checked the house!* The soldier fired again and Lindner replied with a short burst from the MP-40. The soldier slumped to the ground.

Lindner turned and ran for the truck. As he reached the other side of the bridge, the tank drew up in front of the house. "Get in!" yelled Stagg.

"Just a minute," said Lindner. "I want 'em to follow us."

He fired a long burst at the tank. They could hear bullets ricocheting off the tank's armor, followed by the clackity-clack sound as the tank started after them.

"Let's go!" yelled Lindner as Stagg pulled him in.

Kabello fired up the engine and started rolling. They had gone only a hundred yards when they heard a loud crash behind them. The bridge had collapsed into the river.

Lindner started changing into Schweizer's uniform. "We're in big trouble," he said. "We have to stay off the main roads now."

"How much time do you think we have?" asked Stagg.

"I don't know. Maybe that tank just happened to be coming by. Maybe there's an alert out for us. Do we hide or make a run for it? Either way, it's going to be light before we make it to Switzerland ... and we don't even know what direction that is. We could sure use a compass, or a map."

Lindner completed the change of uniform and signaled for Kabello to stop.

"One more thing," said Lindner before he jumped to the pavement, "be sure our passenger comes to no harm. We might need him later."

"Sure thing. He gets the red-carpet treatment at least till we get to Switzerland."

A few hours later, after wandering along the winding back roads of the Black Forest, the truck passed through the village of Hausach. It was almost morning.

"I'm beat," said Kabello. "Do you suppose you could drive?"

"Sure," said Lindner. "Pull over when you get out of town."

At the edge of town, Kabello stopped and Lindner got out and walked around to the driver's side of the truck. In the distance something caught his eye. On the horizon behind the truck was a faint glow. A new day was dawning, and they were headed the wrong way. Lindner climbed into the driver's seat and turned the truck around.

"Where are you going?" asked a surprised Kabello.

"See that light in the sky? That's east, and just on the other side of town is a road that goes south ... toward Switzerland."

"We ain't goin' nowhere unless we get some gas," said Kabello.

Lindner looked down at the fuel gauge. It was quivering on the empty mark. "I didn't see a gas pump in the last town, did you?"

"Nope," said Kabello. "Let's find us a car somewhere. We can probably siphon some gas."

As the truck entered Hausach the second time, they could hear church bells ringing. Lindner looked at his watch. It was almost 7 AM and people would be on their way to mass.

"I wonder if this town has a police force," said Lindner.

"I doubt it," replied Kabello. "Why do you ask?"

"It's simple. Somebody has gas and the police or the mayor can probably tell us where." Lindner noticed a fat woman dressed in black with a large shawl coming down the street. He stopped the truck next to her and called out, *"Hallo! Können Sie mir sagen, wo der Bürgermeister wohnt?"*

In spite of the dim light she could see the *Totenkopf*, the *SS* death head, on Lindner's cap. She was eager to help. Five minutes later Lindner was pounding on the mayor's door. Less than a minute after that, a round bald head with a bushy moustache popped out of an upstairs window. *"Gott im Himmel!* Can't a man get any sleep around here?"

Lindner stepped away from the door so the mayor could have a better view. "Oh, excuse me," said the mayor, "I'll be right down."

A few seconds later the door swung open, revealing a short pudgy man in a nightshirt. "Come in, come in," he said.

"Are you the mayor?" asked Lindner.

"Yes. My name is Ernst Gutmacher. How can I be of service?"

"We need gasoline, *Herr* Bürgermeister, and a map of the area."

"I'm afraid we ran out of gas a long time ago," said the mayor.

"You don't understand," said Lindner, raising his right hand and resting it on his holster, a gesture not lost on the mayor. "I am certain there are automobiles in Hausach. I am equally certain that you would rather help us locate them than make us have to look for them."

"Yes, of course, you will have my full cooperation," said the mayor. *Damned SS*, he thought, *wait till the war is over, then we'll see.*

The mayor threw on a coat and led Lindner to a garage behind the house. An hour later, after several similar stops, the fuel tank was nearly full, a map had been found and the men were preparing to leave.

"Excuse me," said the mayor. "I couldn't help but notice the blood stain on your uniform. If you need medical assistance, we have a very good doctor."

"It is an old wound," said Lindner. "It's the only uniform I have, and you know how short we are on supplies these days. Thank you for your offer."

Lindner got behind the wheel of the truck and started the engine. The mayor came to rigid attention and gave the Nazi salute, *"Heil Hitler!"* Lindner looked at Kabello briefly and frowned. Kabello just grinned and shook his head. Lindner looked back at the mayor, lifted his right arm and half-heartedly returned the salute.

"C'mon, let's go," said Kabello in a low voice. "This place makes me nervous and we've wasted a lot of time."

Fifteen miles to the north a flight of three P-51 Mustangs were descending through six thousand feet. Mounted below the wings of each aircraft were two 500-pound bombs.

For flight leader Captain A. J. Nance, it was just another routine mission. Reconnaissance had revealed only a single anti-aircraft battery defending the trestle. By coming in low they could accomplish two things: pinpoint the target, and avoid the anti-aircraft fire. The German 88 mm cannons were great for lofting shells straight up, but in a level position they could not be turned fast enough to track a high-speed fighter.

"Target coming up on the right," said Nance to the other two pilots. "Follow me in. Two or three passes should do it."

The truck passed the church and headed east. Outside of town the road curved northeast toward a railroad trestle. Next to the trestle the anti-aircraft battery, previously unmanned, now had a crew of three old men, members of the *Volkssturm*, Hitler's last ditch attempt to defend the Fatherland.

The road was wet from the recent rain and the sky was obscured by a high overcast. In the distance Lindner noticed three dark specks against the grey sky. They came from the north and turned westward, coming straight for Hausach.

"What do you make of that?" asked Lindner, pointing at the specks.

"Looks like fighter aircraft," said Kabello.

"Ours or theirs?"

The specks were growing rapidly as the truck approached the trestle. Before Lindner could answer, the lead plane opened fire.

"Those are our planes!" yelled Kabello jubilantly.

"Yeah, but they don't know who we are," said Lindner. "Let's get under the trestle. That's the only cover around."

The second and third planes both strafed the truck before Lindner could get it under cover. Kabello scrambled out the door and under the truck when it had stopped. Lindner ran to the back to help the others. Stagg was hanging over the tailgate, half of his face shot away. Inside, no one was moving. But something was wrong ... Schweizer was gone!

Lindner spun around and looked for the SS officer. He saw him at the anti-aircraft battery talking excitedly and pointing at the truck.

"I am an SS officer," Schweizer shouted. "Those men in the truck are American soldiers who took me prisoner!"

Just then, the planes started another pass. The anti-aircraft crew was too busy to pay attention to Schweizer, but he noticed that they did have rifles. He grabbed one and looked back at the trestle. Lindner was running away from the truck. He had seen the 500-pound bombs each plane was carrying, and instantly realized their true intent.

Schweizer had Lindner in his sights and squeezed the trigger just as the first bomb hit, exploding on the embankment.

The concussion knocked Schweizer to the ground. The second bomb was a direct hit on the truck, sending up a huge ball of fire from the exploding gas tank. Then another bomb hit the trestle. Large chunks of debris flew into the air and rained down everywhere, including the anti-aircraft battery. The planes wheeled around for another pass, dropping one more bomb apiece. Then for good measure, they strafed the area two more times.

As the Mustangs climbed out over the village and headed west, they left behind a scene of carnage that had become so commonplace all over Europe, but until this day totally unknown to the inhabitants of the sleepy little village. On the ground in the vicinity of the trestle nothing moved. In quick succession the tires blew out on the burning truck. Slowly, the people of Hausach gathered at the scene of the bombing. Amid the rubble, the wreckage, and shattered bodies, only one man survived ...

21

The images of the past slowly faded. "Are you all right?" asked Kalt. "You don't look well."

Schweizer felt emotionally drained. The vivid memories that had flashed across his mind like an instant replay were a very heavy burden, for now he knew more than he had ever hoped and much more than he wanted to know. Kalt put his hand on Schweizer's shoulder, a gesture of reassurance. Schweizer had a melancholy look on his face. "I know where the gold is, Friedrich."

"You do?"

"Yes. It's in the cellar of a little house in the Alps, just south of Munich." Schweizer looked at Kalt and smiled. "Shall we go get it?"

"If that's what you want, Karl."

"Yes, I think I've earned it." Schweizer walked back to the car and got in, leaving Kalt by the monument. "What's wrong, Friedrich?"

"Do you remember everything that clearly?" asked Kalt.

"No. But I remember the gold and the house, and with a little luck I think we can find it."

Kalt smiled and got into the car. "I'm very happy for you, Karl, very happy indeed."

Kalt and Schweizer both realized the search for the village where the gold was hidden could take several days, so they decided to use Munich as a base of operation. This time, though, they decided on a less expensive hotel.

In Stuttgart they had had a tough time explaining the bullet holes in the windshield and the door, but after Schweizer offered the car rental agent a hundred dollars they were on their way. They took the *Schnellzug* to Munich, arriving late in the evening. The following morning they rented a car and the treasure hunt was underway.

But always in the back of their minds were the death of Berndt, the beating of *Frau* Nordhoff, and the shots fired at them at the *Autobahn* rest area. Then what about the microfilm records in Berlin? Was it only a coincidence that the microfilm had been signed out earlier that same day? Schweizer had a persistent feeling of being spied upon. Every time he turned around, he expected someone to be there, but there never was.

The most vivid memory Schweizer had of the past was passing a lake. Several were in the Munich area: the Ammersee, the

Starnbergersee, and the Forggensee near the Neuschwanstein castle were the closest, and the first ones checked out. With a Michelin road map they systematically explored the routes that passed near lakes in the area, hoping to find some clue to the location of the village. Finally, on the morning of the fifth day of their search, they drove down into the valley of Tegernsee. Kalt was looking at the map and Schweizer was driving. Suddenly, he pulled off the road and stopped. "This is the lake," he said.

"Are you quite sure? "asked Kalt. "We have looked at a lot of lakes, you know."

"Yes, this is the one. You see those two mountains?" Schweizer was pointing at two peaks to the south. "The road goes up between those two mountains. The village is up there somewhere."

Kalt's face had a flushed appearance. He looked like he had just won the lottery. One could almost hear him counting the money. "Well," he said, "let's go find it!"

Schweizer looked at Kalt, who was smiling eagerly. "You know, Friedrich, we never discussed what we would do with the gold, *if* we are lucky enough to find it."

Kalt's smile faded like a broken light bulb. "Why, we are going to share it aren't we?"

Schweizer had a teasing look on his face. "You've been a big help, Friedrich. Don't worry. I'll be fair. You'll be taken care of."

Kalt was smiling again, but it was a very nervous smile. He wondered ... money does strange things to some men.

The further they drove, the more familiar the surroundings were to Schweizer. Even he was getting excited now. After almost twenty minutes they had covered a distance of about fourteen miles along narrow winding roads up into the Alps.

"It's just up ahead, around the next curve," said Schweizer.

The road curved and they entered a broad valley. Schweizer pulled off the road and skidded to a stop. His look of shock was matched by Kalt's look of consternation. "Where's the village?" asked Kalt. "Are you sure this the right place?"

"I'm positive," insisted Schweizer. "I distinctly remember that peak over there."

The two men got out of the car and walked to the edge of a slope. Below them, stretching for several miles, were the tranquil waters of the Sylvensteinsee. Off to their right the road curved and followed the shoreline. At the beginning of the curve a guardrail, painted with black and white stripes, prevented traffic from going into the lake. Beneath the guardrail, and continuing down to the water's edge, was a paved road.

"It's a reservoir," said Schweizer weakly. "They've built a dam and flooded the whole damned valley!"

"What are we going to do now? "asked Kalt. "How can we be sure this is the right place? I don't see a village."

The wind was blowing down from the mountains and the only things green were the fir trees that made up most of the local vegetation. Spring was beginning to break forth in the lowlands, but still was weeks away in the mountains. Schweizer stood with arms folded and looked out over the lake. He was absolutely sure that this was the place, but after more than thirty years ... he couldn't help but wonder. After all, he certainly couldn't win any arguments about how good his memory was. If the gold were down there, there was only one recourse, go down after it. But how deep, and what about equipment? Scuba gear was the obvious answer, but he had no experience and likely Kalt didn't either.

Schweizer spoke without looking at Kalt. "Friedrich, as I see it, our choices are rather limited. If the gold is down there ... and I'm sure it is ... we have to go down after it. First of all, we should determine if there really *is* a village down there. Maybe I'm wrong. Thirty years is a long time. On the other hand, maybe there was once a village down there, but it was torn down before the dam was built. In that case, we could look for years and never find it. Once those questions are answered and we have a reasonable chance of success, then I suppose we'll have to take a quick course in skin diving." Schweizer turned and looked at Kalt. "You do know how to swim, don't you?"

Kalt was depressed. He was not an excellent swimmer, and besides, the water was probably very cold this time of the year. Still, if the gold were down there ... "Yes, I can swim," he said grimly.

"All right, let's find out more about this lake."

It only took a few inquiries at Tegernsee, the town named for the lake, to determine that a village had indeed been in the valley now filled with the waters of the Sylvensteinsee. The village had been named Fall and had been flooded when the dam was built in the 1950's, the exact year no one could agree on. A new village of the same name had been built about a mile south of the original site.

During the return trip to Munich both Schweizer and Kalt were rather subdued. They had agreed the only course open to them was to go down into the lake to search for the gold, but neither could generate very much enthusiasm for the operation. The weather was cool and windy, and neither had had any previous experience underwater. It was possible they could get someone more skilled in underwater exploration, but that would mean sharing the gold, a prospect that neither man favored.

Schweizer stopped in front of the hotel and left the engine running. "Aren't you coming in?" asked Kalt.

"I've been thinking," said Schweizer. "Why don't we just get some gear and go down after the gold today? It isn't even noon yet. We could at least get a good look at the village. If we aren't successful, we'll at least have a head start on tomorrow. What do you think?"

There didn't seem to be much point in waiting, thought Kalt. On the other hand, he wasn't very anxious to go down into that lake, either. "If you are sure that's what you want to do, Karl, I'm ready."

Schweizer seemed to relax and there was a smile on his face. "Good," he said emphatically. "I'll go look for the diving equipment."

"Do you want me to come with you?" asked Kalt.

"No. No need for that. Why don't you just relax and get some sleep? This could be pretty strenuous."

As Schweizer drove away he caught a glimpse of Kalt in the rearview mirror. Kalt was standing at the curb watching Schweizer leave. He had a very intense look on his face. When the car was out of sight, Kalt turned and walked into the hotel. There was not much time to get ready for the adventure that lay ahead of them.

The nearest place that sold skin diving equipment was the Münchner Sporthaus. It was also one of the most expensive. However, price was not very important at this stage. Schweizer just wanted to get the equipment and get on with the business of finding the gold.

Skin diving was a dangerous sport for someone who knew nothing about it and Schweizer pointed out his lack of experience to the salesman. "It is required that you be certified before making a dive alone," said the salesman. "Scuba is a sport that can hurt you if you are not careful. It is essential to have the proper training. I wouldn't recommend that anyone dive without it."

"I am just a tourist," said Schweizer, "and I really don't have time to take a training course if it lasts more than just one day."

The salesman frowned. He could see an easy sale slipping away. "Usually our course of instruction lasts for eight days, spread out over two weeks. Perhaps we can find a way around it."

"What do you have in mind?"

"I am one of the instructors for the course. Perhaps I could take you on as a private student, an accelerated course, if you will."

"How much will this accelerated course cost me?"

"Two hundred marks."

"I see. And the equipment?"

"The basic equipment, snorkel, mask, fins, and handbooks will cost about two hundred fifty marks."

"What about air tanks and the like?"

"I would recommend you rent those," said the salesman. "Of course, I would like to sell them to you, but the cost is prohibitive for just casual use. About one thousand marks would do it."

"How much to rent them?" asked Schweizer.

"Fifty marks for the weekend with a two hundred mark deposit."

"When can we begin the instruction?" asked Schweizer. "I don't have much time."

"Would this evening be convenient?" asked the salesman.

"Sure."

"I would also recommend that you don't go alone," said the salesman. "Although it is unlikely that you will have any problems it is best to have someone with you. It's safer."

"No problem," said Schweizer. "There are two of us." The salesman smiled. The sale would be twice as big as he first thought.

At the hotel Kalt had tried to sleep, but couldn't make himself relax. He was worried, about the dive into the lake and the shooting at the *Autobahn* rest area. He couldn't put them out of his mind. Just then there was a tapping on the door and Kalt got up to answer it. At the door was a short, grey-haired man with a thin moustache. It was Max Frohm.

Kalt seemed surprised by his visitor. Finally, he spoke: "Don't you think it's risky coming here?"

Frohm shrugged and smiled at Kalt. "Not at all. I saw Schweizer drive away and I wanted to see what progress you have made. You two have had quite an excursion the past several days. It's been difficult to keep up with you at times."

"You have managed to keep up, then?" asked Kalt.

"Most of the time, but it *is* getting tedious. Now, what about the gold? Any luck?"

Kalt looked intently at Frohm, but said nothing. A very distinct image of a bullet hole in the windshield crowded all other thoughts from his mind. "I said, have you had any luck finding the gold?" Frohm asked a second time.

Several thoughts crossed Kalt's mind. Who had taken that shot at him? Frohm? Who else knew about the search for the gold? Obviously, Frohm was a sly fox and thought that coming to the hotel would allay Kalt's suspicions. *Well*, he thought, *it won't work*. "I think we have found the hiding place," said Kalt.

Frohm clapped his hands together and smiled broadly, saying, "Wonderful! Where is it?"

"I'll have to show you on the map. Just a minute, it's in my coat." Kalt went to the closet and looked inside.

"How soon do we dispose of Schweizer?" asked Frohm.

"Just as soon as I get my hands on the gold."

"Do you want me to do it?"

"No, I'll be closest to him. I'll have the best opportunity."

"You know, the worst business deal I ever made was to let you bribe your way out of that POW camp," said Frohm.

"How is that?"

"You took Schweizer with you. After Koerbler told me about the gold I couldn't wait to get my hands on Schweizer. If I had known you were taking him with you, you would have ended up swinging from a rope and I would have become a rich man while young enough to still enjoy it. Oh, well ... better late than never."

Kalt bristled at the comment about the rope, but only smiled in Frohm's direction. He continued rummaging through the closet. Meanwhile, Frohm was growing impatient. "How long does it take to find a map? Schweizer could come back at any time, you know."

Kalt closed the closet door, walked over to the bed and spread out the map. "The gold was hidden in a village that happens to now be at the bottom of a reservoir."

"You don't say? Oh, that *is* interesting. Where's the reservoir?"

"It's called the Sylvensteinsee and it's up in the Alps directly south of here." Kalt gestured toward the lake's location on the map. As Frohm leaned over for a closer look, Kalt reached into his pocket and retrieved the electric cord to his shaver, the item he had been searching for in the closet.

"How soon do you th ..." It took an instant for Frohm to realize what was happening to him. Kalt had slipped the electric cord around Frohm's neck and was using it as a garrote. Instinctively, Frohm clutched at his throat, but it was futile. Kalt was a head taller and outweighed him by at least fifty pounds.

"Jew bastard!" shouted Kalt, grunting from the exertion. "Thought you would kill me and keep it all for yourself? Well, I'm too smart for you!"

Frohm began to thrash about wildly. His right leg jerked spasmodically, kicking over a table with a lamp on it. Kalt doubled his efforts. Frohm's face was turning purple and his eyes were bulging. Overcoming his natural instincts, he reached into his coat pocket for the pistol he had brought with him. He felt the weapon and started to pull it out. Pinkish bubbles were beginning to form on his lips. Just then, Kalt jerked Frohm's head around so he could look into his eyes. "It doesn't matter," said Kalt. "I was going to kill you anyway, after I had found the gold."

The gun was free and Frohm was trying to raise it to fire. He could hear a roaring sound of rushing wind in his ears, and the room was growing dim and beginning to spin. The muscles in his hand began to jerk and twitch, and with a dull thud the pistol dropped to the floor. Frohm went limp, then sagged to the floor pulling Kalt down on top of him. Kalt was sweating profusely and breathing heavily, but he didn't let go. He wanted to make sure the job was finished.

After a few minutes Kalt felt for Frohm's pulse. Nothing. His own heart was beating rapidly. He was in a near panic. Schweizer could return at any moment. Kalt had killed Frohm on impulse, and now he regretted it. He should have chosen a better time and place. The body ... he had to get rid of the body!

Kalt started gathering up the evidence. He folded up the map and put it and the electric cord in the closet. Just then, he heard a key in the door. Quickly he looked the room over. There were obvious signs of a struggle and it was too late to hide the body. He had to come up with a good story, and fast! *On the floor! That's it*, he thought, *the gun*.

Schweizer got the door half open and was removing his key when he saw Frohm on the floor. He looked at Frohm and then at Kalt. He didn't have a look of surprise on his face. It was as if he had expected to find such a scene.

"What happened?" asked Schweizer. Then it hit him. He finally realized who it was lying on the floor. "My god! That's Max Frohm!"

Schweizer quickly closed the door.

"Did you know him?" asked Kalt.

"Sure. Don't you remember? I told you he was one of the people who knew I was coming over here." Schweizer looked around and shook his head. "I never would have believed it!"

Schweizer looked directly at Kalt and said, "Now I understand what's been going on ... Berndt, *Frau* Nordhoff ... but what was he doing here?"

Kalt was nervous and trying hard not to look guilty. He was too close to the gold to blow it now. "When I came up, he was in the room going through the closet. He pulled a gun and I had to defend myself." Kalt motioned toward the gun on the floor.

"Did you have to kill him? He could have answered a lot of questions."

"Are you serious? When a man has a gun in his hand, I don't take time to interview him!"

"All right, all right," said Schweizer. "It's done. I know you're upset, but we have to think clearly. Do you think we should call the police?"

Kalt began pacing back and forth nervously. "No, I don't think we can do that. They would ask too many questions. We have to get rid of the body. "The room was silent except for the sound of Kalt pacing.

"But how do we do it? How do we get the body out of here?"

"We don't have a trunk," said Schweizer. "What about the maid's laundry cart?"

"Don't be ridiculous!" Kalt snorted. "How would it look for two hotel guests to be pushing a maid's cart down the hall?"

"It was only a suggestion," said Schweizer as he drifted over toward the window.

"Try to come up with an idea that at least sounds intelligent," said Kalt sarcastically.

This was a side of Kalt that Schweizer had never seen before, and he certainly didn't like it. However, considering the circumstances, he was willing to overlook Kalt's rudeness. Absentmindedly, Schweizer parted the curtain and looked at the street five floors below. "It's too bad there's so much traffic," he said. "Otherwise we could just drop him out the window."

As soon as Schweizer had said it, both he and Kalt must have had the same idea. Their eyes met briefly, then both men turned and looked at the open door to the bathroom. A glimmer of light was shining through the bathroom window, yet the window faced away from the street. Both men started for the window, but Kalt got there first, threw it open and looked out.

"This is perfect, Karl. Take a look."

Outside the window was a shaft about ten feet square. Above, four floors up, was blue sky. Below was a dark pit. All around the shaft were windows with translucent glass. Schweizer reached in his pocket for a coin and tossed it out the window. A few seconds later he heard it clattering around at the bottom of the shaft. "Give me a piece of toilet paper," he said.

"What for?" asked Kalt.

"I'm going to throw it down there and see if I can see it." Schweizer threw the paper out the window and watched it disappear into the darkness of the shaft. "There's your answer. No one will be able to see him down there. It will be days at the very least, and possibly weeks or even months before he's found, and probably then only because of the smell."

Kalt had a look of relief on his face and he was trying to smile. "Well," he said, "let's get it over with and then you can tell me about the skin diving equipment."

Frohm was heavier than he looked. The two men struggled to get him into the bathroom. As they lifted the body to a sitting position on the window sill, Schweizer finally understood the expression "dead weight." Kalt gave the final push and a few seconds later they heard a dull thump. Kalt looked down for a moment, then closed the window.

Neither man mentioned Frohm again.

After a brief review of his experience at the sporting goods store, Schweizer suggested they keep the appointment for the skin diving lesson in the evening. He had planned to just read the handbook before diving, but considering the body at the bottom of the shaft, he decided to avoid arousing anyone's suspicions. Tomorrow would be soon enough.

22

THE SYLVENSTEINSEE

The weather was clear the following morning and it would have been a pleasant day for diving except for the wind. There was little conversation on the way to the lake. In the back of each man's mind was the nagging fear Frohm's body would be found before they had a chance to conclude their business. They both hoped for a quick and successful dive.

At the lake they wasted no time changing into their wetsuits. Fifteen minutes after they arrived they stood at the water's edge, ready to begin. "I guess this is it," said Schweizer. "I can hardly believe where I am, in view of what I started out to do."

"It's exciting," Kalt said unconvincingly, "but I will be glad when it's over."

Kalt's experience in the swimming pool the previous night had been unnerving. It had been a struggle to overcome his natural fear of breathing underwater.

"Stay close to me," said Schweizer, "and you'll be all right."

With Schweizer leading the way, they waded out over twenty yards before the water was deep enough to start swimming. Schweizer submerged first. The plan was to follow the road through the village and look for the Nordhoff house.

The water was remarkably clear and not as deep as they had feared. Silt was a problem, as was underwater plant life, but not as much as they had expected. Schweizer attributed it to the elevation. Not much silt would be washed down from the rocky slopes.

As Schweizer made his way above the road, the only sound was the rhythmic bubbling of exhaled air. He paused and looked behind him. Kalt was about ten yards back, so Schweizer waited for him to catch up. They were on the northeast edge of the village.

The buildings were well preserved, but some of the roofs had rotted and fallen in. The onion-like dome on the church steeple was still in good shape. Schweizer stopped to inspect it and wait for Kalt, who had fallen behind again. As soon as Kalt caught up, Schweizer pushed on, not allowing the older man a chance to rest. *Damn you,* thought Kalt, *this isn't a marathon race!*

Swimming above the village, Schweizer had an eerie feeling, as if he was walking through a cemetery on Halloween. In a way it was a graveyard, a graveyard of old empty buildings, and forgotten hopes and dreams. What had the people been like?

The village was not as Schweizer had remembered it, and for awhile he began to doubt that he had the right one. Once they had passed through the village the road became harder to follow. They were getting closer to the dam and silt was becoming more of a problem. Ahead, the lake bottom rose sharply and the road curved around it. Past the rise the road continued straight and the lake bottom dropped gradually to the left ... and there it was. The Nordhoff house was rundown and the roof was sagging, but basically the structure was intact. Silt had accumulated to just below the first floor windows. Schweizer turned to Kalt, who was still lagging behind, and pointed to the house.

Kalt caught up and they swam over to the house, which was typical of many Alpine farmhouses. It was a two story building. Half of the lower floor was living space and the other half was a barn. Schweizer remembered that access to the cellar was through the barn. He located a window into the barn, turned on his light, and led the way in.

The door to the cellar was ajar, as if they were expected. Schweizer swam through and shined his light around. The wooden stairs had collapsed and the cellar was generally in disarray. One of the beams that supported the ceiling was split and looked as if it could go at any time. Something was wrong. Schweizer made a circuit of the cellar, shining the light up and down all of the walls. They were made of stone. Schweizer remembered the walls were paneled with wood and there had been several storage cabinets. The gold had been stacked in a hollow space behind one of the cabinets. Slowly, Schweizer drifted to a sitting position, and just as slowly the truth sank in. The gold was gone.

Kalt joined Schweizer on the cellar floor, grateful for the opportunity to rest, and made shrugging gestures. With his finger Schweizer wrote in the muck on the floor: *KEIN GOLD.* No gold. Kalt wrote: *WO IST ES?*

That's a stupid question, thought Schweizer. *How the hell should I know where it is?*

When Schweizer didn't respond, Kalt took the light and inspected the walls himself. Forgetting his fatigue, he swam around like a shark in a feeding frenzy. Schweizer felt a curious detachment as he watched Kalt's efforts to deny the obvious. *It would be funny,* he thought, *if it weren't so disappointing.*

Finally, Kalt, too, accepted the truth and rejoined Schweizer on the cellar floor. After several minutes Schweizer picked up the light and pointed toward the door. Kalt nodded and they started the trip back. It would be longer going than it had been coming.

Schweizer and Kalt emerged slowly from the water. The equipment was heavy, and middle age weighed even more heavily upon their bodies. The sun was slightly obscured by a very thin layer of strato-cirrus clouds, creating a shimmering hue of rainbow-like colors around the solar disk. A brisk wind had begun to blow off the lake, causing the chill they already felt to penetrate through their wetsuits. Kalt had begun to shiver uncontrollably. They were up to knee-depth when Schweizer noticed the Volkswagen parked on the other side of the guard rail at the top of the embankment.

The car was a very deep green with a small pipe curving out and up from just behind the driver's door. At the top of the pipe was a dome-shaped blue plastic light and stenciled on the door in white letters was the word, *Polizei*. Standing by the front bumper of the VW was a solitary police officer, dressed in medium green pants and coat, light green shirt, a black tie, and the characteristic high-peaked cap. He stood in a wider than normal stance and his fists rested casually on his hips, elbows jutting out to either side. If he were trying to look authoritative, he had succeeded as far as Schweizer was concerned. *God, how these Germans love uniforms*, he thought. *He looks like something out of a World War II movie.*

The officer had apparently gone unnoticed by Kalt as he gave a start when the officer called out to them. "Good day to you, gentlemen!" Schweizer's only response was a distinct nod. "Might I ask why you are swimming in such cold water on such a blustery day?"

Blustery indeed, thought Schweizer. It reminded him of a cartoon feature he had once taken his daughter to, called "Winnie the Pooh and the Blustery Day." Kalt turned his head and looked hard at Schweizer. Both men were thinking the same thought: had Frohm's body already been found? Schweizer returned the look and then turned his attention to the officer. "We had heard of the underwater village and wanted to explore it."

The officer eyed them suspiciously. "Couldn't you have chosen a better day?"

Better make it good, thought Schweizer. "My friend is from Zurich and he must return home tomorrow. Today was our only chance."

The officer's questioning look had been replaced with a frown. Here were two men well past fifty looking positively ridiculous in scuba gear, swimming in cold weather on a windy day. The chill factor must have been below freezing. *They must be crazy*, he thought, *or up to something*. The wind began to blow harder, causing him to shout to be heard. "There's nothing of value down there."

"I can't hear you!" yelled Schweizer.

The officer cupped his hands to his mouth. "I said ..." he began, then thought better of it. He stepped over the guard rail and began to pick his way down the slope. About four feet from the bottom, his lead foot lost traction, while his trailing foot held firm. His arms flailed about wildly as he sought unsuccessfully to regain his balance. He looked like a chorus girl doing a split. The subsequent tumble to the bottom bruised more than his dignity. Schweizer had to look away to keep from laughing out loud. Even normally sedate Kalt managed a snicker.

The officer picked himself up and kept his eyes glued to the ground, hoping that by the time he had dusted himself off the blush would have faded. Schweizer pointed to a place twenty yards to the left. "You should have come down over there. It's not as steep."

"I'll go back up that way," said the officer. "Thank you."

"Are you all right?" asked Kalt, suddenly solicitous of the policeman's well-being.

"Yes, I'm fine. What I was trying to tell you was that there is nothing of value in the lake."

"Well, of course we really didn't expect to find anything," said Schweizer.

"There used to be, though," said the policeman.

Kalt and Schweizer couldn't help looking at each other for an instant, but now their attention was riveted on the officer. Kalt forgot he was cold.

"It was very exciting, actually." The policeman seemed to be toying with them. "It was about 1951 or 1952, I think ..."

"The lake wasn't here then," interrupted Schweizer.

"Yes, I know," said the officer. "It was before the dam was built." He paused. "I grew up in the village down there." He nodded toward the lake. "I was seven or eight years old. It was the only real excitement we ever had."

"What was it?" asked Kalt impatiently.

"Gold," said the policeman simply. It was the answer both men had expected, but the one that neither had wanted to hear. "I doubt that I will ever see such a sight again in my life. It seems that some old Nazi had stolen it at the end of the war and hidden it here in the basement of his home. You should have seen old Fritz Greiner, who lived in that house. I can still see him shaking his poor bewildered head as they carried it out. There must have been hundreds of bars of gold. Soldiers were everywhere."

Two hundred twenty-five to be exact, Schweizer said to himself. "How did they find it?" he asked out loud. "And why did they take so long after the war to come for it?"

"Surely you remember how it was after the war," said the policeman. "Everything was a mess. It took years to get records and things like that sorted out. Maybe it was just a guess, but one day they came looking for the gold and there it was."

A brooding silence settled over the three men. Kalt's and Schweizer's eyes were downcast and they both had a faraway look. People had died over a non-existent treasure. It all seemed so senseless. Finally, the officer broke the silence. "Anyway, there is nothing of value down there. You are welcome to swim, if you like, but naturally I am concerned for your safety."

"Thank you, officer," said Schweizer. "I appreciate your thoughtfulness, but we'll make out all right."

The officer shrugged. "If you need my assistance, please call on us. I'm Officer Pfeiffer out of Tegernsee." With that he turned and climbed back up to his car and drove off. The familiar whine of the VW engine faded away and finally the two men were alone with their thoughts.

Kalt lumbered over to a small clump of trees, hoping to find shelter from the wind as he climbed out of the scuba gear. He was in a very pensive mood as he sat down on a rock and shrugged the heavy air tanks from off his shoulders. "I don't think I can remember a greater disappointment in my life," he sighed. "I really expected it to be there."

"I feel the same way, Friedrich. But you know, I have always believed that everyone has one big payday in his life."

"Not for us," rejoined Kalt. "At least not today."

Kalt had kicked off his flippers and was now standing with his back to Schweizer to unzip his wet suit. Meanwhile, Schweizer began rummaging purposefully through his equipment bag. At last he located the item he was looking for.

"On the contrary," said Schweizer as he walked slowly toward Kalt, "everyone gets paid someday and today is your payday."

Kalt froze. Schweizer's voice had a menacing sound to it. "What do you mean?" asked Kalt, trying to sound nonchalant as he tugged at the oversized zipper, which now appeared to be jammed.

"I mean it's time for you to settle up ... *Herr* Wetzel."

A tingly shiver started in the area between Kalt's shoulder blades and rose quickly up his neck to the hairs on the back of his head. As he turned toward Schweizer, the quizzical expression on his face was already being replaced by one of alarmed comprehension. "Then you do remember," he said weakly as he squared around to face his accuser.

The black muzzle of Schweizer's revolver had an almost hypnotic effect.

"Yes, I remember," he said. "I remember every rotten thing about you. I have ever since that day at the railroad trestle. And now it's time to settle up."

Kalt mustered up his most defiant look. "And what account am I required to square with you, Lt. Lindner? You don't mind if I call you by your real name, do you?"

"It doesn't matter. I've been Karl Schweizer for so long I may as well stay with it."

"By the way, "said Kalt," whatever happened to the real Schweizer?"

"Probably killed at the trestle. Does it matter?"

"How convenient for you," snorted Kalt. "Now just what is it that you feel I owe you?"

"For openers, thirty years of my life."

"Preposterous!" said Kalt. "I didn't blow up that trestle!"

"No, but you could have told me who I really was when we were in that prison camp," said Schweizer.

Kalt looked disgusted. "Would you have been stupid enough to do that if our positions had been reversed?" he asked.

Good point, thought Schweizer. *I would probably have done the same thing.* "There's still the matter of Mike Erickson. What about that?"

Kalt had an uncomprehending look on his face. "Mike Erickson?" he said slowly. "Who the hell is Mike Erickson?"

"I suppose that was the worst thing about that dirty business at *Stalag VII-A*," said Schweizer. "We weren't even people as far as you were concerned."

A feeling of rage was beginning to build in Schweizer. All the hurt and frustration that had been tormenting him wanted to get out. "Mike Erickson was my best friend. He's the man you hung from the flagpole."

The color drained from Kalt's face as he realized the impact of what Schweizer had just said. He suddenly felt helpless facing his accuser. "But ... but that was more than thirty years ago," he sputtered.

"Yes," Schweizer agreed, "thirty years you deprived him of, and thirty years more than you deserved."

"Be reasonable!" Kalt pleaded.

Schweizer snorted disgustedly. "No, the time for being reasonable is over. The satisfaction this is going to give me will never make up for what I've been through ... but, by God, it'll sure help." Schweizer raised the gun slowly. "Say good-bye, Friedrich."

The metallic click of the hammer being drawn back seemed to drown out all other sounds as Kalt's every sense was focused on the enormity of what was about to happen. He looked fleetingly at the blue sky, streaked with wind-driven clouds. At the same time he felt both the sun's warmth and the chill of the wind on his face. He thought he heard a bird singing somewhere in the trees.

"Wait," he said quietly. Like the eye of the hurricane, a calmness seemed to have settled upon him. "I have something to say first."

The peaceful look on Kalt's face was unnerving for Schweizer and he hesitated. "All right," he finally said, "but it won't change anything. Your account is still going to be closed today!"

Kalt only nodded. "I have done many wrong things in my life, and I have often wondered if I could find forgiveness in the next world. Now it appears I cannot even find forgiveness in this one."

"Now, really Friedrich ..."

"I know, I know! You think only of the bad things. But there were good things, too. We were good friends after the war, and even now you turned to me for help."

There was merit in what Kalt said, and for a moment Schweizer's resolve weakened. "I'm sure the gold had nothing to do with your friendship," said Schweizer, trying to sound sarcastic.

"Yes, I admit it. At first that was my motivation. But I quickly realized that you would probably never remember, so I put the whole business of the gold completely out of my mind."

"Weren't you afraid that my memory would return someday and that I might then turn you in?" asked Schweizer.

"Of course, that thought did cross my mind, but I wasn't worried. I guess, in view of present circumstances, I should have killed you."

"Why didn't you?"

"We were friends, Karl, very good friends. I just couldn't."

"Very touching."

"Think what you will, but I could never bring myself to do what you are about to do. I was a product of the times. What are you a product of?"

Schweizer's resolve was fading fast. Kalt was now the accuser and Schweizer found his thoughts shifting to his own motives. Kalt had been a good friend in Switzerland and he had sent money to help Schweizer through school. But he just couldn't put the murder of Mike Erickson out of his mind.

"You're wasting your time," said Schweizer nervously. "You're not going to talk your way out of this." Kalt shrugged. "I think you should know," Schweizer continued, "they didn't get all of the gold."

Kalt was incredulous. "What are you talking about?"

"I'm talking about the fifteen gold bars we buried in the woods before we took off for Switzerland."

"Do you think it's still there?"

"Could be. But it doesn't really matter to you, does it?" Kalt's look of surprise had now been replaced by one of anger and frustration.

"My god, man ..." he sputtered.

A sharp bang originating from the trees across the road echoed through the valley. The bullet punched a hole through Kalt's right shoulder just below the collar bone. The force of the impact spun him around and down onto his knees. It was a tossup as to who was more surprised, Kalt or Schweizer. Schweizer dropped into a crouch and scrambled for cover. He was stunned. How could anyone have sneaked up on them undetected? He strained to see where the shot had come from.

Kalt was struggling to his feet when the second shot rang out. The top of his head erupted in a spray of blood and brains as his lifeless body pitched forward onto the sandy beach. Schweizer stared uncomprehendingly, trying desperately to understand and absorb the shock of what had just happened.

"Come out, *Herr* Schweizer." It was a female voice. "Hold your gun by the barrel with two fingers. Hold it at arm's length and step into the open."

Schweizer glanced quickly around for some avenue of escape, but saw none. "Don't worry," the voice called out, "if you do as I say, I won't shoot."

What the hell? thought Schweizer, resignedly, as he rose to his feet.

He stepped into the open, holding the gun as he had been instructed. At the top of the embankment a figure clad in black pants and black coat appeared. It was Erika Koenig and she was carrying a rifle with a scope. It was an AR-15.

"Throw the gun away, now," she ordered.

Schweizer tossed it about ten feet to his right.

Erika worked her way carefully down the slope until she stood only a few steps in front of Schweizer.

"Erika," he asked with some amazement, "how in the hell did you get involved in all this?"

"I was going to ask you the same thing," she replied. "I have been following Wetzel for two weeks looking for a chance to kill him, but you were always in the way. This time I decided to kill him anyway, even if it meant killing you."

Schweizer shuddered. "Well?" he said, "*are* you going to kill me?"

"I don't know. You are a witness. If the police officer hadn't been here when you came out of the water, you would be dead already."

"How did that stop you?"

"When he left, I had to wait for him to get out of earshot before I could fire. By then you were holding Wetzel at gunpoint. I decided to wait it out, but all you did was talk ... and it was time for Wetzel to die."

"You call him Wetzel," remarked Schweizer. "Then you know who he was?"

Erika looked over at Kalt's body. Her eyes were filled with hatred. "Yes, I knew who he was, and what he was. He killed my mother and father."

Suddenly, the murder of Mike Erickson seemed almost insignificant in comparison. A feeling of compassion welled up within Schweizer. "I'm really sorry to hear that. How did it happen?"

"He was at Treblinka when my mother and father arrived. Wetzel met the trains and selected who was to work and who was to die. My mother was sent with the others to be gassed, naked, driven by men with whips along the *Himmelstrasse*." Erika paused, fighting back the tears. "I said I would never cry, and I won't." After a few more moments Erika had regained her composure and continued with her story. "They were so perverse. It wasn't enough to kill people. They had to make a joke of it. So they called the path to the gas chamber 'the road to heaven.'"

"Wetzel selected my father to be a worker. He didn't last a month. His heart wasn't in it after my mother was killed. For some minor infraction, Wetzel ordered him hacked to death with shovels in front of the other prisoners on the assembly ground."

"How do you know all this?" asked Schweizer.

"My uncle Samuel was there. He saw it all."

"He was a survivor of the death camps?"

"Yes. They killed more than a million Jews in Treblinka, but in August, 1943, the prisoners revolted and burned the camp. Several hundred escaped. My uncle Samuel was one of them."

"You're Jewish then?"

"Only by heritage. My parents placed me with a Gentile couple when Hitler began to ship the German Jews to the camps. They wanted me to be safe. When they never returned, I was raised as one of the family. In 1945 the Russians came and my family fled to the west. My uncle Samuel didn't find me until eight years ago. He told me who I really was. I didn't believe him at first, but my foster parents told me about my real mother and father."

"Why did you come after Wetzel?" asked Schweizer.

Erika pondered the question for a few seconds. "Duty, I suppose. Uncle Samuel had grown old, too old to search for Wetzel himself. I began to look for Wetzel, half-heartedly at first. Then it became an obsession. My husband didn't understand and eventually we parted. And then, two weeks ago, I located Wetzel in Zurich, living under the name Kalt."

"I understand your feelings about Wetzel," said Schweizer, "but how do you justify killing Berndt and his wife, and what about *Frau Nordhoff*?"

Erika looked at Schweizer as though he had taken leave of his senses. "I don't know what you are talking about. Who are they?"

"Come on, Erika! Why did you run away from me that day at the train station?"

"I thought you could figure that out for yourself. I had followed Wetzel from Zurich looking for a chance to kill him, and my lover of the previous night comes walking up with him. What was I supposed to think?"

"Wait a minute," said Schweizer. "Something doesn't sound right. You say you followed him from Zurich."

"That's right."

"I met you the previous night, but Wetzel didn't get in on the train from Zurich until the next day, the day I saw you in the station."

A derisive laugh escaped Erika's lips. "He certainly had you fooled," she said. "I was on the same plane as Wetzel the night before. He took a cab to the train station and left his bag in a locker. Then he got into a car with another man and drove away. I walked down to the streetcar stop and then I met you. I went back to the train station the next day hoping to find him."

Schweizer's mind was racing, trying to absorb all this new information. "What did the man in the car look like?"

"Older, grey hair, a thin mustache. I didn't get a very good look."

"Frohm," Schweizer muttered to himself. Everything was finally coming together. He turned and walked over to Kalt's equipment bag.

"Wait a minute," cried Erika. "What are you doing?"

"Just curious."

Schweizer's tone was almost lackadaisical. He tore the items from the bag in handfuls, tossing them over his head. Near the bottom he found it: a .25 caliber automatic with silencer attached. Schweizer pulled it from the bag and handled it gingerly. Erika caught a glimpse of the weapon and brought her rifle to the ready. Schweizer walked over to where Kalt's body lay. He gazed at the dead man as a feeling of weariness came over him. The slug had turned Kalt's brain into jelly and it was still oozing from the massive wound. A fragment of his skull hung down, attached only by a piece of balding scalp. A look of total surprise was forever imprinted on his face. An unspeakable rage began to well up in Schweizer's guts.

"To think you almost talked me out of it," he said bitterly. "You lousy sonofabitch! I should have killed you myself!"

Schweizer flung the weapon as far as he could out into the lake. Then he turned, gathered up his gear and headed up the embankment.

"Where are you going?" asked Erika.

"I'm going home," he replied.

"But what about the body?"

"You killed him. You bury him."

Schweizer tossed his gear into the back seat and slid behind the wheel. As he started the car, he looked back at Erika. In a way, he felt sorry for her. She had been so eaten up by hatred. Now that Kalt was dead, what was there left for her in life? Schweizer raised his hand in a half salute to Erika and put the car in gear. It was time to go home.

23

CINCINNATI

It was dark as the 727 taxied up to the boarding ramp at the Greater Cincinnati Airport. Behind the terminal, Schweizer could see the brightly lit sign of the Americana Inn. Standing at one of the large plate glass windows in the boarding area was a woman who looked like his wife. As Schweizer waited for the other passengers to disembark, he felt in his pocket for the papers to his newly opened Swiss bank account. Getting the gold into Switzerland had been fairly easy, and for a substantial fee a Swiss goldsmith had recast the gold to obliterate the evidence of its origin. No need for a squabble over ownership. He had then decided to leave it in Switzerland rather than give most of it to the U.S. government.

The stewardess at the door vaguely resembled Erika and Schweizer returned her cheerful smile. He walked up the tunnel and into the passenger lounge where Carole was waiting. She threw her arms around his neck and hugged him fiercely.

"I'm so glad you're back," she said.

Then she leaned away and gazed into his eyes. Schweizer noted the sparkle in her eyes and the happiness in her voice. He decided then not to tell her about Eric Lindner. As far as he was concerned, Lindner was dead.

"Before you say anything," Carole continued, "I've been doing a lot of thinking while you've been gone. I just want you to know that nothing else matters, except that we're together."

Schweizer smiled and kissed her.

Carole pulled away, laughing. "Well, darling, did you find your past?" she asked.

"Yes, I did."

"And what did you learn?"

"I learned that everything is going to be all right."

Schweizer slipped his arm around Carole's waist and they headed for the exit.